IN VINDICATION

A Kings of Boston Novel Book 6

COURTNEY W. DIXON

Published by Courtney W. Dixon

www.courtneywdixon.com

Beta Readers: Isabella Martorana, Jeanette Lawson, Deb Richmond, Mary Ellen Dejmek, Kalie Marie, Nicole Arbuckle, Nikki Johnson, Chanel Johnson, Kerrie-Louise Goodman, Rachel Robinson

Editor: Anna Potter - Potter's Editing

Formatting: Aubree Valentine - Beyond the Bookshelf Publishing Services | Facebook

ALSO BY COURTNEY W. DIXON

Kings of Boston

In Silence - Kings of Boston Book 1

In Retribution - Kings of Boston Book 2

In Strength - Kings of Boston Book 3

In Redemption - Kings of Boston Book 4

In Preservation - Kings of Boston Book 5

In Vindication - Kings of Boston Book 6

Ohana Surfing Club

Impact Zone - Ohana Surfing Club Book 1

Pura Vida - Ohana Surfing Club Book 2

Double Up - Ohana Surfing Club Book 3

Standalones

A Home in You - A M/M Stepbrother Romance

Trapped for the Holidays - A M/M Holiday Novella (Read for FREE!)

TRIGGER WARNING

Listed below are the trigger warnings for this book. Reading them may cause spoilers:

CW: suicide, thoughts of suicide, homophobia, drug addiction, death of a loved one, explicit language and sex.

IN VINDICATION SPOTIFY PLAYLIST

https://sptfy.com/InVindicationPlaylist

NOTE FROM THE AUTHOR

If you've ready my other books from the *Kings of Boston* series, then you've met James. He's been in it since book one, *In Silence*. He's one of those characters that you either love, hate, or love to hate. To put it bluntly, he's an asshole.

I've been dying to write his story since the beginning, making him Ronan O'Callaghan's best friend. My goal was to create a man you wanted to throttle sometimes, but like him just enough to keep giving him second chances. But James doesn't achieve his HEA without a shit ton of work and major self-reflection and growth. So, while you may not like him in the beginning, I hope I have you cheering for him in the end.

Thanks for reading *In Vindication*, my last book in the *Kings of Boston* series.

CHAPTER 1

James

THE SMALL, DARK, AND PRETENTIOUS BAR THAT PLAYED THE EIGHTY'S greatest hits over the speakers made me want to lop off my ears. The crowd mainly consisted of young businessmen dressed in their finest with slicked-back hair and the perfect amount of scruff on their faces—basically, clones of myself. And for the first time since I could remember, I felt my age. I practically shared the same generation with these assholes... barely. I wasn't exactly too far away from being forty.

I took a sip of my old fashioned—a pretentious drink to match the atmosphere. With the lack of women present, I doubted my choice of bar selection for my Friday evening. I wanted to get laid and not hang out in a crowd with a four-to-one ratio of men versus women. I didn't pick a gay bar, did I?

The place was new, and across town, so I hit it, hoping I had a fresh crop of women to choose from. Boston had a decent-sized population, but I usually stuck close to home or work, running into the same faces over and over.

And fuck if I didn't miss my best friends, Ronan and Daniel, my old college buds, back from our Harvard days. We'd been friends for nearly twenty years, and now both of them were fucking married with kids, something I vowed never to do. Ever. I had my reasons. Now, I barely saw either of them these days unless it was some fucking kid's birthday party, wedding, or a family gathering for the holidays.

I had a high-paying job as a litigation lawyer, and I was about to make partner. My bank account was filled with more money than I could ever spend, and I had scores of beautiful women to fuck. What would I need marriage and kids for? Marry a woman who'd only end up divorcing me or cheating on me, then take me for all I was worth? Use the kids against me? No fucking thank you.

The triggers suddenly hit me, and I clamped that shit down right fast with a chug of my drink. The burning of the whiskey distracted me, if only for a moment, but it was enough.

I swallowed down thoughts of loneliness along with my drink and sat on a stool facing the front door to stake my claim on the first gorgeous woman to walk in. But the next person who entered wasn't a woman but my co-worker, who instantly zeroed in on me.

Too late to hide now.

Brody Tennyson seemed cool enough, I supposed, and not unlike me in personality, except maybe friendlier. But he always tried to palm off his conquests on me, which was annoying as fuck. I wasn't sure why he felt the need, as if he was doing me a favor or something.

I downed my drink meant for sipping, hiding my scowl behind a look of indifference as he headed in my direction. It wasn't that I disliked the guy, but I wasn't in the mood to chitchat either. I just needed a woman to help me get rid of this funk I was in. With a wave of my hand at the bartender, I lifted my empty glass to order another.

Brody still wore his suit from work, and like me, he was always neatly pressed. He was three inches taller than my six-foot frame, but with the same lean muscle. His hair was a little darker than my dirty blond, with light-brown eyes. I supposed he was good-looking if you liked that sort of thing. The women enjoyed him enough.

Usually, I was more upbeat than this. But Daniel and Luke's wedding last week soured my mood. Then Ronan just announced he and Cat were expecting another baby. God, I wanted them to be happy, and they were, but it left me without my two best friends. Damn, we had some good fucking times. It just made the growing loneliness more crushing.

You're thirty-seven, prick. Perhaps it's time you grew up.

"Funny seeing you here, Clery."

I bit back another scowl at the hard clap on my back. I hated when men did that. "Is it necessary to smack me around, Brody? Can't you just say 'hi' like normal fucking people? What are you doing here, anyway?"

"You can pretend all you want that you're a dick—"

"There's no pretending."

"I'm pretty sure there's a soft spot in there somewhere."

"Keep dreaming."

Fuck, I was in a real mood tonight.

Brody chuckled and shook his head. "Keep telling yourself that," he countered. "You can't fool a lawyer. It's the only reason I put up with your arrogant ass. I see how well you treat your assistant. No dickhead is nice to their assistant."

"Only because she doesn't let me get away with shit, and she'd mess around with my schedules to torment me."

"Sam would never do that to you."

No, she wouldn't. In fact, she was the closest to a confidant I had. I trusted her more than anyone, even my two closest friends. She pulled all my pain out of me like the plucked strings of a guitar. Ronan and Daniel were my closest friends, but we partied more than poured our souls out to each other. Perhaps Sam should've been a therapist instead of my assistant.

The bartender placed my drink in front of me, and I took a sip, refusing to argue about it. I'd given up being nice a long time ago, not that I was cruel, but I told people like it was. No beating around the bush. No pretending to be someone I wasn't. It didn't always make me a lot of friends, and I used to not give a fuck, but with Ronan and Daniel hardly in my life anymore, I grew restless and bored, making me rethink a lot of shit in my life. I'd been comfortable with the status quo for far too long, making change difficult.

Even finding another woman to distract me wasn't helping. Fuck, maybe I should just take a break from sex altogether.

Brody ordered some fancy beer from a tap and took a sip. "I actually had no idea you'd be here. My girl suggested we meet here, saying it was the newest hotspot. But she texted that she's running late."

"Ah. So, she's a girlfriend now, huh? Since when have you decided to do relationships?"

He chuckled and took a sip of his beer. "What's your problem with women anyway?"

"Nothing. I just don't need attachments." I was sure a shrink would tell me I had trust issues, not that it would change a damned thing, so I never bothered shelling out money for one.

He waved a dismissive hand. "Anyway, I think I've found the one, man."

"The one? Surely you jest. You've only known her for what? Two weeks?"

"Three months, which you know damn well since you've met her enough. You can try to dissuade me all you want, James, but she's the one. The first girl I actually see a future with."

"Brody, I struggle to see you with two-point-five kids, a puppy, an expensive van in the garage, and a white picket fence."

"Yeah, me neither. But I imagine myself with a wife who can live in my condo. Maybe start us off with a dog or a plant or something."

"And what happens when she wants kids?"

"Then, I'll fucking give her a kid. I mean, when you find your one, you do whatever you can for them. They'd do the same for you. That's how it's supposed to work."

I rolled my eyes. "You're a fucking divorce lawyer. You, of all people, shouldn't want to get involved."

"See, that's your problem. You see doom at the end of it all. I say it's worth the risk if you love them enough." He clasped me on the shoulder and leaned in. "So, which woman pissed in your Cheerios? What did she do to ruin all other women for you?"

You don't want to know.

Brody wasn't far off, but that wouldn't change who I was. No way would I relive that shit. Been there, fucking done that twice. A third time would turn me into a fool.

"As I said, I enjoy women's company. I just don't need them lingering. I'm fine on my own."

That used to be true, but now I was beginning to wonder if that was a fact any longer.

He snorted a laugh. "Yeah, they all say that until loneliness chokes the life out of them. One day you'll wake up old, dying alone, and full of regrets."

I took a sip of my drink and said nothing, ignoring how much

Brody was mirroring my thoughts. It was better to die alone than in pain from betrayal. I had enough regrets to last a lifetime. What was one more?

I glanced up when a woman walked in. A woman I recognized and who was already taken.

She had her dark blond, highlighted hair in perfect curls bouncing behind her. She wore little makeup other than mascara and bright red lipstick. Her height was average, but she had long legs, especially with three-inch heels strapped to her feet. She wore a modest lavender dress that was all business and suited her.

She was unconventionally pretty. Brody usually preferred the model types, so his interest in her surprised me.

She stepped up to him, kissed his cheek, and wiped off the lipstick she had left behind. Brody wrapped an arm around her waist, brushed away her hair from her neck, and kissed it.

"Hey, babe," he said.

"Hey, back."

"Look who I ran into, Penny?"

"Ah, yes. Womanizer James. How could I possibly forget?"

Her astute observation didn't bother me in the slightest. I enjoyed honest and blunt people. Life was too short to beat around the bush. I especially hated liars. Ironic, considering my line of work. I lied a lot, but only to make money. But I always told people in my personal life the truth, even if it wasn't something they wanted to hear.

"I'm pleased my legacy precedes me," I said, shaking her hand.

"And narcissistic."

I shrugged and took another sip of my overly sweet old fashioned. "It's my best trait."

She snorted a laugh, then turned to the bartender to order a glass of Chardonnay.

After taking a sip of her drink, she set the glass down and narrowed her dark-green, shrewd eyes on me. Eyes that said she had a scheme in mind that I wanted no part of. She was also a lawyer, after all. Family law.

"You know, it's good we ran into you."

"No," I said.

She pouted out her full bottom lip, which told me I was spot on in my assessment. "But you don't know what I'm going to say."

"It doesn't matter. Whatever you want, the answer is no."

"What if I told you I had a job for you?"

I raised a brow, seeing the lie for what it was. "Do you have a job?"

"Well, no. But I would like to ask a favor of you. It won't hurt you to hear me out."

Brody said nothing, watching the back-and-forth volley between his girlfriend and me.

"Fine, I'll hear it, but the answer is still no."

"We'll see... Anyway, my sister Jane needs someone like you."

"As in a lawyer? What legal problems does she have? I thought you said it wasn't a job."

"No, she doesn't need your legal advice. She needs a good fuck."

I choked on my drink I stupidly sipped when Penny explained her favor, spilling the whiskey all over the counter and on my tie. Dammit. Brody slammed my back, but this time I couldn't hide my scowl. As usual, my attitude unfazed him. Laid back motherfucker. Then again, I liked Daniel a lot because of his easygoing disposition. He was always the smartest and kindest out of the three of us back in college. He balanced out my bad attitude and Ronan's temper.

I grabbed some cocktail napkins and blotted up the liquor.

Seriously, the last words I expected Penny to utter was for me to bang her sister. No sister in her right mind would recommend me. I knew myself well enough that I wasn't good for women. I could give them the best orgasms of their lives, but beyond that, you wouldn't want to bring me home to Mom.

My eyes narrowed at her. "Why in the hell would you want me, of all people, to bang your sister?"

Penny took another sip as she gathered her thoughts. "Because she needs it. The last thing she needs in her life is a relationship until her life settles down. She recently started her own business, and it's taking up all her time. Her last job left all of us with a bad taste in our mouths. But my sis needs a fucking break. Literally and figuratively. Some sort of release. She's not the type to settle down any time soon, anyway, being highly independent as she is, which is why you two would be a good fit."

I chugged my whiskey and decided to switch to a Cabernet, mulling the favor over when I sipped my new drink. I didn't exactly struggle to find women to fuck. I was attractive enough and had the money. But having sex with a woman who had no interest in relationships would make things easier.

Sometimes women were okay with a quick fuck. But usually, they wanted more, despite agreeing to my terms.

"Not interested," I said. Not that I didn't want sex, but I didn't like the idea of her sister suggesting it, which could pose problems down the road if this sister wanted more from me. Then Penny would get on Brody's case, who would get on mine while at work.

"I realize it's a weird suggestion coming from a sister." Penny slid a business card my way. "But this would be good for her. She's done one-nighters before, so she won't be weird about it. And this is good for you, too, since you won't need to worry about those pesky little emotions."

I lifted the card, glanced at it, and shoved it in my sport coat's inner pocket. "Why me? What's wrong with her? Can't she find someone for herself?"

"Nothing's wrong with her," Brody said. "She's just…"

"Rigid. Very determined. Very picky. You're highly attractive, James—"

"Hey! I'm sitting right here," Brody said, feigning a pout.

She kissed his cheek and wiped away the lipstick again. "You're adorable, but I'm not setting you up with my sister. She can't have you."

I did a mental groan and eye roll.

"Anyway, you're a good-looking man with a good job, and you make your own money. And just like her, you're also highly independent. Yeah, you're not the warmest person, but you've got one thing that the men in her life didn't."

"Oh? And what's that?"

"Honesty and bluntness. You won't toy with her or play games. She's had way too much of that in her life."

Penny had a point. I never lied to women. There were enough men in their lives that did that. While I struggled to trust them, I wouldn't play with them either.

When I said nothing, she reached across Brody and placed a hand on my arm. "Just think about it."

"I'll think about it, but the answer is still no."

I waved at the bartender for my check to get out of there before I learned Brody and Penny were the next to tie the knot when a stunning dark-haired woman walked in. Even better, she was alone with no ring on her finger.

"Uh, oh. I've seen that look." Brody turned his head to watch the gorgeous brunette. "Well, go get her then. I'll see you on Monday."

"See you on Monday, Brody. Penny…"

"James."

Straightening my tie, I glanced at it to make sure I blotted up all the alcohol, left my drink behind, and ambled my way toward the lovely lady. She glanced over at me with a coy look and a sweet smirk. Oh, yes. She was going to be fun.

CHAPTER 2

Jane

THE BUILDING DIDN'T SIT IN THE BEST PART OF BOSTON, BUT I currently couldn't afford more. It had a private office, a reception area, a small space for files and a copier, and a bathroom. All the place needed was some new industrial carpeting and fresh paint on the walls. Maybe I'd paint them a different color to boost the mood. Something green or blue.

I glanced out through the only window in the place, not including the glass front door, which was large like it used to be part of a store-front, but it didn't have the best view. All I saw, looking out, were old buildings just like this one with brick facades. At least the window had blinds. I'd add curtains to spruce up the place and put a plant in the corner.

At least the big window allowed the sun to stream in. A little cleaning would brighten the place right up.

There was an underground clinic down the street, well-known by the police. The place did a lot of great work for the community, helping the less fortunate, but back when I was on the police force, we often wondered where the money came from. We had no evidence to show it was anything nefarious, so probably some philanthropists who wished to remain unknown funded the clinic. But it was pretty swank considering the area and who they treated.

What I liked even more about this office was the private upstairs leading to a small apartment. I'd been previously working as a private investigator out of my condo, but as the jobs came in, so did the money, and I didn't want strangers in my private home. So, I sold my place to invest in a real office.

The upstairs apartment wasn't nearly as big as my old condo and needed some renovations, but it had the potential to be cute and cozy.

The kitchen and bathroom needed updating, and if I had the time, I'd probably do most of it myself, saving me money. Dad taught his three daughters how to fix things ourselves, so I was pretty handy.

The apartment only had one bedroom, but the closet was big, and the living room was a decent size. Both the living room and bedroom had two tall windows each, nearly reaching the high ceiling, adding the illusion of space. What gave the place character was the old crown molding on the walls, which also needed work, but it was beautiful and a benefit of having a building built in the late eighteen hundreds. But I'd have to deal with the fire escape, making sure no one could open the windows from the outside. And definitely, a security system needed to be installed.

The entire place was for sale and not rent, which I preferred. It gave me more control over the property and no corrupt landlord to deal with.

"So, what do you think?" said the real estate agent with hair too bleached, long red fingernails, and wearing a pantsuit that was entirely out of place in a neighborhood like this.

"I'll take it."

Yep, this place called to me. It wasn't perfect, but nothing was. Just look at my last job. A job I loved until I didn't. After dedicating eleven years of my life to it, the betrayal ran deep.

"Wow, you're easy. This was the first place we looked at. Wonderful. I'll draw up all the paperwork and contract today. And you said you've got the money to put down, yes?"

"That's right." I had good equity from my condo, so I was able to put down money on this place with a little extra left over to fix it up. I also never did anything or went anywhere, allowing me to save my money as a detective.

Ex-detective.

The word ran bitter like a bad taste in my mouth.

I'd worked so fucking hard for that job, fighting less qualified men to climb to the top, but they were always put at the front of the line, so to speak. The tears threatened, and the last thing I wanted to do was cry in front of my agent. I rarely cried and hated to do it. Men especially saw it as a weakness. A weakness I couldn't afford to show in my line of work.

"I should have everything ready for you on Wednesday," said my agent. "How's that sound?"

"Good. What time?"

She scrolled through her phone, biting her bottom lip. "Hmm, how does three thirty sound?"

I checked my own calendar on my phone. I already knew I was free, but it made me seem like I had a well-established career. "Yes, that time works."

"Excellent! I'll put in the offer to the owners tonight and see what they say, but you should be in. You're offering what they're asking for, and they haven't had many people interested in the place. This should be a shoo-in for you."

I took one more walk-through in the office space, smiling. It would soon be all mine. Then I'd work hard on expanding my private investigative business.

It was early evening when I pulled up at my parent's house. We were a close-knit family, and we tried to catch up with each other every Friday. Having dinner once a week solved that.

I turned off the car, pulled out my gun from my holster, double-checked to make sure I had the safety off and locked it in my glove box. Being a cop for eleven years, I never left home without my gun, but I never brought it inside to my parents' house, nor the homes of my sisters.

My parents' place in Westborough, thirty minutes outside of Boston, was a brick colonial, painted white with black shutters. They bought the house after securing good jobs when I was around four years old and Penny had just been born. The house was large but not grandiose and had enough bedrooms that each of us sisters got our own room.

They had a neatly manicured yard with perfectly trimmed bushes surrounded by thick purple petunias. All of it was my mother's doing. She loved to garden when she didn't work as an accountant.

Dad was a professor at Harvard and tenured, teaching art history. School would be out next month for summer break, allowing Dad to hide away in his little studio in the backyard, where he tinkered with all sorts of projects around the house when he wasn't researching.

I opened the front door to smells of garlic and red wine, hoping Mom made her braised beef ribs with mashed potatoes. My favorite.

I loved this house which was filled with comfort, love, and more art than I'd ever seen in one house. There was no rhyme or reason to the furniture and decorating. The place was eclectic and chaotic, but it worked, filled with knick-knacks and books from Mom and Dad's travels across the globe. They tried to go overseas at least once a year.

Judging by the noise, my sisters had already arrived, along with my two nephews.

"Hello!" I called out.

"Auntie Janie!"

A tiny torpedo of a boy with dark hair came barreling at me and landed on my legs, hugging them for dear life. Followed behind him was a waddling toddler, giggling and trying to be just like his big brother.

"What's up, kiddos!"

I lifted Tristan, the smallest, into my arms and gave him a snuffle, making him laugh, then set him down to lift Tyler, whom I carried into the kitchen.

"So, what's the news? Did you get it?" My mom asked, wiping her hands on a dishtowel as I set Tyler on his dad's lap and made my way to the stove. I lifted the lid to the large pot and inhaled. Mmm. Yes, my favorite.

"You're the best, Mom."

She whacked me with her towel. "Out!"

I laughed as Penny handed me a glass of Cabernet, and I sat at the kitchen table with the rest of the family to stay out of Mom's hair as she cooked.

After I took a sip of wine, I smiled and said, "I got it. It's perfect. The apartment's a little small, but with some updates, it'll be cute."

"Oh, that's wonderful news. I'm so glad you're done being a cop. Jerks. You deserve better." Fiona rested a hand on my arm, giving me a sweet smile.

My parents had a James Bond obsession problem. Movies, books. It didn't matter. Of course, Dad's last name was Bond, making me wonder if that wasn't why he got interested in the first place. My name was a play on James Bond—Jane Bond, and people never tired of making jokes about it, and a never-ending annoyance.

They named Fiona after a Bond girl from the movie 'Thunderball,' and Penny after Moneypenny. But no, I was the unfortunate one to have a name that got the most teasing.

While Penny and I got our mousy brown hair and dark green eyes from Mom, Fiona got her dark hair and brown eyes from Dad. Except Penny lightened hers to blond.

"Well, we'll help you move in when you're ready," my brother-in-law, Carter, said. He was a bear of a man, and an entire foot taller than Fiona—than the rest of us, really—standing at six feet and seven inches, looking like a linebacker, but was a construction manager. He and Fiona had been high school sweethearts, and then they got pregnant at nineteen, so they married, and two years after Tyler was born, out came Tristan. And she was pregnant again. They hoped for a girl this time but decided to keep it as a surprise.

"Thanks, Carter. I appreciate any help I can get. There's a lot to move. At least they'll deliver all the office stuff."

"Good for you, honey," Dad said. He looked like the professor he was with thick black glasses, a beard threaded with grays, and thinning hair, but not quite bald. "We're all proud of you, no matter what you choose to do with your life. What a terrible thing it was that happened to you, but I'm happy you took control of your life. Now the police are short one amazing woman."

I smiled and leaned over to kiss him on his cheek. "Thanks, Dad."

Seriously, I had the best and most supportive family, being best friends with my sisters and with loving parents. And Carter was a sweet teddy bear who treated my sister like a goddess. I couldn't forget my adorable nephews.

After dinner, my parents headed upstairs to their room to read or watch a movie, while my sisters and I cleaned the kitchen. And Carter took the boys, who had both fallen asleep, home.

The three of us stepped outside onto the patio under the stars and surrounded by a lush landscape and tall trees. The evening was cool and typical for late April up north. But the days were nice. Penny came out with blankets and a bottle of wine.

"Ugh, I swear this is the last kid I'm having. I'm tired of not being able to drink," Fiona whined.

Penny poured herself and me a glass after handing each of us a blanket. I wrapped myself up in a lounge chair and sipped my wine.

"Have you thought about not having anymore?" Penny asked. "You're only twenty-four. By the time you're thirty, you could have three or more kids. You're like an incubator."

I snorted a laugh. "You do tend to get pregnant easily."

"Ugh, I know! I can't help it. Carter just smolders at me and, *bam!* I'm pregnant."

We all barked out a laugh. In reality, Fiona couldn't take birth control because she clotted easily from having thrombophilia, a genetic disorder, which she got from our grandfather on our mother's side. In fact, it was risky for her to be pregnant, but her doctors monitored her closely while she was on blood thinners. Though she whined about drinking, she was always careful.

Fiona rubbed her growing belly. "After this little punk, I'm going to try an IUD. I didn't want to use it yet because I wanted kids. But I think three kids is enough."

"It's your call," I said.

Penny curled up in a chair across from me and sipped her wine. "So... Jane."

"No."

She huffed. "You don't even know what I'm going to say."

"I know you. You may be a good lawyer, but you're still my sister. I always know when you're about to ask me for a favor."

"Ha! Well, you're wrong this time. It's not a favor. It's… a suggestion."

I sighed and narrowed my eyes at her. She was up to something, the busybody that she was. "Out with it, Pen."

"I may have found someone for you."

"No. Absolutely not. I'm not interested in dating. At. All. I need to get my life together first."

Penny raised her hand to stop me. "I understand that. This wouldn't be a… potential boyfriend. He doesn't do relationships."

"Great, so he's a misogynistic asshole. The very last thing I need, Pen. Especially after what happened that led me to quit my job."

"You do realize that not all men who don't date are misogynistic. There *are* other reasons." She waved a dismissive hand and stared at the blackened backyard. "But you're not wrong."

"There you go. End of story." I finished my wine and poured another glass. I planned to sleep in my old room tonight, so I didn't have to worry about driving.

"I think he'd be good for you to let off some steam. You've been moody lately, and for valid reasons. You're stressed. And he's sexy as hell. Hot in all the right places, plus he works with Brody at his law firm. This would just be for sex. Really, you're an independent woman, and this is the twenty-first century. Live a little. Besides, you've done one-nighters before."

I'd thought about doing just that, so I could let off some steam, but I wasn't the type to go out to bars alone and pick up random dudes for one-night stands. It wasn't my thing. Penny had her own life, and my only best friend, Colton, my ex-partner at the department, was gay and in a relationship. And no way I was doing one of those apps. There were only so many dick pics a girl could stand. Been there, done that.

"I just suggested it in case he calls. He wasn't interested, anyway. I felt he was perfect because neither of you wish to get attached. And I did mention he was hot, right?"

"God, you two… it's always about the sex," Fiona said, giggling.

"Says the woman who's pregnant for the third time."

Fiona burst out laughing. "Fair."

Penny turned her attention back to me. "Anyway, just think about it, in case he goes for it. I have a feeling he'd blow your mind, among other things."

What the hell? Why not? It wasn't as if I was trying, and if she felt he would be good in the sex department, then I trusted her. Penny was pushy and nosy, but she'd never steer me wrong.

"Fine, I'll think about it."

"That's all I ask."

"Busybody."

"Rude."

I snorted a laugh and took another sip of wine, leaning back in my chair to stare at the night sky. I felt freer than I had in a long time. A new career that was all mine, soon an office that I could call my own. Then my life would be fully in my control and not in the hands of the police department, who protected their own until they didn't.

CHAPTER 3

James

I PLACED THE NAUSEATINGLY SWEET AND OVERLY CARAMELIZED COFFEE on my PA's desk when I strolled into the office at eight in the morning. There were very few people in this world that I liked, and Samantha Goffe was one of the best—and one of the few who didn't put up with my shit. Like me, she was never married and chose a life of singlehood. At sixty-two, she never regretted her decision, stating her independence and career were more important. I respected the hell out of her for not bowing down to societal norms.

She wore her gray hair in a tight bun on top of her head today, refusing to color her hair, embracing her natural gray. While she was in her early sixties, she looked no older than fifty and beautiful for her age with bright hazel-green eyes.

"Thank you, James," she said, lifting the lid off of the cup and inhaling it. "Mmm, you spoil me."

"Only the best for my favorite person."

"Ass kisser."

I winked at her. "Only yours, my dear."

"Keep this up, and I'll file a sexual harassment complaint to HR."

"That would never happen. You love me too much."

"You're right. What would I do if you didn't keep me caffeinated with a perpetual sugar high?"

"Exactly. Honestly, it's *you* I can't live without. Any messages?" I asked, sipping my own coffee, straight-up black.

"Not this morning. I've got all your emails cleaned up and ready to be read, and I've sent you your calendar for the day. Oh, and Brody has requested lunch with you."

I rolled my eyes like some petulant teen. "Did he say why?"

"Don't be mean, James. Brody is a nice young man, and it would

do you good to make some friends around here. All your old friends
are busy with family lives now."

Wasn't that the fucking truth? Sam had no idea about what Ronan
O'Callaghan did for a living, being the leader of the Irish mob. Not
only were we best friends, but I also helped him out with legal snags,
which technically made me a part-time lawyer for the mob. And Ronan
compensated me, allowing me to live beyond my means. Even my
employers at Meyers & Levitt, LLC had no idea what I did on the side.
But she knew enough that Daniel and Ronan had been a part of my life
for nearly two decades.

"Don't remind me."

"Go have lunch and make friends, James. I set you and Brody up
over at Bobby's Kitchen. You know that new place that serves farm-to-
table dishes."

"Fine. You're so bossy."

"You love it."

"Only because it's you," I said, making my way into my office.

I removed my suit jacket and hung it up in my small closet. While
sipping my coffee, I stared out at the city from the sky above, looking
down at all the human ants. I only needed one case. That one case
would turn me from being a senior associate to a partner.

I'd been with Meyers & Levitt since I graduated from law school
ten years ago. Many law firms tried to recruit me, being at the top of
my class, and a graduate of Harvard and Harvard Law. But I chose the
smaller firm because it not only held the potential for growth, but I
stood a greater chance of becoming a managing partner. I tended to be
competitive by nature, but a firm with over five hundred attorneys
would have very little growth with the fierce competition. I could stand
out more with only fifty-three lawyers, clambering to the top.

My cell phone buzzed, yanking me out of my thoughts. I walked
over to my desk to see Ronan calling.

It was wishful thinking on my part that he was calling to tell me he
wanted to get out of the house, away from screaming babies and
married life to spend it on a night out with his best friend.

"Ronan."

"James. Listen, I'm calling because we're having a get-together with everyone on Saturday. It will be some outdoor grilling thing. Cat's idea."

I pinched the bridge of my nose. Fucking Ronan, leader of the Irish mob, went from playboy to family man, and now, apparently, a griller. Shit, Olivia wasn't even his daughter. But I'd arranged for her adoption when Ronan asked Cat to marry him. Or was it the other way around? Who the fuck cared? He kept pulling me into this family shit I wanted nothing to do with, and I only did it because I loved him and Daniel. Shit, all the O'Callaghans were my family. I guess Cat was okay, too. But unless he had mob business at the end of it, I wouldn't go to some fucking cookout.

"You've become a family man, and now you grill. Mob bosses of old are going to be rolling in their fucking graves."

"First, you realize I hate this mob shit. Second, I'm not fucking grilling. Fuck that. I'll hire someone to do it. Can you imagine me with a fucking spatula and an apron saying, 'Kiss the Chef?' I'd just ask someone to off me and put me out of my misery."

That was the Ronan I knew, swearing worse than a sailor and always salty like one.

"You aren't about to announce more children, are you? If you are, leave me out of it."

"What the fuck does that mean? You understand Cat's pregnant, right?"

"Never mind. Anyway, I'm not really into cookouts and family gatherings. You know this, Ronan. I've done my duty as your friend."

"Can't you put aside whatever issues you're fucking having for one damned night? I need you here, and I miss my best friend,"

Then you shouldn't have gotten married.

I didn't really resent him for it, but our lives no longer converged, drifting apart because our priorities had changed. Well, his did. Mine had always been the same.

Then Daniel fucking got married. Who knew he was even gay? I sure as hell didn't until he and Luke started having relationship problems, and he finally confessed to me one drunken night. Well, he wasn't gay but said he was pansexual. I still wasn't sure what that meant. He and Luke had been foster brothers together and had always cared deeply for each other.

That he kept his secret from me until he was drunk when he blurted it out, fucking hurt. Like he didn't trust me enough. I was still pissed that he hadn't told me. The three of us used to tell each other everything, and I hated lies. Omitting the truth was a form of lying in my book.

"Ronan, you're dragging me into this family world that I'm not interested in. I love you as a brother, Ronan, and I will continue to do my brotherly duties, but simple get-togethers while all of you have your fucking happily ever afters is… uncomfortable." It was uncomfortable as hell. Ronan wasn't wrong, but I refused to acknowledge the deeper-rooted issue. Nope. Time to fucking lock the door on that bad boy.

"You have the tattoo, fucker. That means you're a part of this damned family, whether you like it or not. How about stop being a fucking manwhore, and a whiny bitch, and grow up? Find someone to be with, so maybe you won't be so fucking resistant to being a part of this family."

I absently rubbed the tattoo on my chest, a Celtic triskelion, meaning family. Ronan and his three brothers got one when something happened to Cian when they were teens, leaving him despondent after dealing with their abusive, prick of a father. While in college, Ronan, Daniel, and I grew as close as any brothers, so Ronan had Daniel and me get the tattoo as well.

That didn't change the fact that I grew more and more resistant to spending time with my family. I knew why, too, but I couldn't go there. If I acknowledged it, then I'd be forced to do something about it. To change. And I didn't want to change.

"I'm never going to do that, Ronan. I'll never be tied down."

He gave me a derisive snort. "Yeah, that's what I said until I met Cat. It's fucking inevitable, brother. Give it up."

"Not if I can help it. I'll see you on the next holiday. Fourth of July, right?"

"Fine. Fuck you. I'll see you then unless we have another fucking catastrophe or attack against the family. Thank fuck, it's been quiet now that we've dealt with our enemies."

Ever since Ronan became leader, other mob families have tried to pluck him and his brothers off, but they'd been fucking lucky and stood strong. Not that Ronan was a fantastic leader. But between him and his brothers, they eked by, barely surviving it, thanks mostly to Cian.

"Call me if you need me before then," I said and hung up, tossing my phone back on my desk.

I felt cornered. Like Ronan was right, and this relationship shit was inevitable. Then I'd have to face my past. I'd kept that shit locked up tighter than a drum for so long, I wasn't sure if I could ever face it.

Fuck it. I'd worry about it if the time came.

————————

Brody was already at the restaurant when I arrived five minutes early. When I reached the table, he stood, and we shook hands. As soon as I sat, a young male waiter approached our table.

"Can I get you gentleman anything to drink?"

"I'll have gin and tonic," Brody said.

"Just water for me."

"Water? Boring," he singsonged.

"I don't drink that much, especially during the day. I enjoy being clear-headed and in shape. Three drinks at a bar are my max."

When the waiter returned with our drinks, I ordered the steak salad, and Brody ordered the fried chicken and waffles.

"Is there a reason behind this lunch?"

"So suspicious. Can't two co-workers have lunch once in a while?"

"They can. You still didn't answer my question. Answering with a question isn't an answer."

Brody gave me a toothy smile and spread his hands. "Well, I *am* a lawyer, after all. A good one, I might add."

"You're still beating around that proverbial bush, Brody."

He chuckled and took a sip of his drink. "There's nothing prover-bial about it. I definitely am. Fine. While I love Penny, she's pushy as fuck. She's determined to see you and her sister get it on for some fucking reason."

I sighed and pinched the bridge of my nose. "Not this fucking again."

"What can I say? I'm kind of in agreement with her, believe it or not. Her sister's had... a rough time. She needs a break. You'd be great for her temporarily."

"Dare I ask? What sort of a rough time?"

Brody spread his hands, giving me a sheepish smile. "It's not my story to tell, man."

"What's this troll's name?"

God, am I seriously contemplating this insane idea?

"Don't be a dick. Not everything revolves around beauty. Regard-less, she's nice to look at. She's no troll. Anyway, her name is Jane."

Our meals came, and we dug in.

"So, with you asking her name, does that mean you'll agree to this?"

"Nope. Not at all."

"I don't get it. You fuck women left and right. What's one more? Besides, it'll get Penny off my back."

"It's not about fucking another chick, but about you *knowing* this chick. If I do something to piss her off, I'm never going to hear the end of it from you and Penny. You two will be on my fucking case to make it up to this Jane for being an asshole."

He snorted a laugh. "Please. Since when have you cared what others thought?"

"I don't. I just don't want to hear it. And it sounds an awful lot like a pity fuck. The last thing I need is some woman crying under me."

Brody shook his head with pity in his eyes. "First of all... you're a real dick sometimes," he said, ticking off fingers as he counted. "But I like you, anyway. You know, not all women are like that when they're upset. Second, she's not the crying type. Third, I thought it was estab-lished that she doesn't do relationships. Besides, Penny chose you because you'll be honest with her sister, and you two will understand your boundaries right off the bat."

I waved a dismissive hand, done talking about it. "Whatever. I'll think about it. That's all I can promise."

"I'll let Penny know."

Friday night sex was aggressive, yanking clothes off, tossing them all over the fuck pad, biting, sucking, growling.

I lifted my woman of the night by her strong thighs, and she wrapped her legs tightly around me. She grunted in my mouth when I shoved her back against the wall. Hard. Then I slammed home with my cock in her wet cunt.

Long nails dug into my scalp as she tangled her fingers tightly in my hair. "Yes! Right there. Right there! Holy fuck, I love your cock."

"Yeah? Do I fill your sweet pussy nicely?"

"Yes…" she breathed.

"My cock loves your cunt, too. So fucking tight and wet."

"Oh god…"

I'd spent twenty minutes eating her out, making her come twice. Now it was my turn. I may have been an arrogant bastard, but I always satisfied my partner.

"Harder!"

Jesus. I wasn't sure I could. I'd been slamming into her as hard and fast as possible already, sweating from my efforts. She seemed to enjoy taking a bruising from my dick. The lady was a wild cat. Who knew when I picked her up at the bar? She seemed shy. The shy ones always had the best cunts. They had this hidden desire they rarely showed unless you could tap into it.

"Yes!" she cried out again. Soon, strong pulses gripped the fuck out of me as she leaked all over my cock. Her body went limp as I took it home, feeling my own impending orgasm. The extra grip had my balls painfully tight, sending me over the edge and spilling my load into the condom.

I pulled out of her and eased her back onto her feet. She gathered her belongings and stumbled into the bathroom without so much as a backward glance, while I headed to the second bathroom to get myself cleaned up. Digging around in the dresser, I pulled out some joggers and put them on commando. She came out fully dressed in her pencil skirt, heels, and retro blouse that was fluffy and tied at the neck. Her hair was done perfectly, as if I didn't just give her three fucking orgasms.

She *should've* been barely able to walk. Maybe I was losing my touch.

She ambled towards me and pressed a kiss on my cheek. "It's been a pleasure, James." Then she left.

She bored me. At least she left me alone when we wrapped it up. But I was still restless and bored. Not to mention, I was the only one using the fuck pad nowadays, which didn't help my mood either. Ronan, his brothers, Daniel, and I all bought it together. We'd bring girls here instead of our homes, so they had no idea where we lived. Though, Cian and Brady never used it that I was aware of.

The place felt unused and a waste. Sure, I used it, but it was missing my friends.

I rubbed the tattoo over my heart, squashing the pangs of loneliness. Fuck that.

Pouring myself a drink since I planned to sleep here, I sat on the sofa and pulled out the business card from my wallet sitting on the coffee table.

Penny—fucking—Bond, Family Law.

Why did that last name sound so familiar? And it had nothing to do with the movies.

I sipped on my bourbon, twirling the card between my fingers. The time on my phone read just after nine at night, and still early enough to call.

Fuck it.

I dialed the number on the card, and after a couple of rings, Penny answered.

"Penny Bond, Attorney at Law," she said.

"This is James Clery."

There was a pause before she replied.

"James. Nice to hear from you."

I wasn't in the mood for pleasantries. "Fine. I'll do it."

"Do what?"

"You're fucking kidding me, right? Don't toy with me. I'm barely agreeing to this crazy scheme you've concocted as it is."

She laughed on the other end, making me want to hang up on her.

"I'm only teasing. Don't get your boxer briefs in a bunch. Anyway, I'm happy you've finally agreed. So, when and where, and I'll make sure to get my sister there. She's as tentative about this as you are."

I sighed, regretting this already. "Tomorrow night, seven pm sharp. Does she like Thai?"

"She does."

"Then she can meet me at The Lotus Room."

"Nice. Expensive. You buying?"

"Of course. And if she's late, I'm leaving."

"She'll be there."

Fuck, it was like we were haggling or something.

I hung up before she talked me into something else, like donating my left kidney.

I'd probably fucking regret this. I felt it in my bones. The only reason I agreed was that it was something different. Plus, I was annoyed and bored.

CHAPTER 4

James

WHEN I ARRIVED AT THE RESTAURANT, SCENTS OF COCONUT MILK, curry, and fish sauce filled the air. It was one of my favorite places, serving more traditional Thai food and less of that Americanized crap. Food at The Lotus Room would guarantee to set your mouth on fire.

"I have a reservation for two. James Clery," I said to the hostess.

"Yes, Mr. Clery." She grabbed two menus and gave me a bright smile. "Follow me."

She set the menus down at a small private booth, per my request.

"My date isn't here yet. Her name is Jane. Would you mind showing her to my table, please?"

"Yes, Mr. Clery."

A Thai waiter greeted me not two minutes later. "Can I get you a drink, sir?"

"Just some water. I'll wait until she arrives, then we'll order."

He gave me a small nod and left.

I glanced at my watch. If she didn't arrive in five minutes, I'd leave. Normally, I wasn't such a stickler for time when it came to dates. I'd give them fifteen minutes, but I really didn't want to be here. Earlier tonight, I had spent it trying to talk myself into going and not canceling.

I glanced at my watch again, and with one minute to spare, I heard, "I'm here! I'm here! I'm not late."

I didn't know if I was relieved or annoyed that she showed up on time.

"Phew, traffic was killer tonight. There was an accident on—" She sat down, and looked at me wide-eyed. "You!" she hissed.

I scanned her features. She looked a lot like Penny but without the blond highlights, and her age looked to be in her early thirties, wearing a plain and boring outfit… atrocious, really. Like what a kindergarten teacher would wear with a simple knit green top to match her eyes paired with some atrocious floral skirt that looked like someone made it from bed linens back in the nineties. She was pretty enough with a button nose, full lips, and a splash of freckles. But her recognition of me told me she knew me, and it explained why she looked so familiar to me, too.

"Did… we share a night together already or something? I usually remember these things," I said.

She gave me a derisive snort and winged brow. "No, and thank god for that. You're that asshole lawyer who showed up at the police station a couple of years ago. Well, not quite two years, but almost."

I scanned her face again when it finally hit me. My evening just got exceedingly more interesting. My mouth curled into a smile as I leaned in, staring at her dead in those dark green eyes. "Well, if it isn't Bond. Jane Bond."

Her eye roll pleased me to no end.

"Yeah, you said that last time, too, as if I haven't heard it about a thousand times in my life. It *never* gets old. I really wish people would get new material."

"Well, it *is* a classic."

Detective Bond had been in charge of questioning Cat, Ronan's girlfriend and now wife, in the early fall of 2020. Her abusive ex-husband found her after she fled from Texas to Boston when she learned she was pregnant. Because Daniel taught her how to fight, when her prick of an ex caught up to her, she fought him, took his gun, and shot the fucker in the face. But the police had no choice but to arrest her.

That was where I came in. Ronan begged me to be her attorney during her questioning. And here sat the very detective from that day. I prevented Detective Bond from ever getting Cat's full story, especially with her involvement with Ronan. No way I would tell the police that she had been dating a mob boss or allow Cat to do so. They never charged Cat since it was clearly self-defense, so they were forced to let her go. Detective Bond wasn't happy with me. I was good at what I did for a living.

"God, I *knew* this was a mistake. I'm going to fucking kill Penny."

"I completely disagree. Before, it was a mistake. Now, it's interesting."

She folded her arms, clearly not amused with my bullshit. "You made my job fucking difficult that day."

"I *did* my job, and you know it. My duty was to my client. Not to you. Besides, you got your story… sort of, and your case closed. We all knew she killed her asshole ex in self-defense. But let's not talk about that and instead discuss more pleasant things, like what our plans are after dinner. Stay awhile, have some amazing Thai food, then we can talk about the rest of the evening's festivities. I'm looking forward to getting to know you, Bond. Jane Bond."

"This is going to be a long night… Fine. I'm only staying because I'm starving. And you're buying."

"Of course."

She smoothed her ugly skirt and placed a napkin on her lap. "Sorry about the outfit. I don't really own anything nice and didn't have time to buy something since you gave me only a day's notice."

Before I could say anything, the waiter returned. "Can I get you and the lady something to drink?"'

I glanced at Jane for her to order first. She looked at her menu for a list of cocktails. "Uhm… do you have anything refreshing that's not too sweet?"

"Yes, our most popular cocktail is the Lotus Refresher with Scotch whiskey, lemongrass, cucumber, ginger, and soda water. It's topped off with a sprig of Thai basil."

"Sounds yummy. I'll take that, please."

"And for you, sir?"

"Smokey Old Fashioned. And we will start out with your larb."

After the waiter returned with our drinks and appetizer, he took our order for dinner and left us alone to get to know each other. Jane stewed while I couldn't stop smirking. I loved little coincidences like this. It showed how small our world really was.

She'd barely spoken to me, probably to avoid as much conversation as possible. To get fed and leave, but not if I could help it. I had every intention of following through with Penny's request, curious to see what was under that horrible skirt.

Jane picked up a piece of cabbage, piled it with the ground chicken and kidney mixture, a slice of cucumber, and sticky rice, and topped it with basil. She took a large bite as I took a sip of my drink, waiting for her eyes to water and her face to sweat. The larb was one of my favorites, but it was also one of the hottest items on the menu.

Sure enough, her eyes popped wide and welled with tears. She fanned her mouth as if that would ease the pain, quickly swallowed her food, and chugged down her water.

"Eat the sticky rice. It'll help."

She ate half of it, much to my amusement, shoving it in her mouth as if she hadn't eaten in days.

"Ugh, stop laughing at me. You could've warned me."

"You didn't give me a chance, diving into it like a starving animal."

"I *am* a starving animal. I forgot to eat lunch today."

I actually enjoyed a woman who wasn't afraid to eat. Jane showed no hesitation in cramming her mouth full of food. Rabbit eaters were boring.

Jane sipped half of her drink down through the straw, and when the waiter returned, she ordered another.

Since she wasn't going to engage in conversation, I would. "So, Bond. Jane Bond. How's detective life?"

When she got her drink, she chugged half of that too. Interesting. I wondered if she was nervous. Or trying to blur her irritation with me. Probably the latter.

She sighed and sat back in the booth, finally looking at me. "There is no detective life. I quit several months back."

I raised a brow. Something must have happened. It took a lot of work to become a detective, yet it's apparently a highly rewarding job. Most don't up and quit.

"What made you leave?" I was honestly curious.

"Man, these drinks are really good." Jane finished her cocktail and waved the waiter over for another. She glanced out at the crowd, lost in thought. "It's a long story," she finally said.

"I've got time."

She turned to me with narrowed eyes, a furrowed brow, and a scrunched little nose. I wasn't sure why that made her cute, but it did.

"Please, you don't really care."

"You're right. I don't. But I am curious."

She rolled her glass between her hands and sighed. "Let's just say, no matter how hard women try sometimes, it's hard to fight fucking patriarchy. This bullshit bros mentality."

I took no offense. I may love fucking women and not commit to them, but I always believed they should be equal in all ways. Many of my acquaintances assumed I had no respect for women. Even my close friends believed it. But the opposite was true. I respected them enough to be honest and upfront. I didn't toy with them. So what if she never wanted to marry or have kids? So what if she wanted only one-night stands or to fuck several men? More power to her.

That didn't mean I trusted them, either.

"I take it some douchebag did something to you? Or maybe several?"

She still didn't meet my eyes, but she nodded. "My, uhm, deputy superintendent. He was always inappropriate with me. It started out as little microaggressions, but because I blew them off, they got worse. Soon, he was touching me. First, it was a touch on the small of my back, then an accidental brush of my breast with his hand. It didn't take long before he was trying to get me in bed with him."

"I hoped you filed a sexual harassment claim on him."

Jane appeared taken aback by my comment. No doubt assuming I sexually harassed women. As if I needed to or wanted to. That shit I took offense to.

"Don't look at me like that. All the women I've been with have done so willingly and voluntarily."

"Right. Sorry, I guess. It's a sensitive topic. And it's rare for someone to believe me. Anyway, so yeah, it got bad. Soon he pushed me for sex and used the job against me if I didn't comply. But I

refused, trying to let him down gently. Then files started going missing, evidence was lost, and he'd dump the worst cases on me. I mean...
I mean, I worked my butt off to become a detective, and why I joined the force in the first place." She finished her drink and ordered another.

"Don't you think you've had enough?"

If a scowl could kill, I'd be dead in seconds.

"Fine, drink up. Please, finish your story."

"Like all women who are faced with this, I was afraid I'd lose my job if I said anything, but fuck that, you know? But he was my boss and the deputy superintendent, making things extra difficult. I ended up filing a sexual harassment complaint against him, but it was useless. No one believed me because I didn't have any proof. So, I started digging around, keeping track of every little thing he did. But he covered his tracks well."

"Surely, there were other women he hurt. Men like him don't target just one woman."

He looked at me and nodded with wide eyes. "Very true. You're right. I found several women who'd gone through what I had. They never filed a formal complaint like me, but there are records of them going from excelling in their careers to suddenly being reprimanded for every little thing. Then they get the shitty jobs, evidence missing... just like me. I reached out to them, but they all refused to talk to me. There was no convincing them. One was a single mom, for example, who didn't want to further risk jeopardizing her career."

I never understood why powerful men took what they wanted when they could easily get whatever they wanted without tricks or by force. But it was usually a power trip for them more than anything. A way to control.

"It ended when the rest of the team got wind of what I'd done, turning their backs on me. No one believed me. Because I couldn't trust anyone to watch my back, I quit. What's the point? Even if they found that he harassed me, the damage was done. The men on the team would always assume I'd do the same to them... as if I wanted to ruin the deputy superintendent. The only one who believed me was my... my... my partner."

And there went the waterworks. I thought she wasn't a crier.

"Oh, god, I'm so sorry. I hate crying."

She blew her nose in the napkin and wiped her eyes.

Christ.

"I'll be back. Stay put," I said.

I left to pay the check and ordered our dinners to go. I may not have done relationships, but I wasn't about to leave my date crying in the middle of a restaurant.

When I got back to her, she had her face buried in her hands, looking entirely deflated.

"Let's go, Bond."

I lifted her by her elbow and helped her to stand, then wrapped an arm around her, so she could hide her tears in me. To anyone observing, all they'd see was an affectionate couple.

When we got outside, she pulled away and wiped her face. "I'm sorry. I don't normally get this upset. It's... taken its toll on me."

"Along with all the alcohol. It's a depressant."

She stared up at the night sky as her eyes welled again with quivering lips. "God, and I'm still hungry."

"That's why I got our food to go. I'm going to call for a car, and we can eat in private."

"No, I... can't do this. This was a mistake, and it's already been a disaster."

"I disagree." I should've let her go, but that little coincidence thing made me interested enough to keep going forward. Maybe it wouldn't pan out, but at least I'd get her fed. I did promise her dinner.

With my free hand, I lifted her chin to look at me. She stared back with fathomless dark green eyes full of water and questions. I leaned in and pressed my lips to hers. And just like that, she melted into me. Her lips parted open, allowing me to enter her with my tongue with absolutely no resistance, tasting like whiskey and cucumbers. That's what you call need right there. It seemed her sister wasn't wrong.

Her moan was that moment she woke up to realize where she was, and what we were doing. She got control of herself, easing me off of her. "No. Please just give me my food, and I'll call for a car myself to take me home. I don't need you distracting me with a kiss."

"How about this? Let's go back to my place and eat our dinner, so we can at least finish our date. If you want to go home after, I'll call a car for you. But I'd rather feed you, get some of that alcohol out of your system, and then blow your mind."

She gave me a snort and folded her arms, quickly recovering from her breakdown earlier. But at least she was thinking about it.

"I didn't think I'd be interested in your sister's scheme, but I am. How about it? Dinner, then see if we want more afterward?"

"Fine. Just dinner. I'll *think* about the rest.

I brushed a thumb across her cheek to wipe away a stray tear. "That's all I ask."

CHAPTER 5

Jane

JAMES-FUCKING-CLERY, ATTORNEY DOUCHEBAG AT LAW. WHEN HE stepped into the interrogation room almost two years ago, Cathryn Ruiz was about to tell me everything she knew about her ex-husband, but James Clery stepped in, only allowing her to explain what he wanted her to. Sure, he did his job, but it was with taunting, smirking, and arrogance. As if he was the prick of the mountain. Seriously, I had to deal with enough of that shit while working on the force.

Don't even get me started on his overuse of 'Bond. Jane Bond.' I worked my ass off to be a detective, and he couldn't be bothered showing me respect.

Not only that, but Cat had a lot of holes in her story. I couldn't fill them, making my position as a detective precarious because that was around the time my deputy superintendent started making his moves on me.

Penny knew I didn't like guys like James. I liked them to be nice, sweet, and patient. James was none of those things. Why would she set me up with him? Fine, he was sex on a stick… but still.

And dinner was a disaster, yet it wasn't even his fault, but mine. I drank too many of those delicious cocktails, and he listened to my sob story without interrupting or making it all about him. Then I cried. How humiliating. All I wanted to do was crawl under a rock and hide with some delicious Thai food. Instead, I let James kiss me, with tears and all. Then he steered me to the car, waiting to take us to wherever. At least I knew he wasn't some deranged serial killer. Hopefully.

The smells of spice and curry wafted through the car, making my stomach growl. Ugh, nightmare. The entire night was a mortifying wreck. Another reason I rarely dated. I not only got tired of men treating me as if I was nothing more than meat, but I wasn't good at it.

And most of my adult life I spent working my ass off in college and fighting to reach detective. I spent the rest of my free time with my family.

"Feel better?" he asked, staring out the window. Did he really care, or did he ask because it was the proper thing to do? There was no denying he was a womanizer. You could smell them a mile away. But he hid me away from others as I made an ass of myself, protecting me. He could have easily left me there alone, wallowing in self-pity and empty drinks, but he didn't.

Whatever. I didn't have time for relationships. He didn't do them either. So, it didn't really matter who or what he was at the end of the day. I'd eat my dinner; then we could see where the night took us. After that, we'd never have to see each other again. Maybe sex was exactly what I needed. Take my mind off of the wreck that was my life.

"I feel like an idiot," I said.

He turned to face me with a sexy smirk and smolder. Penny didn't lie. He was hot as hell. I remembered how good-looking he was when we first met, but I'd been too agitated at the time to care. His eyes had that perfect sort of blue you see on a clear summer day. He kept his dark blond hair neat, without a stray. Even his outfit was precise and wrinkle-free, wearing pressed dark denim jeans with a lavender button-up and a navy sport coat.

And don't get me started on the perfect amount of blond scruff on his face on that chiseled jaw. Jesus.

Unlike me. Even my outfit was a disaster. The skirt used to be my mom's since I didn't have one and always wore jeans. I felt completely out of place, if not a bit out of James' league. He probably slept with every supermodel who crossed his path.

"They told me you weren't a crier. I worried this was about a pity fuck."

"Ugh. Honesty is good, douche head, but no need to be brutal about it."

"Honesty is always brutal."

"That's a terrible way to look at it."

"It's better than the alternative."

What did he mean by that? I turned to face him, but I couldn't see his expression as he stared out at the city as we drove by.

"How's this for honesty?" he asked, facing me again. "Now that I know it's you, Bond, I look forward to our evening. It got exponentially more interesting as soon as you sat down across from me... crying or not crying."

"It would be better if I believed that wasn't some backhanded compliment."

"Gaining my interest is always a compliment."

I rolled my eyes. "Gross."

He glanced at me with that arrogant smirk of his. "You won't think so by the end of the evening."

"Double-gross. God, you can't help yourself, can you?"

"I'm always honest unless I'm trying to win a losing case, of course."

"Let me guess... you never lose."

His blue eyes gleamed. "Never."

Smug bastard.

The car pulled up to a building of luxury condos. Condos I'd never be able to afford in my lifetime.

"Is this where you live?"

"No. I don't take women to my private home."

"So, this is what? A fuck pad?"

"Precisely."

I tried not to let the idea make me feel cheap, reminding myself that I wanted to fuck, he wanted to fuck, end of story. Nothing more. Nothing less.

When we slipped inside the condo, James busied himself reheating our dinner and plating our food. While he did that, I took in the place. It was comfortable, with a fantastic view of Boston, but it had that unlived-in hotel vibe. There was nothing personal in the space.

"Let's eat and stop your stomach from trying to have a conversation with me."

I sat down as he placed a plate in front of me.

"So, what do you do now that you're no longer with Boston's

finest, Bond?" he asked mid-bite after we'd eaten half of our meal in silence.

I chewed on my green chicken curry as I told him with my mouth full. "I'm a newly licensed private detective and recently bought an office in South Dorchester."

"Good for you for keeping up with the independent theme, but you're not working in one of the safest neighborhoods."

"It's affordable. Besides, I can take care of myself."

"I don't doubt it."

"Are you poking fun at me?" I narrowed my eyes at him.

"I'm always serious about poking, but not in the way you think."

The chicken dropped into the pool of curry sauce in my bowl, spattering all over my shirt as I coughed from his comment. My mind hadn't decided if it wanted to laugh or be annoyed. "Dammit!"

I glared at his broad smile, entirely too pleased by my reaction.

"Asshole," I muttered.

That brought out a laugh from him. It was deep and throaty and too damn sexy.

"And here I thought you weren't capable of laughing," I said to turn my lady bits back to the off position.

"I don't do it often enough, but you bring it out of me, Bond."

"Yay me. Another backhanded compliment. This date is going swimmingly if I do say so myself."

At least I felt fed now and not buzzing anymore.

James huffed a laugh, stood from the table, and offered me his hand. When I took it, he pulled me up and leaned in close. I felt the heat from his skin and his breath ghosting my neck. I inhaled some smoky, spicy scent which had my body instantly reacting to him. My breathing and heart picked up a notch in speed. Long fingers grazed down my sides and trailed along the small of my back, slightly tickling me. He then grabbed the hem of my top with both hands and easily pulled it over my head and off my arms.

While holding my shirt in a fist, his blue eyes grew black with heat, and he stared unwaveringly at my body, scanning every inch of my flesh. I liked to take care of myself with Tae Kwon Do and workouts when I could squeeze them in, so I was fit. If I was proud of anything, it was my body. I didn't have the biggest boobs or the ultimate butt, but I was tight.

"You look better already, not wearing this hideous shirt. I'd rather burn your clothes, but I'll just toss them in the wash to remove the curry."

"My skirt is fine."

He glanced down. "No, it's not. You have a large blob of green between your legs. I realize it's hard to tell with that... floral print."

I refused to be baited. "You're just trying to get me naked."

"That too."

James tossed the shirt on the floor and stood toe to toe with me. Reaching around me, he unclasped and unzipped my skirt, letting the fabric pool around my ankles. I closed my eyes to inhale his yummy scent as I suddenly throbbed between my legs. I wanted to resist him, but just his nearness set me on fire. Despite him being an arrogant ass, my body didn't give a shit, apparently.

Hell. When was the last time I even had sex? It must have been a while, judging by my reaction.

With long fingers, he lifted my chin to look at him. "Step out of the skirt, Bond."

He didn't remove his hand as I did as I was told, but his brows furrowed when I bit my bottom lip, glancing up at him through my lashes. With a thumb, he eased my lip out from between my teeth. "Not yet, sweet girl. I've got to throw your clothes in the wash first."

He bent down to pick up my clothes, grabbed my hand, and led me to the living room.

"Stand here, and don't you dare move."

He didn't wait for me to respond, to defy him, or to do as I was told when he left the room.

I stood with my arms wrapped around me and suddenly felt awkward being half-naked.

You know what? Fuck him. If I want to sit, I will.

I plopped my ass on the couch, sinking into it. Oh, that was nice. I wish I could afford a fancy sofa like this.

My hands roamed across the soft fabric as thoughts of being fucked on it by James crossed my mind. It was why I was here, right? It was only sex. Afterward, I'd never have to see him again. Not that I'd want to.

"Is there a reason you're sitting instead of standing as you were told?"

The tone of his voice heated me between my legs, but I waved a dismissive hand, ready to be defiant. It was bad enough that he was arrogant, but bossy too?

Please, your body likes it.

Shut up, body.

"I felt like sitting."

"Is that so?"

"Yep."

His smile was crooked when he grabbed my hand and helped me to stand again, pressing me against his hard body—his really, really hard body—I tried to swallow the sudden lump in my throat at his intense gaze. James reached around me and, with little effort, unhooked my bra and eased it off of me. And I let him, but it took everything I had not to cover myself up.

My eyes fluttered closed when he cupped my breast and grazed his thumb across my nipple. He had my body instantly in tune with him. My panties grew wet, and I groaned.

God, I was so damned touch starved.

"You have a gorgeous body, Bond. It was hard to tell under those ugly clothes." James' voice was deeper, and throatier than earlier, making my body heat even more.

His large hand slid across the small of my back, and his face nuzzled my throat, sending waves of goosebumps across my skin. With his other hand, he slipped it in beneath my panties and slid a finger inside my entrance.

"Mmm, someone's wet for me."

I hid my flaming face in his neck as he fingered me, not used to men talking dirty to me. Sure, I've had one-night stands, but they never talked the way James did, if at all.

And just like that, he removed his hand, and I swear, my body thrust at him for more of its own volition.

He chuckled at my reaction. "Patience. Remove your panties, Bond."

He watched me do as I was told while he unbuttoned his shirt and slid it off his arms. Holy shit, he was cut with rippling abs. Now I understand the term, 'washboard stomach.' And that tattoo on his left pec was interesting. It looked Celtic with three wolf heads. I wondered what it meant.

"Do you like what you see?"

I just nodded like an idiot, not taking my eyes off his stomach and chest.

"What's that tattoo mean?"

His eyes clouded for a second but left just as quickly. "It's not important right now."

James didn't remove anything else and sat on the sofa. With cat-like reflexes, he grabbed my arm. One minute, I was standing there naked; the next, I was sprawled over his lap with my ass in the air and my arms pinned at my back.

"I think you like testing me, Bond, pushing my buttons. You wanted to know how I'd respond if you disobeyed. Do you know what happens to sweet girls when they're naughty?"

I shook my head, suddenly unable to speak.

"They get spanked. Is that what you want, sweet girl? To lie bent over my knee and be spanked until you behave?"

I swallowed hard as my body trembled with need, and I soaked my panties. Holy shit. His words had me on fire as he continued to smooth his hand over my ass. I'd never been spanked before, but why was it suddenly very hot and appealing?

"When it comes to the bedroom, *sweet girl*, I expect you to do as you're told. If I tell you to stand there, I expect you to stand. If I tell you to get naked, you'll do so without complaint. Is that understood?"

What a weird sensation. I wanted to be defiant, yet my ovaries were on fire. How the hell did he do that?

"And you'll spank me if I don't?" My question came out as more of a squeak.

"Yes, I'm going to spank you now. Naughty girls need to be spanked." He smoothed a hand over my ass again, making my body thrum with excitement, anticipation, and heat.

Because I didn't fight him or get off his lap... or tell him no. He gave me one hard smack, testing my boundaries.

I heard the slap before I felt the sting on my ass.

After I groaned and still didn't fight him, he gave me four more slaps. By that time, I was squirming, and my ass was on fire. I wanted to be angry and embarrassed, but fuck... I was so turned on and pulsing with a strong achiness. Who knew I'd enjoy being spanked? No man ever dared before.

His fingers inserted deep into my core, then he used my juices to glaze over my clit.

"Oh, god..."

"I knew you'd like this. You have this look and demeanor that begs to be taken control of. It's okay. Be as defiant as you want, sweet girl. I'm happy to spank you all night until I have you begging me to let you come."

"Yes," I breathed, having no idea what I was saying 'yes' to.

"I can always tell the ones who need to be controlled, and there's nothing wrong with that. In fact, I'm more than happy to give you what you want."

I squirmed on his lap, feeling his erection poking into me as he spanked me several more times. Fuck. Why did I find this so hot? I was completely exposed, vulnerable, and at his mercy, yet I'd never been turned on so much before.

"Are you going to listen and be a good girl now?"

God, I wanted to be defiant, yet give in. When I didn't answer, he smacked me two more times. "My hand prints look amazing on your gorgeous ass. I could do this all night, but I'd rather taste you and then fuck you."

"Yes," I said.

"Yes, what?"

"Yes, I'll… be good." I winced when I admitted that.

I had no idea what to expect from a sexual encounter with James other than to fuck and be done with it. But this was on an entirely different level of sexual fun.

James helped me sit up. I hid my reddened face as I rubbed my sore ass. But, admittedly, it hurt in a good way.

"Take off my pants and briefs."

Without question or hesitation, I unbuckled his belt, unzipped his jeans, and pulled everything off of him as he sat there, including his underwear, tossing them to the side on the floor. But I couldn't take my eyes off his cock. It was long, wide, and velvety smooth, all nestled in trimmed, dark blond hair. I reached for it on instinct, but he grabbed my wrist and pulled me onto his lap.

When I straddled him on the sofa, he reached behind my head, wrapped my hair around his hand, and pulled me close until our lips hovered over each other.

"Kiss me, Bond."

My hands rested on his firm pecs as we pressed our lips together. His lips weren't overly full, but they were strong yet soft and warm. Possessive. He eased his tongue in, exploring my mouth and controlling the kiss with his tight grip on my hair. Shit, he was a good kisser.

I chased his mouth when he pulled me back. My eyes fluttered open, then widened when he slipped a finger into my wetness. I moaned because, damn, I missed being touched down there. He removed his finger and inserted it straight into his mouth.

"I knew you'd be delicious."

Jesus.

In one swift movement, making me yelp, I landed on my back on the couch with James hovering over me. He gave me a brief kiss before he moved down my body with his lips, lingering on my breasts long enough to get my nipples pebble hard.

"Pull your legs apart and hold them open for me."

It was a vulnerable position, but James seemed to enjoy putting me there. Fine, I liked it too.

When I did as I was told, he slid his hands under my ass and lifted me to his awaiting mouth.

Yes!

Fuck, yes!

Holy shit, he was good.

He consumed me like I was his only source of sustenance, dragging his tongue from my pucker to my clit, tongue fucking me. He'd swirled, suckled, and nipped until he had me writhing under him. And as I teetered over the edge, he pulled away, making me cry out for more.

My fingers threaded through his perfect hair, pulling his face back to where I needed it, but he'd only kiss my thigh or lick just outside of my pussy. I fucking throbbed so much for his mouth and to come that it almost hurt.

"No… please."

"Please, what, sweet girl? Tell me what you want."

"You already know."

"Say it."

"Ugh." I tried to ignore the heat crawling up my face and took the plunge. "I need you to make me come with your mouth."

"Good girl."

And for that, he rewarded me with total abandon on my pussy and clit. His blue eyes kept steady on me as I watched him consume me.

So hot.

So sexy.

All his man-whoring paid off, apparently.

That build-up of pressure had my eyes rolling into the back of my head, along with my toes curling, and a second later, he finally let me fall into sexual oblivion.

I barely recognized the sounds coming from my mouth as I thrust into his face. Desperate for more, yet it grew to be too much. The strength of my orgasm left my body shaking from the aftershocks. Wave after wave of them.

Once I came down, my body lay there limply. James hovered over me with a shit-eating grin on his face and lips glistening with my release.

"Proud of yourself?" I asked.

"Yes, now taste yourself. I want you to enjoy what I did."

He thrust his tongue in my mouth, and I could taste my tang and musk, which was arousing as hell.

James pulled away and climbed over me until his large cock hovered over my mouth. His leaking tip brushed my lips, and I licked his bitter pre-come off. "Open up, Bond."

As soon as I opened my mouth, he eased himself inside. At least he took care not to choke me but tested how far he could take it. The skin was velvety smooth, and while he smelled like all man, full of pheromones and musk, he had the lingering scent of his smoky and spicy cologne or body wash or whatever he used. The cumulative scents intoxicated me. Like he spent years perfecting his scent for ultimate arousal of the senses.

My hands reached around and grabbed his ass to do a little teasing of my own, fingering his hole, then I shoved the tip of my finger inside. I secretly enjoyed his hiss, thrusting deeper into my mouth. Breathing through my nose, I swirled my tongue over his fat cockhead when he pulled out. Damn, he had a pretty dick.

"That's enough. Don't you dare move unless you want to be punished again?"

When he climbed off of me, he headed towards his pants on the floor, digging through his pocket for his wallet. I rolled over onto my side to stare at his gorgeous backside full of rippling muscles and a smooth, round, firm ass.

He pulled out a condom, tore it open, and quickly put it on.

"On your hands and knees."

When I didn't move fast enough, he smacked my ass, making me yelp and quickly doing what I was told.

After pressing two kisses on my ass, he grabbed my hips and plunged. There was no easing into it. No adjustment. I took his cock as if my pussy was made for it.

He situated himself inside me without thrusting. One of his hands slid up my back and snaked around my throat, forcing my head back. It was tight enough to make me uncomfortable but not to hurt me. Only then did he pull out and slam it back home.

The way he situated my head made my back arch, giving me no control over my body. James completely owned it as he fucked me hard and deep.

"So, tight… Jesus."

As he gripped my throat tighter, he pounded into me, and with his other hand, he grazed his thumb over my tight hole, sending a wave of pressure and euphoria through me, especially, when he hit that sweet spot. A spot that's never made me come before, but always felt good.

A sheen of sweat glistened over my body as he worked me. Controlling me. Owning me. There was nothing I could do but take his sweet, big cock.

But he kept hitting that spot over and over and over. The pressure built and tingled. And when he forced his thumb deeper inside my hole, that was the end. For the second time tonight, I exploded into another orgasm. And for the first time ever, I came during sex.

"Fuck," I groaned, pulsing all around him.

"Shit, Bond…"

I fell onto the couch as I chased my orgasm, and James loosened his hold on me. He grabbed my hips, lifted my ass up, and slammed back home over and over and over. Deeper and deeper. Faster and faster. There was nothing I could do but take him, leaving me with a whirlwind of sensations, making me dizzy.

James froze as soon as his cock swelled in me and filled me with pulsing heat as he came into the condom.

"Shit, shit, shit…" he breathed.

I had a stupid, blissed-out grin on my face, buried in the pillow at his reaction.

Fine. He was good. Really good. Best sex ever, kind of good.

Instead of pulling out right away, he lingered and pressed kisses to my back as a lover or a partner might, rather than a one-night stand. After he finally pulled out, he gently rubbed my back, digging into knots I didn't know I had.

"Fuck, you were tight as hell, Bond."

I yawned and groaned into the pillow, suddenly sleepy. Between all the hot sex, the relaxing massage—and probably those drinks—that was it. I could barely keep my eyes open.

James got up to do something, leaving me cold, but it felt good against my heated skin. My eyes fluttered closed before I reached darkness.

CHAPTER 6

James

AFTER I GOT CLEANED UP IN THE BATHROOM AND TOSSED THE CONDOM in the garbage, I headed to the kitchen and poured Bond some water. She was going to need it after all those drinks and all that sex.

I called it.

I knew she'd be into me taking control. But after what she'd been through with her deputy superintendent, it could have been a hit or miss, but her body practically cried for someone to take over for a while, and I was happy to give it to her. What a needy little thing she was.

And damn, she was tight, as if she hadn't had sex in a long time. Admittedly, it was hot and felt fucking good. Her little noises when I spanked her were cute, too. At first, it shocked her, but soon it turned her on as she gave in to me.

When I reached her, she was still lying on the couch with ash brown hair spilling in her face. "Drink up, Bond. I need to get your clothes into the dryer. Though I should just make you go home naked instead of putting back on those ugly clothes."

When she didn't move or answer, I combed away the hair from her face to see her eyes closed and her mouth open… fucking sleeping.

Shit.

I gently shook her. "Up and at 'em, Bond. You can't stay."

She snuffled and rolled over in answer.

Women never stayed over. Ever. I always called them a car if they needed it, but they had to leave after the fun and games were over.

I tried one more time to wake her up, but nothing short of a nuclear blast was working. That woman slept like a rock.

I blew out an irritated sigh. Fine. My only recourse was that she apparently didn't want a relationship. So hopefully, no feelings got involved.

I brought her water to the bedroom and set it on the nightstand, tossed her clothes in the dryer, found her purse, and pulled out her phone, which I also set on the nightstand. I didn't know if she had an alarm or not. Then it was time for the boulder herself.

I scooped her up, carried her into the bedroom, and eased her onto the bed. She didn't even flinch. I climbed in next to her and covered us both with the thick comforter. And after some tossing and turning, not used to sharing a bed with someone, I finally fell asleep an hour later.

A strange sort of comfort and warmth woke me up, along with a thin line of light filtering in through the thick curtains. I tried to roll over, but a warm pressure and weight on my chest left me unable to move. I cracked an eye open to see Bond snuggled into me with an arm and leg draped over my body. Her sleeping face was relaxed and soft, making her prettier and younger. She was pretty already, but in that girl next door kind of way. I was more of a tall supermodel kind of guy.

The kind of women that make it easy to not get attached to.

Fucking errant thoughts.

Regardless, I couldn't have her hanging on me. We weren't a damned couple. But when I tried to move her off of me, she clung tighter. Was she messing with me right now? No, her face was too relaxed, and her breathing too steady.

I tried to escape her snuggling clutches again, but she rolled virtually on top of me, and her hand climbed to my hair, where she threaded her fingers through it.

Great. I had a high-maintenance snuggler on my hands. And I was far from being the snuggling type. I didn't cuddle.

"Alright, Bond. Time to stop mimicking a blanket."

This time I wasn't as gentle and practically lifted her off me and back onto the bed. She barely even stirred as she rolled over to her other side.

I breathed out a sigh of relief.

Fuck, that woman slept like the dead. How did she manage to get up on time for her job?

Before I crawled out of bed, her alarm went off on her phone, and she bolted upright. After quickly turning off her phone, she yawned, stretched, and climbed out of bed as if she hadn't been my personal blanket a minute ago.

Still completely naked, she made her way over to the closet and looked around as if she fucking lived here. Then pulled out one of my button-ups, tossing it on.

What the hell was happening?

I was left speechless, not used to waking up with women. Bond then turned to me and gave me a smile and a little finger wave, looking half asleep and cuter than I would have liked.

One minute I couldn't get her off of me, the next, she was bright-eyed and bushy-tailed.

"Morning, grumpy pants. Not a morning person, eh?"

I must have been scowling or something.

Before I could muster a response, she reached behind her to scratch her back and padded to the bathroom.

"Do you have a toothbrush?" she called out over the banging of drawers and cabinets. "Never mind. I found one."

I huffed at her making herself right at home. Thank fuck we didn't stay at my place. Climbing out of bed, I dug around in the drawers, pulling out a pair of boxer briefs, a T-shirt, and a pair of joggers and putting them on.

When I stepped out into the kitchen, I found her rummaging through the pantry, bending over, and exposing her adorable naked bottom. *Adorable?* It was like we were fucking married or something.

"Do you mind?"

Bond looked over her shoulder. "Oh, are you going to make it?"

"Make what, pray tell?"

"Coffee. What else?"

I struggled not to pinch the bridge of my nose. "Yes, I can make it. Then you need to go home."

"Boy, you *sure are* grumpy in the morning, but you're even cuter when you're all rumpled with messy hair. I bet it's a rare treat to see you not completely put together."

"I'm not… never mind."

"Great! While you make the much-needed caffeine, I'll get dressed."

As she headed out of the kitchen, she stopped, grabbed my face with two hands, and pulled me down into a kiss, smelling of toothpaste and the lingering smell of sleep and sex.

Fucking flabbergasted. That's what she made me.

When she pulled away, her smile was bright, and she gently patted my chest. "I had a fantastic night last night. I'm glad you talked me into this. But don't worry, grumps… no feelings are forming on my end, and I know you're itching to get me out of here. Just make sure I'm caffeinated, and we'll call it even."

I rubbed the back of my neck when she stepped out of the kitchen; not used to this at all. Not used to sharing space unless it was for sex. Or kisses in the morning. Or women wearing my clothes. Or fucking snuggles.

Infernal woman.

Even worse? I didn't fucking hate it.

It was chilly at six in the morning as I stretched my legs on a park bench, knowing I'd warm up soon enough. The run would do me good. I needed something to get Bond out of my fucking head. That morning with Bond ran through my mind each day for the past week, looking entirely too cute in my shirt and with sleep-head. And it irritated the hell out of me.

Whatever. It didn't matter. There would be nothing more between us. We both got a fun sexual encounter out of it. End of story.

Yet, she remained rent-free in my fucking brain.

I shoved in my earbuds and scrolled through my music until I found the song perfect for running, then strapped my phone to my arm.

'Tribulations' by LCD Soundsystem was a great song to run to, with its upbeat tempo at just the right speed to keep me going. I started my run at a steady pace, not too fast and not too slow.

There were other joggers out, but not too many, being so early. I loved jogging at Back Bay Fens, also called the Emerald Necklace Conservancy, a large parkland set in the middle of the city, near Fenway Park. It was filled with gardens, trails, ponds, and a few memorials. The place was relatively quiet despite being smack dab in the middle of a city.

Despite the beauty and the music, fucking Bond wouldn't get out of my mind. Flashes of her cute tush bending over as she rummaged in the kitchen, or her sleepy face as she tangled her body around mine. Then my mind went straight to her tight as fuck pussy. All of it seared into my brain unhindered.

Even worse, I struggled not to acknowledge my annoyance when she kissed me, and patted me on the chest like some child, telling me she wouldn't get feelings. What kind of patronizing shit was that?

She called you out on your shit is what she did. That's what you get for fucking a former police detective.

Before I could dwell on it further, my phone buzzed. I stopped and breathed in slowly, in and out, to steady my heart, so I didn't pant on the phone, then I answered.

"What's up, Sam?"

"You may want to head into the office soon. Mr. Meyers has a case for you. He wants a meeting at eight. This could be big, James, and be the break you've been looking for. It's going to be high profile if it pans out."

"Thanks for the heads up, Sam. I'll be in shortly."

I hung up, and as I made my way to my car, I put in a quick call to Callum before I changed my mind. Part of it was curiosity. But the other part? I didn't want to think about why I was really doing it.

"Dude, this better be good. It's like the crack ass of dawn," he said, yawning.

Callum had been through the wringer the past eight months. The Bratva had been after the O'Callaghans, and one of them shot Callum four times. The last bullet landed in his spine. They said it was a million-dollar shot that only left him with a partial spinal cord injury, which allowed him to learn to walk again. He was walking better, but it wasn't without a lot of work from his physical therapist and now girlfriend.

"Who's the deputy superintendent of the Boston P.D.? I believe it's District B-2, Roxbury. He would be the deputy superintendent of the Bureau of Investigative Services, Homicide Division."

"Ugh, hang on... Fin? Can you make some coffee while I work for the early rising asshat on the phone?"

After a minute, he was back. "I should know this as I'm supposed to keep track, but there are a lot of fucking cops in Boston." I heard the clicking of a keyboard as Callum yawned again.

"Here we go... Joshua Eakin. He's got a lot of commendations and shit. Why are you looking into him? I bet he's not as squeaky clean as he looks. He's too perfect."

"Exactly. Apparently, some shit has been covered up. He's a sexual harasser, but I'm only aware of one woman. A prick like that will mess around with several of them. Can you try to dig some shit up on him? Like intentionally giving the shittier jobs to women, removing evidence. Shit like that. I'm sure he tried to bury any complaint as well."

"Is this a case you're working on?"

"No."

There was a pause, then a chuckle. "Oh, is this a *lady* friend we're helping out?"

"It's just a friend."

"By friend, you mean a friend you're porking?"

"Jesus, Cal. What are you? In middle school?"

"Middle school humor is my forte, along with elaborate fart jokes. You should know this by now."

"Just see what you can find, please."

"Absolutely-dilly-o."

How did the O'Callaghan family hacker grow to be such a man-child? Callum took nothing seriously. Except hacking, which he excelled at.

———

I stepped into the office with fifteen minutes to spare, straightening my tie. This time, it was Sam who had coffee waiting for me. I took a tentative sip and sighed. Bless this woman.

"Here's the file Mr. Meyers wants you to scan over before the meeting. It's a potential divorce."

I winged a brow. "Isn't this Brody's normal territory?"

"Mr. Meyers wants you personally on this one, besides, Brody is tied up with several cases as it is. But this one is especially tricky with a potentially hefty payout."

Interesting. It must be tricky and worth a lot if Leo dumped it on me.

"This is why I think this could be the big one. Look at the name."

I opened the file to see Ms. Rikke Madsen, who was a Hollywood darling, as the plaintiff... sort of. She hadn't brought a case against her husband, Anthony Newall, yet, who was a big-time architect here in Boston. A quick scan claimed he was cheating on her, and she basically wanted to take him for all he was worth.

"What's the story?" I asked Sam, knowing she'd already read the file. "Why hasn't she hired anyone for evidence?"

She shrugged. "I'm sure Mr. Meyers will let you know."

I took my coffee and the file and headed to the small conference room where Leo was already waiting.

"Morning," I said.

"James, good to see you."

Leo Meyers was a criminal attorney who looked more like a pit bull than a lawyer. He was fifty-eight, with an expansive gut, and about three inches shorter than my six feet. He had dark hair and a thick beard, both sprinkled with gray. And in the middle of his craggy face were dark brown eyes.

We shook hands, and I sat next to him, opening the file.

"I trust you've looked over it."

"I scanned it. Why does Ms. Madsen believe her husband is cheating on her?"

"I'll let her explain all that to you this afternoon. She's coming in to meet with us at two."

"And is there a reason she hasn't hired a private investigator to follow him around? Where's the evidence?"

"Unfortunately, it's all circumstantial, but she suspects he's actually having an affair with a man, and she's pissed. Not only would he be cheating on her, if it's true, but he's lied to her the entire time they've been married for the past eight years."

"I would be, too." And this was why I'd never marry, but I didn't tell Leo that, who'd been married for over thirty years.

"If we catch this bastard in the act, the settlement could be in the millions for us. This would put Meyers & Levitt on the map, especially with the famous name attached to the case."

"I understand. I'm curious, though… Why us? We're small in the grand scheme. She could afford a much bigger law firm."

He smiled and patted my back. "And this is why I need you on this. You pay attention to important details. Yes. Ms. Madsen wants to keep this as quiet as possible. There's a bigger risk of a leak with bigger firms."

I leaned back in my chair and took a sip of my coffee, hashing out details and potential consequences. The first consequence to pop into my head was to hire Bond to track Newall, the husband. It was more of a consequence on a personal level rather than a professional one. Regardless, Bond was an ex-detective, and on the police force for over a decade. She'd be more than qualified, and this would jump-start her business.

Why the fuck do you care? You rarely reach out to women you fucked for a second go around.

I tried to convince my mind, telling it she was the best qualified, but my mind told me to fuck off.

The truth was, I wanted to see her again. Maybe have one more fuck, and get her out of my system. I had no idea why she was even in there in the first place. Then fucking Bond in my button-up hit me at the most inopportune time. I shoved away the arousing vision and focused.

"I know someone. An ex-cop. Detective, actually. She's now a private eye. I'll hire her to track Newall."

"Perfect. Keep it quiet, James. We don't want her husband to find out he's being followed and spook him. There's a lot riding on this."

I nodded. "Understood."

CHAPTER 7

James

AS SOON AS I SAT BACK DOWN IN MY OFFICE, I REALIZED I NEVER GOT Bond's number because I never get women's numbers. I never even asked for her business name.

Shit.

That meant I had to talk to Brody.

Double-shit.

With a sigh and a mental eye roll, I picked up my phone and texted him to meet me in my office. Five minutes later, there was a knock on my door.

"Come in," I said, reading over the Madsen file, needing to be ready for our meeting this afternoon.

"So, are you going to tell me how it went with Jane?" he asked, plopping down in a leather chair in front of my desk for unwanted guests. He crossed his leg over his knee and threaded his fingers together behind his head.

"No."

"Come on… you need to give me something. Penny's been nagging me all week to ask you. I was about to hop on over here before you texted me."

"Get over it. I'm not the type to kiss and tell."

"Oh ho! So that means you kissed… and more, knowing you."

I glared at him, mentally begging him to shut up. "Other men may love to brag about their conquests. I have no need to brag. My mind and looks speak for themselves."

I swear, the man pouted. Penny was rubbing off on him with her nosiness. Brody had become that damned elderly neighbor with nothing better to do than to butt into everyone's business.

"Well, shit. Why am I here, then?"

"I need Bond's... ah, Jane's phone number."

Brody's eyes literally popped out of his head. "Ho-ly shit... are you going to see her again? That's a first."

I waved a dismissive hand. "Absolutely not. Well... not like that. I need to hire her."

"Disappointing, but promising. She's going to get under your skin. I can feel it."

I scoffed at him. "That's a reach. Project much? Fine. She's... interesting. Little did I know we'd met before, and not under pleasant circumstances. Needless to say, she instantly disliked me. She was interrogating my best friend's girlfriend... long story."

I rolled my eyes at his continued shocked expression. "Seriously, if you keep bugging your eyes out like that, they're going to fall out."

His smile was wicked and way too knowing. "I won't say it."

Did I really want to know? "Say what?"

When he said nothing, I narrowed my eyes at that humorous face I was itching to suddenly punch and rolled my hand for him to continue.

"Fine. I'll say it... You two are going to be a match. It's like fate, man. You've met before because of your best friend, now I happen to be dating her sister, who happened to talk you into taking Jane out. Sorry, but there's some divine intervention going on here—or karma. Depending on how you look at it."

Brody threw back his head and bellowed a laugh. He was the only one who currently found humor in this.

"Jesus, I just need her damned P.I. services, not her sweet cunt."

Shit.

His smile was crooked, which only pissed me off more. The one drawback of always being honest was it affected me, too, leaving me subject to incessant teasing. *Oh, look at arrogant James getting his karma on.* Another reason I didn't share my personal life with others.

Fucking annoying.

"Smile all you want, you smug bastard. At the end of the day, I don't do relationships. Besides, I'm no good for women on a permanent basis, and they're certainly not good for me."

Brody's smile dropped, and he shook his head with pity. Fuck his pity. "What did they ever do to you, man? Something happened. My divorce lawyer's nose smells a story."

There were two, but I wasn't about to tell him that. "Can I please have her number? I'd rather get it from you than Penny, who will push my buttons more than you. The woman is relentless."

He winked. "I know. How do you think I got suckered into a relationship? But damn, I don't regret a second of it."

"Give it time."

"It's a risk I'm willing to take. A life without risks is no life at all," he said, grabbing my pen and some paper to jot down her number.

"Finally. Thank you. You can go now."

When he reached my door, he turned and winked at me again. "Go get 'em, tiger."

"For fuck's sake…"

He shut my door behind him, drowning out his booming laugh.

My work phone buzzed, and I put it on speaker.

"James, Ms. Rikke Madsen is here to see you."

"Thanks, Sam. I'll come out to greet her myself."

I put back on my suit jacket and straightened my tie. In the mirror, I fingered back my hair to make sure everything was in place. Satisfied, I left my office and headed toward the reception area.

Rikke Madsen was shorter in person than she looked in the movies, standing at about five foot three inches, but she had a couple of inches in height from wearing heels. Her hair cascaded down in long, bleach-blond waves. She wore a one-piece jumpsuit in silky green with gold shoes and gold jewelry. Her biggest accessory was her damned Yorkie, resting its head on the edge of her massive purse.

To say she was stunning was an understatement. If I had met her when she was single, I would have fucked her.

Though I rarely watched movies, I knew she had won two Academy Awards. One for *'Time Back to the Beginning,'* an epic love story through the century between fated lovers. The other was *'Primed for Death'* set right here in Boston, where she met her now husband, Anthony Newall.

"Ms. Madsen," I greeted, holding out my hand to shake hers.

"Please call me Rikke."

She had cold and soft hands, giving me a small smile, and scanning me up and down. I grew used to men and women looking at me like that. "Well, aren't you in the wrong business? You're handsome enough to be an actor."

I forced myself to smile. "Thank you, but I'm terrible at acting."

She scoffed. "Please, as if lawyers don't act all the time."

I offered a fake laugh. "Fair. Let me take you back to our conference room. Can I get you something to drink? We can have anything you want to be brought to you."

"I'd like a glass of Krug Clos D'Ambonnay, please."

I nodded and guided her to one of our smaller conference rooms we decked out in comfortable furniture for high-end clients. Once I had her seated, I buzzed Sam to bring us drinks. The champagne was expensive, but we already knew what she drank and had it ready before she arrived.

Rikke sat on the cushioned sofa and pulled her dog out to sleep on her lap. I never understood pet accessories, like they weren't even living animals but decorations for handbags. Annoying.

After Sam handed Rikke her bubbly, Leo came in and introduced himself.

"Why don't you tell us why you've hired us?" I asked. "In your own words."

"There's something going on with my husband, but I don't have proof. First, I think he's gay or something." She rolled her eyes and picked at her finely manicured nail. "Second, I think he's cheating."

"Why do you think that?"

The woman had plenty of money, but judging by her file, she had plans to destroy him. If he was guilty, I'd be all for it, but if he wasn't, she'd pose a problem for us and this law firm. Plus, her husband was wealthy and well-known in this city. He was respected with his own powerful lawyers.

She raised her nose in the air and sniffed. "For one, in the past eight years, we've hardly had sex. Sometimes he has to take a blue pill to get it up. I mean, look at me. I've never had men having trouble getting it up."

"Mr. Newall is what? In his mid-forties? That's not unheard of," I said.

Leo coughed and leaned back in his chair. "All sorts of health circumstances could cause those problems. That doesn't mean he's gay."

"He smells different sometimes. Like from another man's cologne. I am familiar with all his scents. There's one, in particular, that isn't his. Then there are the growing late hours working. I realize he gets lots of messages from work and friends, but he frequently deletes his phone of texts and calls. I've walked into rooms with him suddenly hiding his phone. He wipes his computer clean, and I'm not smart enough to dig through it."

I steepled my fingers under my chin and nodded. "It's all definitely circumstantial. Let me ask you this, Rikke… why not just divorce him and get it over with? Why all the added stress of sneaking around?"

"Because I hate being lied to," she snapped.

Wasn't that the fucking truth?

"Cheating is bad enough, but if he's gay, he's used me as a tool to cover up his sexuality and I just wasted eight years of my life. That pisses me off. If word got out, which it will, I'll be a laughing stock." Her little dog whined and looked up at her when her voice raised. "Don't worry, schnookums, Mommy's just upset but not at you."

No, I wouldn't have slept with her. Not after her little show. But I didn't blame her for being upset if what she said was true.

"Why didn't you hire a private investigator?" I asked.

"I don't want to hint that I've been spying on my husband, or to have anything come back to me that will ruin my chances of destroying him. If you do it, it will seem like part of your regular service to get all the evidence I need to file for divorce."

I sighed and stared out the window. This was highly unusual for a law firm. Her husband would probably find out regardless, and I wondered if she planned to spring it on him. That it wouldn't matter if he found out, as long as it shocked him in the worst way. Perhaps she wanted a leak from our law firm after all.

"I have a firm in mind," I said. It wasn't an outright lie. Bond had a business and an office. Just because she didn't have employees, didn't mean she wasn't qualified. "I'm sure she can find dirt on your husband if there is any."

I may have to bring in Brady, Ronan's brother, to pull out information from her husband if need be. Once I had all my cards in place, I'd confront him, weaken him, and help him lose once the divorce goes to trial. Perhaps come to a hefty settlement without getting the court involved. It would save us all time and money. Though, admittedly, I loved the theatrics of a courtroom. To stand out in full display, winning my case.

We spent the last hour hashing out the details and discussing anything that could be gleaned from her to use against her husband. Nothing was too trivial. Then, once I got proof, I'd sort through the mess and build my winning case, or a settlement. Regardless, if all went according to plan, this would make me. Finally.

Now to call Bond and give her a high-paying case.

I ignored the niggling thought telling me I wanted to see her again.

CHAPTER 8

Jane

IT WAS A GOOD THING I WORKED OUT AND PRACTICED MY MARTIAL arts. Even with all the exercise I did, my arms still burned, rolling on the pale sage-colored paint in my brand-new office. I needed to get it done before they installed new laminate flooring since I opted out of carpeting.

I stood back to look at my handiwork. It already looked better and brighter. I still needed to paint the edges, but the walls were almost done. At least in the front office. I still had the rest of the office and apartment to paint. Perhaps I should have hired a painter, but I tried to save a few bucks wherever possible. Who knew how long my savings would last me?

My office furniture had arrived, and once the flooring got installed, I'd put it all together. In the meantime, I continued to work out of my apartment upstairs. Because I had renovations, it didn't mean I wasn't working.

The buzzing of my phone in my back pocket startled me. I set down the paint roller in the paint tray and wiped my hands before pulling out my phone.

"Bond Investigations," I answered.

"Well, that's boring. I thought you would have chosen '007 P.I.,' or 'Shaken, Not Stirred Investigations,' or—"

Ugh. Thanks, Mom and Dad, for the never-ending Bond jokes.

"James! One, how did you get this number? And two, why are you calling? I thought you didn't *do feelings*. You stalking me says otherwise, Clery."

"No worries. We're both safe from emotional attachments. I got your number from Brody because I want to hire you."

I snorted a laugh. "Seriously? You have a plethora of investigation firms in the city, and you chose me, who's barely started? You're showing your stalking colors, bud. Worst pickup line ever.

He scoffed over the phone, making me smile. Now that I'd recovered from my sex high with James, which had been phenomenal and knocked my ass out for the entire night and into the next morning, I could make light of it. I just reminded myself that because he was good in bed didn't mean he was a good person. Though, it was hard to ignore the little things he did. He had such a big and domineering personality, so when he did kind things, no matter how small, it was hard not to take note.

That didn't change the fact that he was still a freakin' narcissistic, arrogant snob.

It didn't matter, anyway. Neither of us wanted a relationship. I wasn't against them and actually wouldn't mind having one, but I didn't have the time. My focus had to be on my career.

"You've yet to experience my pickup lines. But, yes, I could've hired anyone, though you have police detective experience. You're already skilled, even if your business is barely getting off the ground. I can give you an extra push to help you succeed."

"That still doesn't answer why me. Plenty of skilled PI's for hire."

"Bond, I'm surprised I need to tell you this, but pushing clients away isn't how you run a successful business."

My eyes rolled so far back into my head that I saw blackness. "No, shit, Clery. I'm just trying to figure out your true motives here. Former detective, remember? Again, there are plenty who are just as qualified. Surely, you'd want someone more experienced."

"I'm paying fifty bucks per hour."

The silence was long, as calculated in my head. That was just over twice my going rate. Holy shit. That still didn't answer my question, but... holy shit!

"Judging by your silence, you're either amazed, or you've passed out."

When I still didn't respond, thinking about all the extra equipment I could buy, he said, "Look, this is a sensitive case, and needs to remain quiet. If you're anything like the woman I assume you to be, you'll be discreet. I'd rather hire someone I know."

"You don't know me at all," I said, finally finding my words.

"You'd be surprised how much I know about you. You may be a former detective, but as a lawyer, I'm also trained to read people to help win my cases."

He went silent for a moment, and after his next words, was probably smirking something awful. It was all in his smug tone. "Need I remind you of how you gave in to my hand smacking your ass, *sweet girl*?"

I inadvertently shuddered. Thank god he couldn't see me. "Bastard," I said, but I had no bite to my bark. I was sure I added some unintentional heat in it, too, unable to forget the amazing sex, no matter how hard I tried.

"Is that a yes, Bond…. Jane Bond?"

I was going to strangle him the next time we met. *If* there was a next time. But there probably would be because I could use fifty bucks per hour.

"No. It's not a yes until I see the case file."

"No can do. You need to trust me that this is big and needs to stay quiet. It's a lot of money for you. It could also put your newborn business on the map. Take it or leave it. If you accept, you'll need to sign an NDA."

I sighed, knowing I'd have to spend more time with him if I accepted. Maybe it wouldn't be so bad if I got more sex out of it. Make it worth dealing with his ass-holiness. My vibrator was on its last legs, anyway. It wasn't very professional, but owning my own business let me do whatever the hell I wanted.

"Fine, on one condition."

"What?"

"No more Bond jokes."

Silence.

"I'm sorry, but that's where I draw the line."

"Are you being freakin' serious right now?"

"Allow me to counter your offer. I'll relinquish all my Bond jokes, except I still get to say, 'Bond. Jane Bond."

Yep. I was going to strangle him. "Fine, but I get to punch you every time you do."

"So violent. As long as I can spank you back for your naughtiness, sweet girl."

Shit, his words went straight between my traitorous legs as I pulsed with heat. How the hell did he do that?

Infuriating.

"Not happening. I'm always a good... girl..."

Fuck. Me.

I facepalmed that I blurted that out, waiting for James' comeback. I could practically hear him smiling on the phone.

"Oh, I'll make sure you're a good girl."

"*Anyway...* When and where do you want to meet to discuss the case?"

"Your office, tonight. I'll bring dinner."

I looked around my sparse office and was about to say no, but realized I'd enjoy seeing Mr. Attorney Douchebag on his knees, sitting on old, dirty carpeting.

"Okay."

I recited my address and hung up.

A knock on my glass front door startled me, despite expecting James. I dumped the paintbrush I was using to paint the trim into the tray and wiped my paint-covered hands on my paint-covered cargo pants.

I quickly tried to fix my messy bun but gave up. I had to face the reality that I looked like hell after painting all day. With a quick whiff of my pits to make sure I didn't stink too badly, I rushed to unlock and open the door.

The stunning blond stood, instantly taking in the wreck that I was, with a twinkle in his blue eyes. The day was waning, and he glowed with the sinking sun behind him. He looked gorgeous with his perfect hair, clothes, skin, and body… ugh. If he wasn't such a schmuck, I'd be drooling all over him.

Fine, I was drooling a little in my mind, but he didn't need to know that. He looked good in his pressed jeans—who pressed jeans anyway—and a deep purple v-neck sweater with a white v-neck T-shirt peeking out. Both of them stretched over his tight body.

An unexpected sense of insecurity filled me about my appearance. I always felt I was the least pretty out of my sisters, with my mousy brown hair, bland face, bland everything. Now I was without makeup and a wreck on top of it. I shoved away my doubts and stepped aside to let him in.

He raised two large bags. "Dinner."

When he put the bags on the ground, he looked around at my handiwork. "Had I known you were busy painting, I would have done this tomorrow. And… you have no furniture."

"I just signed the contract a few days ago. All my furniture is still in boxes in the next room, waiting to be put together. You could always help if you want to sit."

"No, thanks. Not my idea of fun."

"Suit yourself. The floor it is then."

I sat cross-legged on the old carpeting and dug in the bags with a growling stomach. Why, oh why, did my stomach always talk when James was around?

"Forget to eat again, Bond?" he asked with a smirk as he sat next to me. I thought he'd complain about the dirty carpeting, but he didn't seem to care in the least.

"Maybe."

"It's a good thing I brought a lot of food, then."

"What is it?" I asked, pulling out several containers.

"Sushi, sashimi, and miso soup."

I looked up at him and blanched. "Er, raw fish? Couldn't you have gotten me some noodles or something?"

"Please tell me you've had sushi before."

I shrugged, and he gave an exasperated sigh. "Trying new things is good for the soul."

"So says, Mr. I'm Resistant to Change?"

"I'm quite adaptable, thank you. But why fix something that isn't broken? Anyway, try it. I'll make you into a sushi lover by the end of tonight."

James opened up containers full of displayed rolls of fish wrapped around rice and sauces. There was another tray with perfectly sliced raw fish. That was it. Nothing else. I wasn't so sure about this.

Then he handed me a plastic container filled with warm soup and a spoon. I inhaled it and took a tentative sip. Okay, now that was good. It was salty with a light briny broth filled with seaweed and bean curd.

I set my soup down and grabbed my chopsticks to get it over with. Besides, I was starving with little else to eat. I picked up some green goop and spread it on my roll, and brought the piece to my mouth. James grabbed my arm before I could shove the sushi in.

"I refuse to have you accuse me of allowing you to set your face on fire like the last time. That green stuff you so generously put on your roll is wasabi. If you want to keep your sinuses intact, I suggest you don't eat it like that. Here…"

He poured some soy sauce into a small container, picked up a dollop of wasabi, and mixed the two together. Then he layered a thin slice of ginger on top of a slice of white, fatty fish, and dipped it into the soy mixture with his chopsticks.

James lifted the tender fish to my mouth. "Escolar is a type of tuna. You'll like it, Bond."

I opened my mouth, and he shoved it in. I slowly chewed, tasting all the flavors, while the wasabi slightly burned my nose.

"Actually, it's tasty," I said with my mouth full. I could admit when I was wrong.

"See?" He smirked and reached for my face. His thumb brushed the edge of my mouth and brought his thumb back to his mouth, sucking on it. "Soy sauce."

I swallowed the fish before I finished chewing, unable to take my eyes off of his mouth, sucking his thumb. Shit. There went my lady parts in an inferno of heat. And he knew exactly what he was doing if the knowing light in his blue eyes were anything to go by. Why did he have to be sex on a stick? Let's not forget his arrogant smile. Asshole.

"Do you need me to keep feeding you, Bond?"

I narrowed my eyes at him as I reached for a piece of sushi, dunking it in the soy sauce and shoving it in my mouth. Okay, so sushi was pretty good. It was a little spicy but the right amount. The fish was fresh, and I liked the touch of cucumber and cilantro.

Yeah, he made a good call. So what?

"I can handle myself," I said when I finished chewing.

"I know you can."

Shoving away lustful thoughts, I sighed. "I thought you were here on business. Can you turn off the flirting for five minutes?"

"Well, I could, but you don't want me to. I'd rather turn you on."

Bastard. He could fucking read me like a book. He would've made a great detective.

James reached over, curled fingers inside the neck of my paint-stained T-shirt, and pulled me toward him. Our faces were barely an inch apart when he pressed his lips to mine. And like the sucker I was, I fell right into his trap. I completely melted into him, like the escolar melted into my mouth earlier.

"I thought we were going to do business," I repeated, trying to catch my breath when we parted and bringing my brain back online.

"Eat up, Bond. Then it will be all about pleasure. Afterward, we can get down to business."

CHAPTER 9

James

THERE WAS SOMETHING ABOUT THIS PAINT-COVERED GIRL, WITH HER cute blushing, while shoving a large piece of sushi in her mouth, that had my dick instantly on alert. If I were being honest with myself, my reaction to her should've been worrying—a red flag—but my second brain kept pushing rationality to the side. My second brain wanted another taste of her.

Bond was a simple little thing, not standing out in any way other than her smarts and wit. She was quirky, clumsy, lacking in refinement, with average style and average height, and did little with her appearance. She was no supermodel, though most women weren't. And while she was definitely pretty, the more time I spent with her, the more attracted to her, I grew. I noticed she had flecks of yellow in her forest green eyes and a splash of freckles, ever so faint, on her nose. When I had her naked last time, she had a sweet little birthmark on her only a few inches from her pussy. And damn, when she gave herself over sexually to me, a woman always in control, she had me wanting more.

Let's not forget her lack of a chase, promising me she wouldn't give in to the feelings. It was exactly what I wanted, yet here I was, wanting more of her. I didn't have any strong emotions towards her other than the need to fuck her brains out. Yet, I tried not to think about why. I rarely asked for seconds. It wouldn't have been the first time, but a second time could lead to a third or more.

When I told her we were going to have pleasure first, I smirked, seeing her mind war with itself. Bond wanted to give in, but she fought it too. It was cute that she thought she could resist me when I wanted something.

I internally smiled when she let me pull her by her shirt and take control of her mouth. Her willingness, despite her resistance, was intoxicating. My easy girl, ready to let me take over and give her the pleasure of her life.

My girl.

Fuck.

Fine. She was mine… for now. Temporarily, as we worked together, with some fun on the side. I just had to make my boundaries clear.

Once we finished eating, I rinsed my mouth out with the water I had brought with the food, and she did the same.

"Get undressed, Bond. We're going to have a little play time before we work."

She folded her arms, trying to be defiant, but I knew she wanted to give in. "No. Work first."

I raised a brow. "Oh, so you *do* want some fun. I love being right all the time. Have you been thinking of me? Hoping I'll fuck your tight little pussy again?"

She scoffed and stood to pick up all the trash from our dinner, unable to hide the red blooming across her cheeks and to her ears. "No… Maybe. It doesn't matter because you won't get any if you're going to be an arrogant ass about it."

You can play all you want, my little P.I. I know you want it. You want my hand marking your pert little ass.

"Get undressed, Bond. I won't ask you again. If you don't, I'm going to teach you how to do as you're told… again."

Oh, so slowly, she walked over to the trash can, dumping our dinner containers into it… *not* doing what she was told. It was all a game, of course. A way for her to resist me while allowing me to take what I wanted. I'd been with many women, learning all their nuances. Bond was no different. Try as she might, she couldn't hide what she wanted.

I stood, dusted off the back of my jeans, and headed over to her. As soon as she dumped the trash, I wrapped my arms around her and pressed our bodies together. My lips grazed her neck as I unbuttoned and unzipped her pants. "I told you, you were naughty. Now you have to be punished."

Her breath hitched, and her body froze. "I was just throwing out the trash."

"We both know what you were really doing. It's okay to admit you want my hand marking you... owning you."

"I-I haven't showered."

I pressed my nose to her throat and inhaled. She smelled a little sweaty but with a fuck ton of arousal and a hint of some cheap body wash, probably with the word 'ocean' on the label.

I slid my hands up her T-shirt and cupped her breasts. "You smell fine to me, Bond. Now, are you going to make me strip you down? Or are you going to do what you were told? No matter your choice, you're still going to be punished for disobeying me. But if you don't strip down now, your punishment will be harder."

Her body shuddered against mine, and her breathing picked up the pace. She didn't move, debating.

"You have five seconds to act. Five... four... three... two..." My smile grew broad. My naughty Bond. "One," I whispered and nipped her ear.

I headed over to the light switch to turn it off, plunging us into darkness. She had no curtains on her office windows, so I didn't want people peeking in; not that many people walked around this particular neighborhood at night.

I stood behind her again and squatted to remove her shoes. Once they were tossed aside, I pulled down her pants, already unbuttoned, and slid the legs off. Next went her panties. My fingers trailed up her thighs, leaving goosebumps in their wake until I reached her ass. She flinched, but I only grazed the skin. My fingers continued their upward movement until I reached the hem of her shirt, pulling it over her head. I tossed it to the ground, then unclasped her bra.

Bond stood there naked with her back turned to me, trembling in anticipation and probably a little fear. That was the beauty of sexual punishments and humiliation. This handing over your control to someone else could be terrifying for someone who struggled to let go. But oh, how they wanted to.

I threaded my fingers through her hair, then suddenly gripped it and yanked her head back. She bit her bottom lip and groaned. There was my naughty girl. I slid my free hand in between her legs and dipped a finger into her hot pussy. "Mmm, so wet for me already."

When I pulled out my finger, covered in her juices, I slipped it into her mouth. "Suck." She closed her eyes and suckled my finger, and fuck if that didn't have me busting through my jeans.

I withdrew my finger from those full lips, and with a firm grip on her hair, I forced her towards the wall. "Brace yourself, Bond. It's time to accept your punishment like the good girl I know you can be."

When her hands rested on the wall with no complaint or resistance, I smiled and bent her over. Fuck, it was hot how easily she yielded to me. She was clay under an artist's hands. Her resistances were barely that. She *wanted* to give in. To give me all of herself. Sure, I've had other women who gave in, but they came to me for it. They already knew what they wanted, making the game less interesting. But with Bond, this was new to her. She couldn't quite understand what to make of it, but her body knew perfectly well. And that right there was sexy as hell.

And having me fully dressed still was also intoxicating, giving her that additional humiliation and vulnerability.

My hand traveled along her back and to the soft globes of her ass. She flinched, but I didn't spank her yet. It was all about the anticipation. The wondering when the first smack would come.

With my hand still fisted in her hair, I pulled her head back, forcing her back to arch. "Are you hot for this, sweet girl?"

"Y-yes."

"Hmm, I know you are. Good thing you didn't lie, or else it would really hurt."

Smack. Smack. Smack.

The sound reverberated across the empty room, followed by a moan.

Bond squirmed, but didn't move from her position.

"Yes, take your punishment like a good girl."

I rubbed her heated and reddening skin, then slipped a finger inside her cunt to feel how wet she was, dripping down her thighs, and so turned on for me. She couldn't fake this level of arousal.

"What a sweet girl you are to be so wet for me."

Smack. Smack.

I added four more to the count.

She writhed, groaned, moaned, and her body trembled, but she held still to take her punishment.

After several more spankings, Bond keened, whined, and leaked like a sieve.

"Don't move from that position."

I pulled away to eye my handiwork. The only light filtering in was from the streetlights, but it was enough to see her gorgeous reddened ass. As she remained bent over, exposing her tight and wet pussy to me, my cock ached and throbbed. I slowly peeled off my clothes, folded them neatly on the floor, then rolled on a condom I pulled out from my wallet.

"What are you doing?" she asked, still out of breath.

"Did I say you could talk?"

She shook her head.

"I can't hear you?"

"No."

"No, what? Who's in charge here?"

"You are? Uhm… sir?"

"Good girl."

I headed back to her, and combed my fingers through her silky hair, then trailed them down until I reached her hips, which I gripped tightly. Then I slammed home.

Fuck.

She was so slick; I met no resistance despite how tight she was. Her back arched, forcing me deeper inside. I'd been so turned on by doling out her punishment along with her reaction and unable to do anything about it, so the first tingles already traveled down my spine.

Way too early, buddy. Slow down.

I pulled out of her, and Bond literally whined, making me chuckle.

"Don't worry, sweet girl. You're going to have my greedy cock back inside of you soon enough."

I lifted her up, flipped her around, and slammed her back into the wall. She could take it. She loved it and groaned when I thrust my tongue into her mouth. Our kiss was quick, so I could lift her, wrap her legs around my hips, and glide right back into her.

She tossed her head against the wall and groaned as her nails dug into my shoulders.

"Fuck…," she mumbled.

"You like my big dick in you? Fucking you?"

She nodded with her eyes closed. "Yes…"

I pressed my face against her throat, inhaling scents of sex, musk, sweat, and body wash. All enticing. All arousing. All Bond. She clung to me for dear life as I pounded into her.

"Get yourself off, sweet girl. Come for me. I want to feel your cunt grip the life out of my cock. And don't worry… I've got a hold of you."

Her hand slipped down between us, and she wasted no time rubbing her clit. It took less than a minute before she was squeezing the life out of me while her orgasmic sounds reverberated throughout the room.

"Shit, shit… You're so damned tight."

"James…," she cried out, pulsing around me that sent pressure straight to my balls and right out of my cock. I spilled my load into the condom as she became dead weight from her sexual high.

With my last thrust, we slid to the floor in a sweaty heap. I held on to her until we both settled our heart rates. Once she recuperated, she pulled away and stood up, reaching a hand down to me. I grabbed it, and she helped me stand.

"Let's go upstairs and get cleaned up, then we can go over the paperwork," she said as if I didn't just fuck her brains out.

Was she fucking kidding me right now?

I mentally huffed, irritated, but I didn't know why. I wanted her indifferent, yet when she was, I found myself irked. That was some fantastic sex, and she acted as if we had just finished a round of checkers.

"And maybe if you're going to be my client, this should probably be our last time for some fun. It's been great, but it's probably a good idea for us to remain professional."

Fuck that.

I wasn't done with her.

When she walked away to grab her clothes, I pulled on her arm and pressed her close to me. With my fingers fisted in her hair again, I pressed our lips together and consumed her mouth as if it was life-sustaining. Our tongues explored, tasted, and licked.

When I pulled away, her eyes were closed, and her mouth was still open, with lips swollen from our recent sex. *That* was what I was going for.

"I'm far from being finished with you, Bond. Now, let's get you cleaned up. We'll work, and if we can wrap it up early, I may just devour your sweet pussy as a reward."

She bit her bottom lip, trying not to smile.

Gotcha.

No, we are far from being done, my sweet girl.

CHAPTER 10

Jane

I CHEWED ON THE SIDE OF MY MOUTH, FILLED WITH DOUBT. TONIGHT was so damn hot. James was the puppet master, and I was his marionette. He easily got me to do his bidding, and I did it happily. Why did that turn me on so much, along with his dirty talk?

At first, I thought we'd work and have some fun, but after tonight, I wondered if it was such a good idea. James screamed red flags, but if we kept going, I worried about keeping the emotions at bay. He pulled things out of me sexually I had no idea existed, so I worried about what else he'd pull out of me.

Despite my initial resistance and telling him we were finished, he had other plans. I didn't think he was the type to want more from any woman, but he wanted to continue, which also confused me.

We headed upstairs to my apartment because I really needed to take a quick shower before we started working. It was embarrassing enough having raunchy sex after painting all day. Surely, I didn't smell so good, but James didn't seem to care.

At least I had my apartment relatively put together. I had tons of boxes to unpack, but my furniture had been moved in, thanks to my family. I still had a lot of work that needed to be done, but getting my office ready first was a priority.

I unlocked the door, and we stepped inside. "Make yourself at home while I take a quick shower," I said. "I have some wine chilling in the fridge if you want, though I'm sure it's not as good as what you're used to. I've also got some beer, sodas, and juice."

"Do you want a drink?"

"Sure, a glass of wine would be nice."

After my shower, I threw on some joggers, and a worn and loved UMass T-shirt I still had from my college days, put my wet hair up in a clip, then padded out to the living room. James sat on my sofa, one of my better pieces since I recently bought it, and sipped on some of my wine.

"Not bad, but a bit flowery for me," he said, glancing up at me over the rim of his wine glass.

Shit, that smolder alone could make me come. I coughed back my arousal and ignored his smirk. "Let's get started."

When I sat on the other side of the sofa, he slid over some documents on the table and placed a pen on top. "This is the contract you need to sign, plus an NDA. The client is well known."

I quickly scanned the paperwork. It was all relatively standard, but it was the name of the client that drew me in. Rikke Madsen. Interesting. I'd seen most of her movies. She was gorgeous and a fantastic actress.

A strange surge of jealousy hit me. A feeling I had yet to experience, but I recognized it for what it was. Did James sleep with her? She seemed more his type than I was, with long wavy gorgeous hair, perfect skin, perfect body, perfect everything. Did it matter that she was married? Did James care about such things?

How about I stop caring? He's not mine. We're just having fun. That's all.

But damn if his sudden possessiveness after I tried to stop whatever was going on between us didn't make me question everything.

That's his game. That's all it is. This is what players do. Just roll with it, Jane.

"Why do you look like that?" he asked. "Is there something wrong with the documents?"

"What do you mean?"

"You seem like you're pissed off."

"No, your documents are fine." *Calm those features, girl.*

He narrowed his eyes at me but didn't push. Thank god because I had no idea I revealed so much. I knew better. As a detective, I had to keep emotions at bay. Not show my hand, especially during interrogations. But around James, I was an open book, apparently.

I quickly signed the paperwork and handed it back to him.

"Great, now the real work begins," he said, handing me a folder. I opened it and scanned the contents. "Rikke is growing to be a bitter woman. Can't say I blame her if what she says is true. Not just with the cheating, but lying about his sexuality, and basically using her as a beard to protect his image."

"I'd be pissed too if factual."

"Agreed. I need you to follow him. Where does he go? Who does he meet with? Who are all his friends? Are any of them old lovers? I'm sure you get the picture."

"Yep. I assume you want pictures too?"

"Definitely. We'll need images of everyone he interacts with so Rikke can verify who they are to him."

"It won't be easy. Newall is a well-known architect around here. Even *I* know who he is, and I don't get out much. He's going to have a lot of connections. Do you have any background on him? I'm going to dig anyway, but I'll take whatever you've got to get me started."

James handed me another file labeled *'Anthony Newall.'* I opened it and perused through the papers.

"Here's the USB drive for your computer. You can dig to see what you can find, but I have someone already researching for me who does this for a living. Whatever he finds, I'll send your way."

I nodded and tucked my feet under me as I read the documents in more detail. To my surprise, James pulled out my feet and rested them on his lap. I glanced at him with furrowed brows as he began rubbing them.

Okay then... I was a damned detective not long ago, yet I struggled to get a bead on James. Once I thought I had him all figured out, he'd do something surprising. Rubbing my feet on his lap felt awfully intimate and personal, but what did I know? It wasn't like I had tons of previous relationships to reflect on.

"You have cute toes," he said.

Huh.

"Uh, thanks."

He wiggled each one, inspecting them. Weird. What was going on with him?

I grabbed my wine glass, shrugged, and took a sip, as I continued reading.

Anthony Newall, forty-six years old, had dark hair, dark brown eyes, and handsome, judging by his photo. He grew up in Boston, went to Harvard, then attended Cornell in New York because of its excellent architecture department. So the guy was super smart. He worked his way up at an architecture firm until he got his break, designing a bank building downtown that was nearly all green in construction. He eventually opened up his own business called Newall Architecture Group, a small firm with only a few designers on hand, but he preferred it that way.

He married Rikke eight years ago when she was filming in Boston. The two hit it off instantly and married six months later. No kids.

He did a lot of charitable work and some pro bono work designing buildings for the less fortunate, such as affordable housing and… Huh. He designed that underground clinic down the street.

"Interesting," I said.

"What is? Did you find something?"

"No, nothing incriminating per se. But that clinic down the street was designed by Newall pro bono. When I was a detective, we'd been trying to find a connection to the clinic and those who fund it, but we'd never been able to find any details. The clinic's paperwork is on the up and up, but… my gut told me something was off. That place is too well-equipped for a community clinic. But I guess I have my answer. Newall funded the place as a philanthropic endeavor. That explains everything.

James put my feet down and stood, heading to my kitchen. "Yep. Interesting. Want a beer?"

"Uh, no, thanks."

He came back and popped the top off the bottle. "I think he likes to do charitable work, and it's good for taxes."

"Maybe, but that's not the vibe I get from him. He seems to be genuine. From what I've read, he comes across as a great guy. Likable, kind, and gives back to the community. Then again, while he doesn't come across as a liar, people change, and anything can happen to turn someone to a darker path."

"I'm aware. Just when you think you know a person…" He didn't finish his words, taking a sip of his beer.

I set the files down on the coffee table and took another sip of wine. "Is that what happened to you? Is that why you like to keep intimacy out of it?" Which would make sense. Depending on the cheating, it could have long-lasting effects on the person who was cheated on.

"Isn't that what you do, Bond?" he retorted. Such a damned lawyer.

"First, no, I don't mind intimacy. I just… My life is disorganized right now. Second, nice deflection. So, you've been cheated on."

His brows furrowed ever so slightly, but he tried to hide it as he took a sip of beer. "Hasn't everyone?"

"No. I haven't."

"And when's the last time you had a relationship?"

"Fair. It's been a while, but I've had them."

He put down his beer on the table, grabbed my legs, and pulled me until my back was on the seat cushion, then he grabbed the waistband of my joggers to pull down.

I grabbed his hands to stop him. He was clearly deflecting. "James…"

"I'd rather devour your pussy than talk about relationships. It's a fucking bore. After all, I promised you some pussy eating if we wrapped up early."

If he didn't want to talk, who was I to make him? I had to remind myself we weren't an item, and it wasn't my business. Besides, oral sex *definitely* sounded more fun.

Off went my pants and panties, leaving my T-shirt and bra on, but James shoved them over my breasts. He tweaked a nipple as he went to town on my clit.

And damn he was good at it.

Instead of teasing me and prolonging the torture, he focused on making me come quickly. Once I toppled over the edge, chasing my orgasm, I was dead. Dead. Two orgasms in one evening were more than my poor sexually depraved body could take.

James shimmied up my pants because I struggled to move. He smiled at me, then pressed his lips to mine. I tasted myself on his tongue, which I never thought I'd like, but did.

"You good, Bond?"

"Barely. If you see my bones lying around, can you tell them to go back into my body? Thanks."

He chuckled or laughed at me. One of the two.

"I need to go. Can you stand, so you can lock the door behind me?"

"I think I can manage."

We walked downstairs, and I unlocked the front door, opening it for him. He plucked my chin between his fingers and gave me a small kiss. "I'm not done with you, Bond, but my view on relationships hasn't changed."

A surge of anger hit me. As if I even wanted something serious with him. "Way to ruin a perfectly nice evening, James." I shoved his hand away, then shoved him out the door. "Don't worry. I don't get attached to Douchebags at Law. Oh, and we are *so* done. I'll send you my reports. No need to meet up again."

He said nothing when I shut the door that I wish I could've slammed. I locked it behind me, and went back up to my apartment, not turning around to see if he was still standing there or not. I didn't want to fucking know.

Dick.

CHAPTER 11

James

I DRUMMED MY FINGERS ON MY DESK, RE-READING MY TEXT FROM Bond as the irritation traveled through my veins. It had been four days since we'd fucked in her new office. And apparently, I pissed her off. All I did was remind her of my boundaries. We had already agreed to that, so why did it piss her off this time? If she claimed she wouldn't develop feelings, then why get angry with me?

And why did I fucking care?!

The better question was, why was I still harping on this for four fucking days?

Every time I tried to call, she'd text me back, saying she couldn't talk. She'd only send periodic emails with status updates on Anthony Newall, which wasn't much. Bond had spent most of her time following him and taking pictures, but had found nothing incriminating.

I shoved my phone away and tried to focus on work. I had several cases I'd been working on, but nothing I couldn't handle. If I only had something complex going on—a difficult case to distract me from Bond that I was strangely obsessing over. I needed to stop this. To do something that took my mind off of her.

Before I could stew any longer, my phone buzzed.

My stomach fluttered when I reached for my phone, then it was filled with a bottomless pit of disappointment reading Daniel's name on the screen and not hers.

I really needed to get her out of my fucking system.

Maybe one more fuck would help. I never slept with a woman more than three times. That was my max. Once I did, I'd wash my hands of her and focus on the Madsen/Newall case.

"What?" I said when I answered. It wasn't quite a bark, but it wasn't pleasant either.

Daniel huffed a laugh. "Someone's pissy."

I still couldn't believe my best friend was married, to a guy, no less. Daniel had always slept with women for as long as I'd known him. Not that I didn't like Luke. He was a pretty good guy, I suppose.

"Sorry, I was expecting someone else."

"Who?"

"It doesn't matter. What's going on?"

"I sent you a text about Georgie's birthday party and never heard back. It's this weekend. You're coming, right?"

"Do you really need me there? You all are a family now. You, Ronan... hell, even Cian, the last person I'd expect to find love, has a girlfriend. I'll just be a fifth wheel, as they say."

"Fuck you, James!"

I pulled the phone away from my ear, shocked. Daniel never yelled or got angry. He was the most laid-back person I'd ever known unless someone was messing with those he loved.

"Excuse me?"

"You heard me. You're fucking family, James, and you know it. So what if we're married, dating, or have kids? That's fucking life. Get over it. Now, if you don't want to be on my bad side, I expect you to be at Ronan's place this weekend at noon. Georgie likes you for some strange reason. And here I thought kids sensed evil."

"Hardy har. Georgie likes everyone."

I tapped my pen on the desk, suddenly filled with a strange sense of guilt. What the hell was going on with me? He was right. I'd been avoiding my family like the plague. The same thing I'd done to my parents.

"Yes, she does, and while Callum is her favorite, you're a close second."

"She's like a cat. You ignore them; they bug you the most."

"You don't fool me for a second. I've seen you playing with her."

"Fine, she's okay, I guess."

"So, you'll be there?"

I gave a dramatic sigh, playing my role. "I suppose."

"Good, and bring her something big and expensive."

"Jesus, fine."

And that gave me an opening to Bond. It hit me like a hundred-watt light bulb.

What better way to get her to talk to me than by using a child. It was devious, but I was desperate and tired of being ignored.

I hated these new feelings. Despite that, I still avoided looking too deeply into them. It changed nothing.

I sent out a quick text to Bond, then I waited.

James: I need help with a little girl.

It didn't take long, thank fuck. I knew it'd work.

Bond: Let me guess. You got a woman pregnant and just found out you're the baby daddy?
James: Har har. I'm way too careful with that.
Bond: Whatever. I'm busy. What do you need?
James: She's turning 7, and I have no idea what to get. Come shopping with me.

I sent her several praying emojis, hoping to get her to loosen up. It was usually Sam doing the shopping for me. She was better at sentimental gift-buying than I was. My gifts were too practical and boring.

Bond: Don't you have an assistant to do these things for you? You're paying me to be your PI, not your PA.
James: Think of the children, Bond.

She sent me several eye roll emojis.
Come on, Bond… do it. Say yes.

Bond: You didn't answer my question.
James: I do, but Sam is tied up with other things right now.

Plus, she's tired of shopping for me. The little girl is adorable...
Bond: I'm charging extra.
James: Deal.

Gotcha.

Bond: Fine. There's a cute place called Frogz & Rabbitz near Fenway.
James: When are you free?
Bond: When's the party?
James: This Saturday.
Bond: Tomorrow during lunch.

I had a work meeting, but I'd have Sam reschedule.

James: See you at noon tomorrow.

All she gave me was a thumbs-up emoji.
See you then, Bond. Then I'd work in my last fuck with her and finally end it.
I could do this.

I stood in front of the ostentatious toy store. It screamed expensive. Well, it was what Daniel asked for, and I could afford it. Hell, he and Luke weren't exactly poor, either. They set up the store on the outside like an old-fashioned store, with the wood facade painted in lime green. The displays had assorted toys that were surprisingly more gender-neutral than I would have expected.

"You're here," said a voice behind me.

I turned to find Bond, but... not. What just happened? Her hair was covered in blond highlights, she wore makeup, and her clothes were...

moderately cute. Tight jeans, a blouse half-tucked in, some earrings, and heels.

"Bond, you look…" Her brow raised, probably expecting an insult. "You look beautiful."

She softened and gave me a genuine and radiant smile. "Thank you. See? It wasn't that hard to be sweet."

"I only speak the truth."

"Harsh truths aren't quite the same as being honest. Harsh truths, tell people *your* truth. That's not necessarily being honest."

I never really thought about it that way, but I brushed it off. I still didn't lie, but I ignored my little trickery to get her here.

"Anyway, thanks for being here. I'm not good at… gift giving, especially for children."

"You're welcome. Do you have a picture of this little girl? And how old is she?"

"She's turning seven." I opened up my phone and scrolled through my pictures of Georgie that I never asked for, but Daniel insisted on sending them to me, anyway. I found one from their wedding last month dressed in white since she was their flower girl. Her strawberry blond hair was up in pigtails with flowers in them.

Bond took my phone to look at it. "Oh my god, she's adorable. I love those glasses on her. What a cutie. Do you have any idea what she plays with?"

"How should I know? Dolls?"

Bond rolled her eyes and grabbed my hand, yanking me into the store. "Come on, terrible gift giver. Let's go get this princess a present."

Fuck, the place was loud, full of little toddlers either screaming in delight or throwing temper tantrums while nannies or mothers tried to calm them with bribes, or chased them across the store. However much they paid the employees, it wasn't nearly enough. On top of all that were the incessant children's songs playing through the overhead speakers.

By the end of it, I had a headache and was irritable, but at least I had some presents, after spending over a thousand dollars on the rug rat. We picked out a realistic doll that had special adoption papers with clothes, accessories, a pet, and thanks to me, her own bank account. Bond felt it was perfect since Georgie was also adopted. She also picked out several age-appropriate books and a couple of learning games.

We headed out of the store full of bags, and I shoved on my sunglasses to the glaring sun.

"Thanks, Bond. You did good, though; I'm a little poorer for it."

"You're welcome."

We stood there for a moment in awkward silence, driving me fucking nuts. I always knew what to do around women, but now I was drawing blanks.

"So, what's with the change? You were already pretty."

"Penny talked me into it. I have a date tonight."

My heart stopped beating.

The hell she does.

For the first time since college, jealousy reared its ugly head. My heart rate picked up, and my gut clenched. I didn't bother to figure out why. All that mattered was that she wasn't going on a fucking date.

And, what the fuck, Bond... you got your hair done, and put on makeup for some douche canoe you don't even know?

"No, you don't."

Her hands on her hips and anger flaring through her green eyes was sexy as hell, and I didn't fucking know why. Then she crossed her arms and scoffed. "I am *so* going on a date."

"No, you're not. Cancel it. Now."

"Who the hell do you think you are?"

"I'm not done with you."

She threw her head back and laughed, only making me question everything. Doubting my sanity. With any other woman, I'd simply walk away and never look back.

"What you don't understand is that *I* am done with you."

"Look... I'm... sorry I said that to you... from before. It was..."

"God, that must hurt for you to apologize. Do I need to call you an ambulance, Clery?"

"Ha ha ha. Hilarious, Bond."

She laughed and shook her head, her anger quickly evaporating. "Whatever."

"Cancel the date with that d-bag. Then come with me to Georgie's party on Saturday."

I quit questioning my sanity, and apparently, my mouth was just rolling with my new brand of crazy.

When she didn't answer, I winced, and said, "Please."

I swear to god, this woman had me by the fucking balls. I shoved away the memory of telling Ronan that very thing when he met Cat.

Nope. I wasn't going there. I only needed to fuck her out of my system.

"Fine. But you're driving. My car's in the shop."

Now I just hoped she didn't know who the fuck Ronan was. The O'Callaghans hid their identities, thanks to his youngest brother, Callum. They all had false I.D.s, passports, bank accounts, portfolios, and even jobs with valid addresses. Callum also spent time with a team of hackers, keeping most of the evidence against them hidden or outright destroying it. Regardless, the cops knew of their father, but the boys stayed under the radar. Their father was a piece of shit abuser, but he had specific plans for his sons he carefully laid out since their birth. He would've protected them if only to protect himself.

Bringing Bond to the party will be a test of Callum's abilities.

I better give Ronan a heads-up.

CHAPTER 12

Jane

JAMES DROVE US IN HIS FANCY BLACK GLE COUPE MERCEDES. ABOUT as pretentious as he was, though I had to admit, the ride was relaxing as we drove out of the city and into the countryside.

The day was pleasant and in the high seventies. The trees had all their leaves finally, bringing the land to life, full of new growth. The music was low, playing a variety of indie music. So much for my detective skills. I would have pegged him for a jazz listener as he sipped his brandy neat, overlooking the city with power-hungry eyes with plans of taking over the world. Then again, James had surprised me a few times.

I glanced over at him as he drove, looking too handsome for his own good, wearing a blue button-up that matched his eyes and his usual pressed jeans. He had his hair perfectly fingered back, with just the right amount of blond scruff on his jaw.

"Who are these people to you?" I asked.

"Family."

"Oh, I didn't know I was about to meet your parents and siblings. A warning would've been nice."

"You're not. They're my… brothers, so to speak."

"Where are your parents?"

"Here in Massachusetts."

I rolled my eyes. "That's rather vague. You might as well say they're here in the United States."

He sighed. "They're in Lawrence."

Interesting. Lawrence was one of the poorest towns Massachusetts had to offer. "Any siblings?"

"No."

"Did you go to school there?"

"Yes."

"Great conversation, Clery."

He glanced at me through his sunglasses. "I... don't enjoy talking about my youth."

"Fair enough. Where did you go to college?"

"Harvard."

"Impressive. You left Lawrence to go all the way to the big city and to Harvard. Now you're a wealthy lawyer. You've made it. Few people can say that. Leaving small towns is never easy."

"I worked my ass off to get where I am." His hands fisted the steering wheel so tightly, that his knuckles turned white. It was clearly a difficult subject for him to talk about.

"Hey, I'm serious. I'm impressed."

He loosened his hands and visibly relaxed.

"Are you close to your parents?"

"God, Bond, what is up with the interrogation?"

"I'm not... never mind. I just thought I'd get to know you since I know literally nothing about you, and I'm about to meet your second family."

He smirked at me, and I wasn't sure if he was masking his earlier discomfort or if he turned it off that easily. "You know some things about me. Like how my hand feels on your ass. Or my tongue on your—"

"Got it!" My face blushed, and I looked out the window, smiling. "I can't tell them those sorts of details, James." Regardless of my embarrassment, I wondered if James used sex as a barrier to hide behind.

"That's fine. We can relive it later."

Forty minutes later, we pulled up to a long drive flanked on either side by thick trees. That didn't scream rich at all. The house rose over the distance, and I had to admit that it was magnificent, with immaculate landscaping. The massive house was white stone and was able to fit twenty of my offices inside.

"Wow, that's some house."

"Yeah, it's nice if you like that sort of thing."

"You don't?"

He shrugged. "I prefer city life, and my condo."

"I like the city, too."

When James pulled to a stop, he turned off the car, hopped out, and opened my door for me. With his hand, he helped me out. Standing, I brushed a hand across my skirt to smooth out any wrinkles. It was a good thing I went shopping.

"This skirt is much better than your last one."

I stuck my tongue out at him, making him laugh. "Promises, promises." Then he opened up the trunk and pulled out all the gifts. "Shall we? Fuck, I hate these things. Be prepared for lots of teasing that I'm sure will be headed our way."

"Oh?"

"I've never brought a woman to meet them before."

He walked off, leaving me jaw dropped. I didn't get it. He wanted no feelings, no attachments, yet he wanted me to meet his second family, a family who's never met any of his girls before. The man perpetually left me confused. Was he interested? Did he want more? Was this for show?

"You coming, Bond? Oh, and there's someone here you might know," he said, winking.

What now?

I had little time to take in the sights of the gorgeous and comfortable home as we quickly made our way out back to the large yard and veranda. Kids screamed everywhere, and a little black-haired toddler tried to keep up along with a chocolate lab, corralling the kids.

They filled the place with flowers, balloons, and a bouncy house. As soon as we neared the group of parents, everyone turned to us and froze with ping-ponging eyes between James and me. Shock was the most apt word for their faces. I wasn't sure if I should've felt honored or horrified that he chose me to be the first woman they'd met.

"Everyone, this is Jane Bond. We're working on a case together. She's a P.I. You can all quit staring now."

Well, that answered that question. No girlfriend status, though I couldn't understand why that bothered me. We weren't exactly a thing, or that I even liked him all that much. Still, this entire situation left me wondering what the hell was going on with him.

"Cat, you remember Bond, don't you?"

Cat?

A beautifully tall, black-haired, pregnant woman came up to me with curious eyes. "Detective Bond, right?"

"Catherine Ruiz. I remember you. How have you been holding up?"

"Great. Married with another baby on the way." She rubbed her growing belly as pregnant women did.

Surprising me, she wrapped her arms around me and pulled me into a small hug. "How do you know James beyond my case?"

"Purely a coincidence. As James said, he hired me for a job, and my sister is dating his friend from work."

She smiled, guiding me to the group by my arm. "Well, let's meet everyone."

Those were a lot of good-looking men. Good grief. Did James know anyone who didn't look like a damned model?

I recognized three of them as brothers because they looked alike with their fair skin and dark, wavy hair.

"This is Ronan, my husband." He was the tallest of the three with piercing green eyes, paler than mine. "And the twins are his youngest brothers, Cian and Callum." I gave them a quick wave. Callum wore forearm crutches from some sort of disability.

Cian didn't even smile, but gave me a curt nod. Callum, though, was full of white teeth from his broad smile. "I can't believe James brought a girl. Holy shit. This is one for the history books."

I snorted a laugh. "Well, it's not like that."

"Oh, it's so like that. James can lie to himself all he wants. But he hasn't taken his eyes off of you since you got here."

I glanced over at James, who had lifted Georgie into his arms as she chatted animatedly at him. He wasn't smiling, but the little girl had his attention. Then he glanced over at me before he looked away.

"See? This will be so good for him. James needs to be taken back to this planet. His ego has its own space station."

I laughed again. "Noted."

"Jane, this is my girl, Finley. And the petite blond with the pink in it, is Addy, Cian's girlfriend."

The two women smiled and shook my hand. Just like Cat, their eyes were curious, uncertain of what to make of me. Hell, I was uncertain of what to make of me. Why did he even bring me here?

A young blond man came up to me and shook my hand. "I'm Charles, Brady's husband. He's the giant redhead over there and the fourth brother."

"Pleased to meet you, Charles. I'm Jane."

After some small talk, I made my way toward James, still having his ear talked off by the birthday girl.

James set her down. "Bond, this is Georgie."

I squatted in front of her. "Hi, Georgie. I'm Jane. It's a pleasure to meet you."

"Hi, Jane! You're really pretty. I like your outfit. Your hair is really pretty too.

"Why, thank you. You look gorgeous yourself."

Georgie beamed at me, then looked back and forth at James and me. "Are you James' girlfriend? Are you going to get married? I think you should get married. Come on. Let's meet my daddies."

She tugged on my hand, and as we walked off, I looked back at James who was twirling a finger around his ear, showing she was nuts. I rolled my eyes and laughed.

"Daddies! Daddies!" Georgie yelled out, dragging me to two more handsome men. One was taller than James, but the other stood a couple of inches shorter.

"I'm Luke," the taller one introduced, holding out his hand. I took it, and we shook. He had some intense hazel-green eyes. They were hardened, as if he'd seen more than he should've in life. I'd seen it before, back when I was a cop.

"And I'm Daniel," said the dark-haired one with soft brown eyes. "Has Georgie talked your ear off yet?"

I laughed. "No, she's adorable."

The two men wrapped their arms around each other and smiled proudly at their daughter.

After eating some cake, watching the kids play, and getting to know everyone, it felt awfully comfortable. Like James and I were a real item, which we weren't. I wasn't about to kid myself.

"Come with me, Bond," James whispered in my ear, threading our fingers together, and pulling me towards the house.

"Where are we going? Are you going to show me your favorite spot to drop your pants?"

He turned his head to look at me with a raised brow, but he wore a smirk on his face. "I knew you were smart."

I rolled my eyes but didn't protest. I only had to remember that we were having fun. Although, his jealousy over my date that he made me cancel, and then with what Callum said, tugged at my mind in the other direction, wondering if *he* was the one developing feelings. Or perhaps fighting them.

When we reached a comfortable but masculine office, James closed and locked the door behind him.

"Take off your panties, lift your skirt, and lie back on the desk."

"Uhm, I'm not sure the person this desk belongs to will appreciate me being naked on it."

"Oh, I intend to fuck you on it. I've been dying to fuck someone on Ronan's desk. He's done it to me often enough, fucking girls on my bed or desk, before the days he decided on the ball and chain."

"It's called marriage, Clery. Perhaps you've heard of it."

"Getting sassy with me will earn you spankings and no coming, sweet girl. Do. As. You're. Told."

Jeez, why did I find his controlling me so damn sexy? My panties got soaked in moments.

I lifted my skirt and peeled off my panties as James leaned against the door with folded arms, making sure I complied.

"Put your panties on the desk, and lift your skirt, so I can see your pussy."

My heart rate and breathing accelerated as I slowly lifted my skirt. I'd recently shaved, too, so I was neat and trimmed.

"Good girl. Now sit your naked ass on the desk, lie back, and spread your legs."

I didn't need to take off my panties. His smoldering stare and intense posture would've melted them off. After lifting my skirt, I sat on the neat desk and lay back, spreading my thighs.

"Lift your legs and expose your pussy more to me."

My body trembled with arousal and a healthy dose of humiliation, but I liked it. A lot. And James knew it. I raised my legs by lifting my thighs. Once I was ready, he walked over to me and dragged a finger through my entrance.

"I love how you get so wet for me, Bond. So responsive."

I stared at the ceiling, listening to him sucking my juice off his fingers, then to the sounds of him loosening his belt and unzipping his jeans.

"Shit. I forgot to put a condom in my wallet."

"Crap… Well, I'm clean and on the pill, and I've been recently tested."

"I'm tested regularly. You sure about this, Bond?"

"Yes… just do it."

"Hmm, I love your desperation for my cock. Next time, I want you on your knees to see how far you can take it inside your mouth."

Next time? So he *did* plan to spend more time with me. This was definitely no longer a one-night stand, and growing into more of a friends-with-benefits thing. One thing I understood for certain was the longer we spent together, someone was going to develop feelings. At first, I would have assumed it'd be me, but now I had doubts.

Not that I was overly insecure, but why me? There were thousands of women who looked like supermodels across Boston. I just didn't seem like his type, so why did he keep coming back for more?

Shut up, Jane, and enjoy the damned moment.

"Fuck, you have a gorgeous cunt. I could look at it all day, but I'd rather be inside you."

With that said, he slammed home. James did nothing delicately. It was always rough and aggressive, but hell if I didn't love that. My back arched off the desk, and I may have groaned too loudly because he shoved my panties in my mouth.

"Let's not drag the families in here, yeah?" he whispered in my ear. "We don't want to shock children."

James slowly pulled out and slammed back in again. I was so wet for him, that despite his size, there was little resistance. His long fingers clawed at my hips and pulled my ass off of the desk as he thrust hard and fast into me, hitting that gorgeous spot, already feeling an orgasm coming on. What a rare treat.

He moaned quietly and moved his hand to my clit, rubbing it with his thumb. "I want us to come together," he panted. "Tell me you're close because your tight cunt feels too damned good. It's a fucking vise. And with no condom on, I'm going to blow."

I could only nod with my panties in my mouth.

He rubbed and pounded. Rubbed and pounded.

"Come on, Bond. Do it. Do it," he ground out between thrusts.

I threw my head back and arched my back, shoving him deeper into me as the pressure grew too much. Like an overfilled water balloon, I exploded with a muffled moan.

"Fuck!"

His cock burned like fire inside me, swelled, then the warm wetness filled me.

When he pulled out, I heard him curse again. "Fuck me... watching our come mingle and slide out of you is... surprisingly sexy as hell."

James zipped up, pulled my panties out of my mouth, and slid them on over my legs and around my hips and ass. Then he lifted my limp body upward, holding me close.

"Hold my come in those panties, Bond. Don't take them off until tonight. I want you to feel my cock inside you every time you drip into them."

"Holy shit..."

"Your pussy is my new religion."

CHAPTER 13

Jane

A WEEK HAD PASSED SINCE THE BIRTHDAY PARTY, AND JAMES STOPPED by nearly every night after work, helping me put together my office as long as I helped him with his incessant horniness. The man was insatiable. When I didn't see him, I tried not to imagine other women he could be seeing. It shouldn't have bothered me, yet it did, not that I had a leg to stand on to ask him about it. We weren't exactly an item. Sure, we fucked all the time, but James hadn't made any move toward anything deeper, leaving me perpetually confused.

I needed to talk to someone, and at first, I almost called Penny, but she'd blab to Brody. Then Brody would blab to James. No, thank-freakin'-you. Instead, I called Colton, my old partner from work. I trusted him as much as I trusted my family. He was the only one who stood by me when all that sexual harassment shit went on, and virtually the only person who believed me. I would forever be grateful to him for helping me not be so alone. Even then, it wasn't enough for me to stay.

Before Colton showed up at the bar we agreed to meet at, James texted me. Because, of course, he did.

James: Where are you?
Bond: Out.
James: No shit. Where are you?
Bond: You know, I'm entitled to not be at your beck and call whenever you're horny, which seems to be daily.
James: Last I checked, you had no problems coming all over my cock.

Good grief. I laughed and shook my head at no one, unsure if it was from humor or exasperation.

Bond: Regardless, I'm out and meeting someone.

There was a long pause, and I saw he was trying to type with the three dots showing up. Either he had a lot to say, or kept deleting and starting over. And... apparently, it was the latter.

James: Who?

I rolled my eyes.

Bond: None of your business.

Yeah, I wrote that on purpose to annoy him, knowing how controlling he was.

James: This better not be a date.
Bond: And what if it is?
James: Where are you?
Bond: Again, none of your business.
James: Oh, you're getting punished the next time I see you. Hard.

And... there went my damn panties. How the hell did he do that all the time?

Bond: Oh, I'm so scared.
James: Your ass and pussy are going to be begging and hurting at the same time.
Bond: Relax, Clery. I'm meeting my old partner, Colton.
James: He better be an eighty-year-old hunchback.
Bond: He's actually really tall, muscular, tattooed, and sexy as hell. He could literally bench-press me.

James: Tell me where you are… now.
Bond: Did I mention that wherever he goes, people want him? Men and women alike. I'm flustered just thinking about it, and my panties are soaked.
James: You're messing with me, aren't you?
Bond: Boy, you're quick. Oh, and I forgot to mention that he's gay. You're safe, Clery.
James: You're not going to be able to sit for a week for that little game.
Bond: Promises, promises.

Before he said anything else, Colton walked in. I waved him over, and when he found me, he gave me a beaming smile. He wore a black Henley that was tight across his broad body, worn jeans, and well-loved boots. His hair was cropped close to his scalp as always, and he had piercing gray eyes. I laughed as every woman in the bar, along with some men, turned their heads to gawk at him.

"Hey, Jane," he said, kissing my cheek.

"How's my favorite person?" I asked.

"He's good. How's *my* favorite person? I miss you."

"I miss you too… and the job. But it is what it is. How are you and Brice? Any wedding bells yet?"

He blew out a laugh and blushed. "We're good. Nah, nothing like that. We're in no hurry."

"Well, tell him I said hello."

"I will. So, how's the P.I. business going? Any clients?"

"Yep, but my biggest job is under an NDA, so I can't talk about it, unfortunately."

He waved the waitress over and ordered a beer, and I ordered another margarita. "Interesting. Someone well-known?"

"Yes. But it's… complicated. I was hired by this lawyer, and, well… we sort of met before. From a, ah, date."

Colton winged a brow. "Don't tell me you're still dating him. You realize it's risky when you combine pleasure with business."

"Ugh, I know! We aren't really dating. Mostly just, you know…" I waggled my brows for effect. "Honestly, I'm not sure what to do. He's an arrogant ass, and if you look up *'red flag'* in the dictionary, it has his face on it. But he's... growing on me. I didn't want anything serious, but there are things about him that he shows more and more. Things that aren't so... red flaggy."

The waitress delivered our drinks and left us. Colton took a long sip of beer, thinking about what to say. Probably ready to tell me to end things, which would be the smart thing to do.

"I never pictured you liking some bad boy, Jane."

"I usually don't. But he's growing on me."

"And he hasn't told you how he's felt?"

I shook my head. "No, but he tries to see me every day, and he gets possessive. It's... confusing, especially after declaring his boundaries of not getting involved at all with women."

"Hmm, and how long have you two been going at it?"

I shrugged. "A couple of weeks? But our date was over three weeks ago."

"If he hasn't made his interest in you beyond sex known in another week or two, dump him, especially if you're getting the feels. If he feels the same, he'll tell you by then."

I nodded and sipped my drink. "You're right. That's a good plan. See, what would I do without you?"

We clinked glasses to good ideas. After catching up and a few more drinks, we called it a night. I really needed to spend more time with him. Perhaps once I got settled, I'd invite him and Brice over for dinner.

I sat in my car with a pair of binoculars, a camera, and cold coffee, scoping out Newall's home in Beacon Hill, one of the wealthiest neighborhoods in Boston, with homes averaging three million dollars. It was one of the oldest neighborhoods in the city and beautiful. It's the place the rest of us plebs envy, and I got to sit there and admire the view.

Brick and stone paved the streets with antique gas lamps, like the days of old, and filled with Federal-style row houses. If you were lucky, you'd have a view of the Charles River.

It was dark out as I observed the home of Anthony Newall and Rikke Madsen. She headed out with some friends while Anthony remained at home. Things had been slow trying to catch Anthony in the act, and I stressed that there was nothing to find. Surprisingly, James hadn't nagged me about it. Then again, he got laid on a regular basis, and I kept him up to date whenever I worked with a detailed spreadsheet of my hours and expenses.

A tap on my window startled me, and I reached for my gun in my holster. Looking at the passenger side, I saw James leaning down, smiling through the window.

How the fuck did he know where I was?

I unlocked my door, and he climbed in along with a bag of food.

"Are we stalking me now? That's low, even for you, Clery."

"I need to protect my investment. You don't come cheap, Bond."

"That's not what you said the other night."

He barked out a laugh. "Touché!"

"How *did* you find me?"

"I have my ways."

"Stalker…" I said, lifting the binoculars to my eyes and pointing them at Newall's house, not that I could see anything. The curtains were drawn, and there was no sign of life.

"I don't know why I'm here. If he's cheating, he's really good at covering it up, so I doubt he'd bring a lover home while wifey poo is out."

"True."

The rustling of bags dragged my attention back to James as he handed me a sandwich. "Eat, Bond. I brought sub sandwiches."

"That's peasant food. I'm surprised you didn't bring escargot."

"Aren't we in a mood tonight? You seem rather… grouchy."

I scoffed and took a large bite of the sandwich full of cheese, a variety of deli meats, and cherry peppers. "That's what happens when a girl is stalked," I said with my mouth full.

"Are you still harping on that? I brought you dinner and entertainment."

"I'm just bored, and nothing's been happening. I'm thinking Ms.
Actress is wrong or wants to hurt her husband for another reason."

"It's possible, but I don't think so. She's certain."

I glanced over at Mr. Gorgeousness. "What entertainment?"

"Hello, delayed reaction. Me, of course."

"You're insatiable," I said, but I couldn't help but smile as I took
another bite of my sandwich. I had to admit, it was nice to be wanted.

"I swear, you must put opiates in your pussy."

"Or, maybe you just like me." My heart stopped. I hadn't meant to
bring this up, but it slipped out. I played off my mistake by taking
another bite, staring off at the large brick house.

"You're okay, I guess."

I blew out a laugh and whacked his shoulder with the back of my
hand. "Way to make a girl feel wanted, Clery."

He leaned in and pressed a kiss to my ear. "How about how I make
a *woman* feel wanted?"

Goosebumps traveled down my arm from his words and his light
breath on my skin. "Now?" I wanted to sound more defiant, but my
voice came out a mere whisper. How did he just switch me on like
that? One minute he annoyed the hell out of me, the next I wanted to
climb him and make him mine.

"Eat first, then you're going to take my cock down your throat like
the good girl I know you are."

After we washed down our food with water, I already had that
tingling pressure that had me aching to thrust my hips at anything, even
the air, when he slid his hand up my shirt and tweaked my nipple
through my bra.

His other hand traveled to my hair and fisted it, as he loved to do.
Taking full control of my body.

My puppet master.

With his tight grip, he pulled me towards his bulge. "Unzip me and
pull me out."

"What if we're caught?"

"You have tinted windows, and I'll keep watch while you make a meal out of my dick."

I couldn't say no to him even if I wanted to, so I did as I was told, unzipping his pants and pulling out his engorged cock. Apparently, it didn't take much to turn himself on, either. Once he was free, James pushed my head down. I opened my mouth and took him in as much as possible. He was too big, but we'd been practicing for me to take him further each time, loosening my throat, and breathing through my nose to control my gag reflex. I was getting better, but still only reached two-thirds of the way.

"Good girl. Take my cock... Mmm, just like that."

Normally, I would've licked the underside of his length, swirl my tongue around his head, and shove it into his slit, but he was content to use my mouth how he saw fit, pulling and pushing my head, and doing more work than I was.

"Fuck, you've got a nice mouth, sweet girl." He shoved my head further down, so he went even deeper. I gagged, and he lifted me up again, but wouldn't release me. "Yeah, take it deeper. I know you can do it."

Despite his ability to talk, his voice grew hoarse, deep, and strained. He definitely felt the arousal consume him.

Meanwhile, I was leaking all over my panties from his control and dirty talk.

He pushed me further down. The deepest I'd ever gone. I gagged and drooled, making my eyes water, but I didn't fight it. A groan escaped, making his cock burn and swell.

"Yes, deeper. Gag for me, baby."

Before I couldn't take anymore, he cried out and exploded down my throat. His hand released me, allowing me to pull up and suck him dry.

"Fuck... you're so good at giving head, sweet girl," he panted.

When I pulled up, he took my face and wiped away the tears. "So beautiful. Look at those tears. Those swollen lips." Then he leaned in and licked the corner of my mouth. "And dripping with my come."

God, I'd never been with a man like James. He made me feel like a dirty whore, but I liked it, as if it was an honor to be his dirty whore. I was revered.

He leaned over and unbuttoned and unzipped my jeans, then slipped his hand underneath my panties, fingering my clit until I cried out and came all over his hand.

The entire scene was filthy, raunchy, and heady. I loved it. What I didn't love was my growing affection for him.

CHAPTER 14

Jane

James: What are you doing tomorrow?

HE WASN'T GOING TO MAKE IT EASY ON ME, WAS HE? GROWING affection meant impending doom and heartbreak, but I couldn't drag myself away either.

Jane: Training.
James: Vague. Can you be more specific, or are you going to make me guess?
Jane: Tae Kwon Do. I like to keep up with it whenever I can.
James: Need a sparring partner?

Interesting. I knew James was fit, but I had no idea he could fight too.

Jane: You know martial arts?
James: More like MMA. Ronan and Daniel taught me.
Jane: Sure, why not. Usually, I just practice my moves or spar with a bag, so this will be a nice change.
James: When and where?

I texted him the address and time.

Jane: Be prepared to have your ass handed to you.

He sent me a few devil emojis.

James: Oh, sweet girl. Your ass belongs to me.

A shiver traveled down my spine as lust coursed through me. How the hell did he do that? It was like his superpower.

I walked into the gym to find James already waiting for me. He was scrolling through his phone, shirtless and wearing only gym shorts. I tried not to ogle his body with those cut, lean muscles, but it was nearly impossible.

"Like what you see?" he asked, catching me staring.

"You trying to distract me while we spar? Worried that you'll lose?"

He gave me an evil grin. "I like your competitive nature, Bond, but you don't stand a chance."

"I'm a second-degree black belt."

"Which will make my win even more delicious."

Sparring with men could be a challenge sometimes. During my years taking classes, they either went easy on me or turned into cavemen if I got in a good hit.

I sparred with one man who cheated when I got in too many hits, so in retaliation, he clipped me in my knee with his foot. Another time, he kicked me in the head hard enough to put me in physical therapy. Both were against the rules. I refused to spar with him again after that.

Hopefully, James would be a better sport.

I wrapped up my hands in sparring gloves, and James did the same. This was for practice, not injuring each other. Regardless, we'd still walk away with bruises.

After some stretching and warm-ups, we stepped into the sparring ring I had reserved. Because it was after dinner, the place wasn't crowded, which I preferred, not wanting to draw in a crowd to watch me. I was decent, but I hated being stared at while I worked out, especially being one of the few females in the place.

I made my stance, keeping my legs loose and shoulder width apart, and lifted my hands, palms facing out. James made his own stance, which was a little different from mine.

Fighting someone who knew MMA could be a challenge. I wouldn't know all the moves, so I'd have to quickly adapt. But James would be faced with the same dilemma.

"Ready to get your ass whooped, Bond."

"You talk too much, Clery."

We put in our mouthguards and started. At first, it was all about sizing each other up as we circled, ever ready, tense, looking for openings and weaknesses. The key was to maintain eye contact, not the hands and legs. You needed to see their reaction before they moved and use your visual periphery to react to their attacks.

James was strong, so I prepared to be hit hard... unless he was one of those who took it easy on me.

"This foreplay is taking too long," he taunted.

"Foreplay is what you do best, Clery."

"Oh, sweet girl, I'm best at a lot of things, as you well know."

He couldn't push my buttons. Once I was in the ring, I was in the zone.

James suddenly came at me with flying fists, which I deflected, blocking with my forearms. Blocking sometimes hurts as much as being hit since you're basically smashing bone against bone. Muscle against muscle.

A quick kick from his long leg had me jumping back. He was definitely taking it easy on me. He could have thrown a lot more.

He kicked out at me again, and when I blocked it, I hit him in the stomach and jumped back.

Soon we were flying arms and legs, neither of us getting much hitting in. Both of us spent more time blocking. Sweat gathered on my body, and I tried not to focus on James' gleaming muscles.

When he did a high kick, I ducked and swiped his other leg out from under him, knocking him on his ass. Something possessed me, and before he could recover, I pounced on him, straddling his body with mine. I leaned in and kissed him, throwing him off guard. He was salty from sweat, and I probably tasted the same.

"Ready to yield, Clery?" I asked when I pulled away.

With a cocky smile, he wrapped his arms around me and flipped me onto my back, pinning my arms down. "I never yield, sweet girl."

God, whenever he called me that, I always got wet, like he trained my body to respond to it. I tried to fight him off, but he was too heavy. Then again, I didn't exactly try that hard, either.

"How about a wager?"

"I don't have a lot of money, Clery."

"Not all wagers have to do with money."

"Fine, what do you want to bet?"

"It's simple, really. The winner gets blown in those showers over there."

My stomach twisted with arousal and the idea of possibly being caught by the few people still here in the gym.

He leaned into my ear. "... sweet girl."

I swallowed and struggled not to let him see how aroused he got me. "Deal."

His smile was broad, with a look of self-congratulations on his face. I rolled my eyes as he helped me stand.

We took our stances once more, ready. Now that we had a bet in place, I knew James wouldn't hold back. He proved to be a challenge and much better at fighting than I had expected.

He blocked my sidekick, but he couldn't stop my jump kick, hitting him in the chest. He staggered backward, and after quickly recovering, he didn't hold back at all. Our shins collided with blocks, my forearms were bruised and aching, and we both quickly grew tired.

I threw one more kick at him, and he caught my foot mid-air. Bastard. So, I leaped off my left foot and swung, hitting him in the shoulder mid-air. He staggered again, but this time he retaliated and kicked my feet out from under me as soon as I landed.

I fell onto my back, and he pounced on me as I did the last time, straddling me. He grabbed my hands and pinned them to the mat. "Ready to choke on my cock, sweet girl?"

I fought him off, but again, he was too damned heavy and strong.

"You can fight all you want, but I'm not letting go until you cede."

I squirmed, but I had one last trick up my sleeve. I pumped my hips high and forward, banging into him. He would have a choice of letting go of me and landing forward on his hands or falling on his face.

He chose the former. Once he let go and fell forward, I rolled out from under him, leaving one leg underneath while my other leg smacked him on his back. Wrapping my ankles together, I squeeze. Sure, it wasn't a Tae Kwon Do move, but it worked. My ability to win depended on the strength of my legs, and they were very strong.

"Fuck, Bond… you're going to… crack a rib," he gasped.

I squeezed my thighs tighter.

"Okay, okay… Jesus."

"Do you yield, Clery? I mean, I know how you hate to lose."

Another squeeze had him wheezing.

"Fine… you… win."

I let him go and smiled. James fell onto his back and rubbed his ribs. "Fuck. Remind me not to get on your bad side, Bond."

I straddled him again, unable to hide my smug smile, and leaned into his ear. "I, too, hate to lose."

"I'd say that was kind of hot, but I still can't breathe."

"Don't be a baby." I stood and offered my hand. He took it, and I helped him up.

"You should see me when I have a cold."

I barked out a laugh. "Ready to rock my world, Clery?"

"I'm always ready for that."

We removed our mouthguards, and James pressed his lips to mine, consuming my sweaty mouth and uncaring a few stragglers who remained in the place.

After climbing out of the ring and removing our gloves, James wasted no time dragging me to the women's showers. There were no women around tonight, so the place was probably safe to have fun in without being caught, but that didn't stop my nerves from flaring.

I double-checked to make sure the bathroom was empty, then waved James inside.

He turned on the shower and let it get hot as we undressed. God, he was already hard as a rock. I watched his cock bounce around as he moved about, getting us ready. Why did that make my mouth drool?

James stepped into the shower and did a quick rinse-off, then he turned to face me and put on a show of stroking himself. "It's time to collect your prize. No time like the present. Want me on my knees before you, Bond?"

I walked into the steaming water and grabbed his cock, and gave him a few tugs.

"Yes. That's a good spot for a playboy like you." I wasn't sure where that line came from. I guess James was rubbing off on me. He gave me a broad smile and dropped to his knees.

"I want your eyes never to leave mine," I ordered. "I want to see those pretty blues staring up at me as you worship me."

He raised a brow. "I'm rubbing off on you, I see," he said, reading my mind.

"Maybe a little."

James spread me and ran his thumb over my clit. I shuddered and fell back against the cold tiles, so I didn't fall.

"Shouldn't I wash up first?" I asked as his face inched closer to me.

"You're killing the vibe, Bond. And no. I quite enjoy pussy tasting like pussy, and not flowers.

With his eyes gazing up at me, he leaned in and ran his tongue in my entrance up to my clit. Though I ordered him to look up at me, I wasn't sure I'd be able to keep my eyes on him.

My body shuddered again when he suckled my clit. And when he inserted two fingers deep inside me, I took fistfuls of his silky hair and moaned. Then with his other, he used a finger to graze my tight hole.

God, the stimulation from his tongue on my clit, fingers inside me, and touching my hole sent waves of warmth through my body and straight to my face. Pressure slowly built between my legs, and I almost thrust for more, but I wanted to prolong this.

"You're so hot down there, Clery," I said to distract myself from the inevitable plunge.

His mouth moved away from my clit, and I nearly cried out, but a whimper escaped me. I didn't miss his smug smile. So damned full of himself. But when we were like this, it was the only time I liked it. There was something to be said for having sexy fun with a confident man who knew what he was doing.

His mouth attacked my clit again, and as soon as his finger slipped deep inside my tight hole, I came. No, I didn't just come. I exploded. I smacked my hand against my mouth as I cried out while pulsing and leaking all over his mouth.

As I chased my orgasm, the only thing keeping me upright was James still attacking my clit. My body nearly convulsed as he kept hitting those sensitive nerves.

"Stop… please."

He finally pulled away, but not without one last lick, making my body jump.

"Asshole."

"You love it."

When he stood, I reached for his cock to give him some release since it was still hard as hell, but he grabbed my wrist, stopping me.

"You won the bet, Bond. You can serve my cock later."

James guided my numb body into the water and lathered it up, taking care to wash every inch of me. After he quickly lathered and rinsed, we dried off and got dressed.

"Let's get you fed, sweet girl."

"Okay." I was too tired to argue.

My body ached and was growing bruises, as was his, and my mind was sex-drunk, so he led me out of the gym and into his car.

"After food, then I'll feed you dessert," he said, winking. "And not the sweet kind."

I rolled my eyes and shook my head, but I was smiling too.

CHAPTER 15

James

"JAMES? RIKKE MADSEN IS ON THE LINE," SAM SAID, CALLING ME over my intercom.

Shit. I had nothing for her yet, and if we didn't find something soon, she could go to another firm, and I'd lose my chances of becoming a partner. Or worse.

I pushed the intercom button. "Thanks, Sam. Send her through."

When the call came in, I lifted the receiver. "Rikke, what a pleasure."

"Enough pleasantries. I'm getting impatient, Mr. Clery. Where is my proof? I know my husband is cheating."

I had to be careful with my words because I was doubting her claims. If Newall wasn't cheating, I'd lose anyway, not that I would ever fabricate something. That shit could come back to bite me in the ass.

"We're working on it. I assure you, he'll slip up. But he's very good at hiding his indiscretions. My P.I. has been on his case, following him everywhere, but all his meetings are held with clients and friends. Nothing out of the ordinary yet. I apologize that it's taking so long."

"Find it. Find something. I mean it, or I will find someone who can."

"Ms. Madsen…" *Careful, James.* "It's your choice to hire someone new. No matter whom you hire, they will have the same problem. There just isn't anything yet. He *will* slip. I promise you that. Cheaters always do. They're always found out, eventually."

"Very well. I'll give you two weeks, Mr. Clery," she said, temporarily mollified.

I hung up the phone, ran a hand through my hair, and sighed. Fuck.

Time was running out, and I felt the noose tighten around my neck. I'd be out of a job if this didn't work out. If she left for another firm, that'd be the end of me. Dammit!

And that wasn't the worst of it.

Fucking Bond. She wouldn't leave my goddamn mind. I thought I could fuck her out of my system a third time, but after that, I kept coming back to her pussy over and over again.

"Or, maybe you just like me."

That's what she said. The truth of the matter was I did like her. I enjoyed her company. She was smart, sassy, and had a mind of her own. While she loved being controlled in the bedroom, she never gave me an inch outside of it. Always calling me out on my shit. She wasn't as desperate for my attention as I apparently was for hers.

Psychologically, I wondered if that was her biggest lure. Oh, sure, other women didn't care or wanted anything more to do with me after one night. But they weren't interesting. Surely my interest in her ran deeper than some reverse psychology shit. Surely I was smarter than that.

The biggest problem was I didn't do relationships, but Bond kept pulling me back to her like we were tied together in this world. Once we found our way together, life didn't want us apart.

Nonsense.

I didn't believe in that fate drivel.

Still...

A knock on my door yanked me out of my worries.

"Come."

Sam stepped inside, bringing me my afternoon coffee and setting the steaming cup on my desk. "What happened to your hair? It's never a mess. Let me guess. Rikke gave you an earful?"

"Thanks," I said, blowing the hot brew and taking a tentative sip. I put it down and sighed, fingering my hair back in place. "Yeah, she's threatened to pull the plug if I don't come up with something soon. She's given me a two-week deadline."

"Maybe he's not cheating."

I nodded. "The thought crossed my mind."

"What else is bothering you? You've never been overly stressed with a tight deadline before. Usually, you have things under control and thrive when things become tense. You'll figure it out."

Sam understood me all too well. That's what happens when you work closely for years with someone.

She sat across from me, crossed her long legs, and folded her hands in her lap, waiting me out.

"It's a woman."

Thank fuck, Sam knew enough not to smirk or tease me at my expense. I wasn't in the mood. If she were Ronan or Daniel, I'd get an earful and a lot of 'I told you so's.'

"I assume it's someone you're interested in. Which begs the question, why now? You've never been interested in women for the long haul, James. And we both know why. So what's changed?"

Sam wasn't only my assistant, but she was like a mother to me and the only one who knew about my past, things I hadn't even told Ronan or Daniel about. I didn't like talking about it. At. All. Or even thinking about it. Perhaps I should've gotten therapy, but ignoring it had worked so far. My assistant should've been a therapist. It wasn't hard to open up to her. I also trusted her explicitly, even more than my friends, who would needle me. Sam would never do that.

"Jane Bond. I ran into her almost two years ago, when she was a police detective. Some bad shit happened to her, and now she's a P.I. The very P.I. that I hired for the Madsen/Newall case."

"Seems like a conflict of interest."

"Oh, it is. She was only supposed to be a one-night stand, but she wasn't one of those typical models or businesswomen I took to bed."

"Yes, you like them powerful and uninterested in you. You also find them boring, which you do intentionally."

I looked at her knowing hazel-green eyes. I swear Sam could see into my soul. What I liked about her was that she didn't shove my issues in my face. "Bond isn't like those women. If I had to compare her to anyone, she resembles you a bit in personality."

She smirked. "So, basically, she doesn't put up with your shit."

"Basically."

"Which makes you want her more."

"In a weird way. God, and the sex. Despite my need for detachment, she sucks me in. It's so real and visceral."

"I guess the question you need to ask yourself is, do you want to continue things with her and trust a woman for once in your life? Or, do you want to end things before you get too involved with her... or before she gets too involved with you."

I nodded. "The million dollar question."

"I can't answer that for you, James. Only you can decide the direction of your life."

"I was afraid you'd say that."

"You understand better than anyone that life is full of difficult questions and choices. Ask yourself if being with her and giving her— and you—something real is worth it."

Sam stood and brushed imaginary wrinkles from her skirt. "I'll leave you to it, James. You know where to find me if you need to talk."

"Thanks, Sam."

As soon as she stepped out, my phone buzzed with a text from Callum to meet him at his house regarding Bond's sexual harassment claims.

Callum's place was hard-wired to open doors or go on lockdown with a simple hit of a button on his computer. After spending years researching the dark web, he'd grown a little paranoid. So, he'd already unlocked the door for me after seeing me arrive on his security cameras, and I walked inside.

He sat in his chair, with a white calico cat draped over his shoulder, in front of his computer monitors in the living room that he turned into hacking central. It was full of wires, computers, servers, and electronics I couldn't begin to name.

At least he didn't need a wheelchair anymore. He still walked with some difficulty, but he improved more and more, thanks to his girlfriend and physical therapist.

"What's up, Cal? Do you have anything for me?"

"James. How's your girlfriend?"

"She's not my girlfriend." This was why I didn't open up to people, especially the O'Callaghan brothers. If anyone was notorious for teasing and rubbing it in your face, it was Callum.

"Sure she's not, then why are you so hot on this topic of finding the truth about her harassment claims? Why bring her to the birthday party?"

"It's just sex, but we're friends, too. I want to get this asshat out of his job if he's doing this to women. Bond shouldn't have had to quit her job because she didn't want to fuck him."

"Fair enough."

He ticked away on his keyboard, opening up some screens. "So, I couldn't find a whole lot. I mean, the deputy superintendent was a detective at one point, and he's got a lot of bros on his side. All that I've been able to find so far is a lot of circumstantial shit. When you look at it all together, he's looking guilty. But sporadically over the years? Nah. No one's going to pick up on it. And it looks like Bond was the only one to go out of her way to file official charges against him."

"So what do we have?"

Callum opened up seven windows on the monitor with pictures of women. Female cops, specifically. All of them were relatively attractive.

"All of these women sent complaints to their captains, but nothing ever happened."

"Jane mentioned she tried to reach out to several women who refused to speak up."

"It doesn't surprise me. There could be even more women, but none have come forward. You see here," he said, pointing to the data on the screen of each woman. "These are awards or commendations they'd received. But you'll notice an influx of reprimands, horrible case assignments, and lost evidence or misplaced paperwork. They all coincide with the time they complained. Suddenly, no more complaints. This spans across a decade, so no one's picked up on it, obviously… except for your Jane. Or, maybe they have, and Eakin made it go away. Detective Bond is the only one who's quit over it, and more power to her. The other women are still working on the force in various departments. Some have a lot to lose, so I'm not surprised they didn't come forward again."

"Regardless, he's guilty. Even worse, he's done this to many women. This fucker needs to go down. Do me a favor and organize all this into a nice, neat little package along with Bond's charges. Then dump the data anonymously to HR and Internal Affairs. Let them see the pattern you found."

"You got it. Your girlfriend is going to be excited to see this asshole fired."

I blew out a dramatic sigh. "One, she's not my girlfriend. Two, she's not to know I stuck my nose in this."

"Keep telling yourself that, James. We all know and love you. You don't do this shit for any woman—friend or otherwise."

I waved a dismissive hand. "Project all you want, Cal. Anyway, I'm out of here. Thanks for your work on this."

"You got it. Let me know if you want this Josh Eakin destroyed. If this doesn't pan out, I can plant some shit on him."

I gave him a curt nod and left.

CHAPTER 16

Jane

I ADJUSTED THE SMALL SOFA AND TWO CHAIRS IN THE FRONT ROOM. The credenza had a vase of fake flowers and a coffee pot for clients. After I hung up two pictures on the walls, I was done. The front office was finished. Everything had been painted, but I still had to put together my own office in the back.

Once I grew in business, I'd eventually be able to afford an assistant, and I could put a desk in here for them.

I had worked on a couple of jobs, but nothing to rake in the cash. James was paying me, but I needed a few more jobs to start bringing in a regular paycheck. Business cards had been passed around, and I had a social media account with a few people following. If I wrapped up this job with James, he'd put in a good word for me for future jobs with other law firms.

Speaking of the devil, he walked in and looked around the room. I'd gotten used to James stopping by unannounced. I wasn't sure why he did that. Maybe he was afraid I'd say no if he asked.

"Nice digs, Bond. Not too shabby for someone who just started their business."

"Thanks. It's a start. At least it's mine, and I have no one to answer to other than myself."

"Well, and me. I *am* paying you after all."

"Don't remind me." I teased him, but I appreciated the work.

He shoved a heavy box at me, wrapped in pretty striped paper in a rainbow of colors.

"What's this?"

"What does it look like? It's a present. Is it, or is it not, your birthday tomorrow?"

"Yes. How did you... never mind. I guess you did some digging of your own."

"Sam, my assistant, did."

I smiled at him as I tore the package open to a large book. I pulled it out of its box and flipped it over to the front, then rolled my eyes, snorting a laugh. "Seriously?"

He shrugged with an impish smile. "I figured you could put the book on display in your office here."

It was a book containing photographs from all the James Bond movies. '*Bond: Movie History in Photography.*' I flipped through the pages, shaking my head. "This is pretty nice, actually, even if I *am* sick of James Bond crap. Thanks."

I glanced up at him, watching me with a look I struggled to figure out. He wasn't smiling, and his brows were furrowed a little. Hmm. "I thought you weren't good with gifts. Or did you have your assistant pick it out?"

His face brightened again. "You know, I can do things on my own sometimes."

"You can?" I teased.

"What are your plans for tomorrow? Can I take you to dinner?"

I hugged the book to my chest and winged a brow. "James Clery... Are you asking me out on a date?"

"Correction. A birthday dinner."

"I can't, anyway. I always go to my parent's place to celebrate."

"Ah. Well, I'm sure that will be quite... enjoyable."

Should I ask? Dare I ask? What the hell?

"James... would you like to come to my birthday party?"

He glanced at me through his thick, dark lashes. "I'm not good at parties... or with parents."

"We could have sex in my childhood bedroom." I waggled my brows for effect. "You can help corrupt my innocent youth."

He gave me a broad smile, which was nice to see. Usually, I got the smirks. It was rare to witness all his straight, white teeth. "In that case..."

"Is that a yes?"

"I suppose. Your sister Penny won't give me any grief, will she?"

"Like?"

"Oh, I don't know, like try to swindle me into marriage or something."

I snorted a laugh. "It's possible. She's quite pushy. Don't worry, I'll tell her to behave."

I drove us to my parent's house in my well-worn, well-loved Honda CRV. Honestly, I couldn't believe James didn't scoff at it. Then again, he'd been in it before and ended up putting a hot memory inside. Even more unbelievable was James agreeing to celebrate my birthday with my family. I invited him under the assumption he'd turn me down. I mean, we made no promises to each other. We weren't committed.

Weren't we, though?

The more time I spent with him, the more I questioned our boundaries. The drawn lines were seriously blurring. I wanted to ask, but I was sort of afraid to. Surprisingly, I had been enjoying his company, even beyond the fantastic sex, despite his red flags. What we had, I supposed, was a true friends-with-benefits relationship. We weren't affectionate like other couples, but we seemed to have a growing friendship... right along with my growing feelings. Fuck.

If he wanted to meet my family, and he introduced me to his, perhaps there was more going on. And every time I had a chance at a date, he'd flat-out deny me. Did that mean he stopped all his sleeping around? Should I ask? No. I didn't want to know.

"Maybe this wasn't such a good idea," he said, staring out the window when we pulled up to my parent's house.

"I'm not turning around."

Although I couldn't see his face, he seemed nervous, with a clenched hand sitting in his lap.

"I realize that."

"Just don't be a dick to them, and they'll love you. Besides, Penny already knows you."

He turned to face me with a raised brow. "Thanks for the bout of confidence."

"James, you can be a great guy when you want to be. You just need to learn to filter the truth sometimes. There *is* such a thing as too much honesty that it borders on cruelty." Before he interrupted me and argued, I raised my hand to stop him. "It's great you're an honest person. It leaves no room for confusion. But... just tone it down. My family is sweet."

"Give me more credit than that, Bond."

I softened and nodded. "You're right. I'm sorry."

As soon as we walked in, two little monsters bombarded us. "Janie!" They squealed. Before they hugged me, they stopped in their tracks and looked up at the big man they didn't know. Both boys moved behind me, peeking out behind my legs.

"Tristan and Tyler, I'd like you to meet my friend James."

"He's a friend?" Tyler asked.

"Yes, he's my good friend."

Just when I thought James couldn't surprise me anymore, he squatted to their level and held out his hand. "Which one of you is Tristan, and which one is Tyler?"

Tyler let go of me and slowly came up to James, taking his hand to shake. "I'm Tyler."

"Nice to meet you, Tyler."

Tristan always copied what his big brother did, and also shook James' hand.

The boys ran off, and I led James to our kitchen, where we always gathered. Mom stood by the oven, pulling out a roast when we walked in.

I pointed at each family member. "James, that is my mother Camila, but she likes to be called Cami. My dad, Gordon. You already know Penny." She and James nodded to each other, but my sister didn't even bother to hide her knowing smirk. Ugh. I was going to get an earful later. "And this is my very pregnant sister, Fiona, and her husband, Carter. Everyone, this is my friend and employer, James Clery."

After my family said their hellos, dinner was ready, so we all took a seat at the large kitchen table.

"Where's Brody," I asked Penny.

"He had to work on a case. He sends his birthday wishes."

Dinner was full of light conversation and a strangely quiet James. If they asked him a question, he'd answer, but he didn't engage as he normally did. Was he still nervous? I gave him the benefit of the doubt. I knew he didn't like gatherings like this, but that he chose discomfort for my birthday kind of flattered me. Maybe his discomfort had to do with family issues. He rarely talked about his parents, so I assumed they were estranged or something.

"Well, James, I thank you for giving Jane her first big case," Mom said, pouring him another glass of wine. "She's going to be fantastic as a private investigator. My daughter is smart and a hard worker."

James raised his glass in a toast and took a sip. "I couldn't agree more."

Mom just beamed at him, as I rolled my eyes, smiling.

"It was terrible what the Boston P.D. did to my daughter. She worked so hard to achieve her dreams, only for some jerk to harass her." Mom shook her head and took a sip of wine. She probably resented it even more than I did.

"Surely, something can be done with that pig. He shouldn't get away with his behavior," James said, looking directly at me. "I know you've reached out to other women, but why not try again? Maybe things have calmed down for them enough to push forward."

I nodded. "No. I'm done. I wish something could be done about him, but at the end of the day, it wasn't only about Eakin."

"The lack of support from people you thought were family," he said.

"Exactly."

Penny leaned back in her chair and took a large gulp of her wine, eyeing James. Uh, oh. I didn't like that look. She was going to stir up trouble. I tried to get her attention without drawing attention from everyone else, but she ignored me. Rolling my eyes, I said, "Penny…"

Again, she ignored me. "So, James. What are your intentions with my sister?"

Ugh. Why did she have to be such a busybody?

"That's none of your business, Pen," I said.

"You're my sister. Of course, it's my business."

"I don't have intentions, Penny. My primary goal is to get this case settled. Secondary?" He shrugged. "We're simply enjoying each other's company."

Her eyes narrowed. "Are you sure about that?"

"Penny," I warned. "Drop it. That's all that's going on between us. We are working together and are friends. Nothing more. Leave it alone."

She shrugged, but her shrewd eyes showed she didn't believe it for a second. Honestly, I wasn't sure I believed it either, simply because I didn't know what James and I were to each other.

"If you say so," she said.

"Pen, enough. You need to learn to mind your own business," my father said, finally saying something. Fiona remained silent, clearly curious about James and me too.

Then the most unlikely person butted in. Carter sat holding Tyler, who fell asleep and eyed James. "Jane is a great woman, and as part of her family, and not trying to be some caveman, I'm going to say this nicely. Please, don't hurt her."

"I can promise you I'll always be honest."

"Fair enough."

"Now that we're done comparing pen-, er, leg sizes, can we drop this now? Thanks."

I stood from the table and tapped James on the shoulder. "Come on. I'll show you around."

"But we still have cake," Mom said.

"Fine… we'll take it with us."

After singing me happy birthday, my face stopped flaming red like I was a child. I hated being sung to. Mom gave James and me a slice of cake on plates. I handed them to James, who stood with me. Then I refilled our wine glasses, grabbed both, and led us to my old bedroom, which hadn't changed since I moved out. Mom and her sentimentality.

"Sorry about that. Nothing short of a muzzle will silence Penny. Though Carter was a surprise."

He put our plates on the dresser and shoved his hands in his jeans pockets, looking at me through hooded eyes. At least he had a small smile on his face.

"It's to be expected. And I definitely expected Penny to grill me."

"Still…"

"So, you're thirty-four now? My assistant got your birth year correct?" He asked, quickly changing the subject.

"Yep."

To say my bedroom was dated was an understatement. The drawback of sentimentality. The bed had a fluffy cream comforter covered in flowers with heart-shaped pillows and a couple of stuffed animals. Shelves had trophies from high school track and Tae Kwon Do, along with framed pictures of my family and old friends from high school I rarely talked to anymore.

"See, innocent childhood. The room needs some serious corrupting," I said.

James' look was evil and mischievous. "That can be arranged."

"Just don't tell Mom."

We took off our shoes and sat cross-legged, facing each other on the bed as we ate birthday cake, which was only my mom's famous chocolate layered cake with buttercream icing and writing on top.

"I'm surprised you came," I finally said.

James reached over to my face, swiped at the corner of my mouth with his thumb, and brought it to his mouth, sucking off the icing. "Promises of chocolate and corruption are worth it."

"I didn't promise you chocolate."

He shrugged, taking a bite of cake. "Semantics."

James was still being James, but he wasn't. He was off somehow, and I couldn't pinpoint what exactly. My detective's brain struggled to analyze exactly what was going on with him.

You could ask him, idiot.

Hell, no. Sometimes it was easier being a detective than dealing with personal shit. He'd probably be honest in his brutal way, and I wouldn't like what he had to say. For now, I ran with the status quo.

James reached over, set his plate on my dresser, and grabbed mine, placing it on top of his, though I hadn't finished my cake.

"It's time for corruption, Bond."

For the first time since I met James, my stomach fluttered. Things were feeling awfully intimate, and I wasn't sure what to do with it.

CHAPTER 17

James

MY BRAIN AND HEART BATTLED IT OUT WITH EACH OTHER. I NEEDED TO stop this and pull away from her. I shouldn't have agreed to go to her parent's house, knowing threads of feelings tugged at us. It was awkward and unlike me. I couldn't figure out what to talk about; not used to the sweet and comfy family. Sure, I had a family with Ronan and Daniel… sort of, but they were killers at the end of the day. That right there was another problem. How would Bond react if she learned who my friends really were?

That was the least of my worries currently. Why did I struggle so hard to pull away from her? Who cared if we worked together? That didn't mean we had to fuck every time we saw each other. Yet, that was all I wanted to do.

I wasn't a stupid man. Deep down, I understood what was going on, and I understood my issues, but I didn't want to face them. Even deeper, it might've even scared me a little with those unwanted triggers. What a strange thing to see a woman so different from my usual choices. How I interacted with Bond, this inability to get her out of my head. I didn't like it one fucking bit.

The woman fucking grew on me. I kept making excuses about fucking her out of my system, but my system kept changing the damned rules on me.

At dinner earlier, I had flashes of the blond teen girl from so long ago, so full of life… so full of love. But none of it was real. Betrayal wound in lies.

Shit. I kept my past locked up tighter than Fort Knox, but around Bond, she chipped away at my walls like a thief in the night, ready to steal my soul. And she did it without even trying.

And instead of turning it all off and shutting her out, I leaned in and tasted her sweet, chocolatey lips. Her sugary tongue. Her birthday mouth. The things I wanted to do to Bond...

"We can't be loud," she whispered, hovering over my lips with a breath that smelled of intoxicating chocolate and red wine.

"Mmm, so we're to be naughty teens, are we? To not be caught by Mom and Dad?"

"How does that sound gross yet enticing?"

"It's a gift."

She pressed sugary kisses on my lips, jaw, and chin.

"James?"

"Hmm?" I asked, tugging at her shirt to take a peek at her cleavage. It's what naughty teens did, right?

"Do you know what I never got as a teen?" she asked between kisses.

"I'm smart, Bond, but not a mind reader."

She gave me a playful shove and giggled. "Good virgin sex."

I pulled away, seeing her stare at me through thick lashes. Her eyes turned coy, teasing, taunting, especially biting that full bottom lip of hers. "I'm capable of many things, but I can't bring back your virginity."

She rolled her eyes, making me grin. "No shit, Sherlock. I'm talking about the experience. My first time was lame and awkward as hell and lasted for about five minutes with only Mark getting to come."

"Mark? I hate him already."

Her fingers walked up my chest, to my throat, and bopped a digit on my lips. "Can we role-play or something?"

"Darling, the only role-playing I do is me marking your sweet ass when you're being a bad girl."

"Come on. It'll be fun. A perfect way to corrupt my childhood."

"Did *Mark* take you here with all his fumbling and promises of a good time?"

She snorted a laugh. "No, that happened in the back seat of his mom's minivan. This bed is as virginal as I was then."

"Not a visual I wish to have of you, Bond."

Her smirk grew sinister and bold. "Then let's make a new visual."

"You're a villainous Bond girl."

She rolled her eyes. "Is that a yes?"

"So basically, you're looking for missionary style, huffing, and puffing, one-and-done kind of sex?"

"No, I already had that. I don't... James, I love what we do. It's so damn hot, but..."

Bond glanced at me with earnest eyes. Shit. Was she saying she wanted to make love without spelling it out? When had I last made love to a woman? College? That was the last time. Another life. Another James. It was after...

I was treading on dangerous waters, and if I wasn't careful, I could get pulled under and drown. I wasn't keen on reliving that shit from my past. But if I did, that could be the final push I needed to separate myself from her.

Making love wasn't my thing. I avoided it religiously. Maybe that was what I needed to finally get over this 'Bond' infatuation I had going on and to finally go back to my old life.

Who's the one who dragged her into your life in the first place?

I enjoyed it while regretting it. My infernal conundrum.

This was what I needed to get over whatever this was with her because something had to be done. We were getting too close, and I was too cowardly to walk away. I sensed the feelings coming off of her, though she fought them. That should've had me running right there. Other women would've tried to have more with me and tried to talk about it, but not Bond. For that, I appreciated her. But after meeting her family... It all felt a little too much like a relationship.

Let's do this. Do it and move on, finally.

I lifted her knit top over her head, tossing it to the floor, then leaned in and pressed kisses on her throat and collarbone as I unclasped her bra. Her tits spilled out as if desperate to escape their confines, and I hardly blamed them. Many women I'd known complained about bras.

Easing her back on the bed, I stood and pulled off her pants and panties, leaving her naked on the bed as I undressed. Climbing back in bed, I hovered over her as she stared up at me, biting that sweet lip of hers. I nearly reminded her of my boundaries, but those rules fled when

I kept going back to her. And I liked where my balls were. The last time I pulled that stunt, she refused to talk to me. I should've let her go then, but she kept sucking me back with her inaction and disinterest.

"Are you wet for me? Or do I need to suck on your sweet pussy?"

Her smile was crooked, and she smacked me playfully on the chest again. "No dirty talk. We're inexperienced, remember?"

"Right..."

I kissed along her throat and her chest, then took one of her nipples and rolled it between my teeth. Her eyes fluttered closed, and a moan escaped her. Her responses were always genuine. That was one thing I could count on with her. Other women sometimes faked it, despite my being good at what I did. Oh, they enjoyed it, but their fake groans and screams grew annoying after a while.

I eased my body on top of hers, testing my weight to make sure she could take it. Her eyes opened, and their green gaze blackened with lust. Parting her lips, she took a breath and threaded her fingers through my hair.

"Ready for me?" I whispered in her ear, then nipped her lobe.

She simply nodded.

I spread her legs with a shift of my thighs and then took the plunge. She was already wet for me, as I knew she would be. Bond was always ready for me. I wasn't sure if she'd always been tight or from her lack of sex before me, but her hot core hugged my cock in a strong grip. A grip as if trying never to let me go.

I hated the thought, but we fit together pretty nicely. Hate may have been a strong word. It was more like I loved it but didn't want to understand what it all meant. But realistically, there wouldn't be a relationship between Bond and me.

And what the fuck do you think this is, asshat?

It was nothing. Just sex. Sex with a female friend, and only that.

I buried my face in her neck with scents of arousing musk and her cheap body wash. I took a deep breath of her as I slowly thrust. There was no hammering, claiming, or owning. I did this solely for Bond. Her hands wrapped around my shoulders to my back, dragging blunt nails across my skin. That was another thing about her. She didn't go overboard with the makeup, manicures, and high-end clothes. She couldn't care less about those things, and I didn't know why I found that so appealing. And why I got pissed off when she did her hair and makeup for another man a while back.

Fingers trailed up and up to my hair, where she fisted it when I plunged deeper inside, wiggling just so to hit that special spot. When she groaned, I kissed her to swallow the sound. She pulled away and threw her head back as she wrapped her legs tightly around my waist, pulling me deeper inside.

"James…"

I closed my eyes to her throaty voice, saying my name. It was the sound and the way she said it that made me both want to run yet absorb everything so deep inside me that it would be forever branded into my soul.

And that fucking terrified me.

I clenched the pillow on either side of her head and sped up my thrusts.

Harder. Deeper. Faster.

Sweat beaded on my skin, but Bond didn't seem to care when she pulled my face into a deep, slow, and languid kiss which meant more than I wanted to know. The sex and kiss were too intimate. How could such a basic sexual position mean so much?

The feelings threatened to consume me as threads of pressure and tingles traveled down my spine.

"Oh, god…" she cried out.

"Come for me, Bond. Touch yourself."

Fuck, my voice was hoarse and deep.

I shook my head as if I could shake the emotions right out of me. A useless endeavor.

Her hand left my hair and slid between us as she went to town on her clit. With every thrust I gave her, she rolled her hips to me, and we met together in deepness and arousing slaps of our bodies.

Bond's swollen, full lips parted as her eyes fluttered closed when the orgasm came. Her body racked with shudders, squeezing the life out of my cock. For a blissful moment, I forgot all about my fears and growing feelings, allowing me to be consumed by her climax. Her tight, pulsing squeezes sent me over the edge, spilling into her over and over and over in an orgasm so strong, and I should've been ecstatic to have such a strong one, but it had me doubting everything.

I quickly pulled out, refusing to stay inside her any longer. When I fell onto my back in the bed, she curled into me as if it was the most natural thing in the world. Perhaps it was for other people, but not for me. Yet I didn't move as her fingers languidly trailed along my chest.

"Now, *that's* how I should have lost my virginity. Not in some stupid mom car that was uncomfortable as hell."

"Mmhm."

"Thanks, James."

"Sure. Happy birthday, Bond. Jane Bond," I teased to hide my growing apprehension.

I was afraid to say anything more, not wanting her to hear my disappointment in myself and the situation.

So much for my fucking brutal honesty.

I was a goddamn coward.

CHAPTER 18

James

IT HAD BEEN A LONG WEEK, AND I WAS RUNNING OUT OF TIME ON THE Madsen/Newall case. Bond had been working her ass off following Newall, but as time passed, the noose of time tightened around my neck, strangling me. If something didn't happen soon, I'd lose not only my chance at a partnership but quite possibly my job. And I never lost, always accepting sure to win cases. But even the more difficult ones, I manipulated to win. There had yet to be a case where I lost, putting me on such a fast trajectory to partnership and eventual senior partnership. I brought in millions to the smaller law firm.

For the first time since I became a lawyer, the chances of losing closed in on me, and it was suffocating. I wasn't used to losing.

And my growing connection to Bond didn't fucking help.

I should have left her that night after she dropped me off at home, telling her it was straight back to business. But I was addicted to her fucking pussy. Not even that fucking intimate sex pulled me away from her. It was meant to ruin things between us, and all it did was drag me fucking closer. And those sounds she made. Her calling out my name. It had been so different from what we had shared before. And the addiction grew so strong that I struggled to detox her from my life.

Brody and I sat at the bar at the restaurant, waiting for Penny and Bond to show up. A fucking double date, he called it. Why did I even agree to do this? Oh yeah, I hadn't seen Bond since her birthday because she'd been so busy doing the job I hired her for. I almost wanted to take the job away to spend more time with her. But that was fucking stupid. One, I'd lose my job. Two, I should've been pulling away from her, not dragging her closer. Regardless, I missed her every hour I was without her. Before, we'd seen each other nearly every day; now, I hated not being around her. Don't even get me started on how I kept calling her Bond as a term of endearment. At first, I meant it to keep a wall between us. Now? It was affectionate.

Our table wasn't ready, so the two of us grabbed some drinks while we waited for the ladies.

The place was some fusion shit of South American and Asian foods. I preferred more traditional cuisine, but the restaurant had good ratings.

"How's the Madsen/Newall case coming along?" Brody asked.

I chugged my whiskey neat, feeling it burn straight down to my empty stomach.

"It's not."

"Uh, oh. What's going on? Usually, you have this shit all wrapped up in a neat little package with a shiny red bow on top."

"Fucking tell me about it. I just don't think there's anything to find. I'm sure Bond would've found something by now."

"Or he's super careful."

"Yeah."

I lifted my tumbler to the bartender for another. He poured it straight from the bottle and into my glass.

"But you might be right. I heard from Penny that Jane was a good detective. She moved up the ranks pretty fast with her high case-closing rate. If anyone can find anything, it's her."

"How about you? Any interesting cases?" I didn't really care because who wanted to talk about divorce? But I was ready to change the subject, which soured my mood further.

"Yeah, I've got a particularly brutal one."

"Aren't they all?"

"Nah, some are strangely amicable, and they hire me only to mediate. But this one's got little kids. Both parents are being shits, using the kids against each other. Those are the worst. Like, can't you get past your own pettiness to realize you're hurting your children? But they're wealthy fucks, with a nanny. Sometimes I wonder why people even bother."

I raised my drink in toast. "Exactly. The shit people do to each other while married is rough enough, then you add kids into the mix? No, thanks. If I had kids, I'd probably fuck them up for life."

I stopped myself before I talked anymore, ignoring Brody's stare that I felt drilling into my side. It wasn't like me to think badly about myself. I wore confidence as armor.

"Why would you think you'd fuck them up? Jeez, James. You have no idea until you actually have one."

"What the hell do you know? You're only now finding a relationship and have no kids."

Brody sipped his gin and tonic, shrugging. "What I do know is if I had kids, I'd love them. I have no desire to have any, but if it happens, I wouldn't hate on them, for fuck's sake."

I recalled a couple of years ago after Cat had her baby, Olivia. She and Ronan had been attacked by his father's second in command to take out Ronan. Instead, he kidnapped Cat, and the trauma forced her to go into labor early. It was touch and go, but they all survived. After Ronan called me for support, I headed to Dr. Miller's clinic to visit the baby out of respect for Ronan. The same clinic that Newall contributed to for its reconstruction. Newall had no idea that the mob paid for it. Thank fuck, Bond didn't look deeper into it.

But I didn't get it at the time. The baby wasn't even his. But seeing that black-haired infant, so tiny, so innocent, so fragile, so... I rubbed my chest from the sudden ache and pain and shoved away the thought. No. I couldn't do kids.

And that was one of the reasons Bond and I had to stop. But fuck! I couldn't let her go.

Brody bumped my shoulder to get my attention. "What's up with you, man? You seem broodier than normal. I know. I know. You're not a date kind of guy. That you and Jane don't have a real thing going on, but you two are friends, right? This isn't that big of a deal. This is more for Penny, anyway."

"It's not just that."

"What is it, then?"

If I talked to Brody, would he blab my shit to Penny? Who would then blab to Bond?

"It's a lot of things," I said, shrugging.

"If you're worried, I'll tell Penny; I won't. We, lawyers, are good at keeping things tight and secret. We have to be."

I glanced over at him, and he seemed earnest. I really should've been talking with Ronan and Daniel, needing my closest friends. But they were fucking busy playing house. Who had time for their old playboy friend anymore?

"It's the Madsen/Newall case primarily. I sense failure at the end of this. This case is going to burn me in the ass. I should've thought harder before I took the case. But all I saw was a partnership in my greedy eyes."

Brody gave me a bro pat on my back. "It's not over yet. Jane will find something."

"I hope."

I downed the rest of my drink and ordered another. Wine this time, since whiskey was heavy.

"It's... also Jane. Please don't fucking say anything to Penny, or I'll have to send the mob after you." Joking, not joking.

He gave a hearty laugh, though it wasn't that funny. "Promise."

"It was only supposed to be one night with Bond. One fucking night. Simple, right? But her pussy sucked me in. I can't stay away from her. I told myself that I'd fuck her one more time. That was all I needed to get her out of my system. But that didn't work even after she dragged me to her fucking parent's house and asked me to make love to her. Make love! Shit, I went into near panic mode after that. I can't do this. One more. That's it. One more to feed my fucking need. I have to—"

"Fuck me out of your system?"

If there's a god up there, please strike me down now. Screw a partnership at work. Just kill me now.

I closed my eyes, knowing Bond and Penny were behind us.

Now, I wished I'd stuck with whiskey and brooded in silence.

Oh, so slowly, I turned toward two angry women.

Before I could say anything, Bond raised her hand to silence me. I swallowed hard, ready for her to rip into me. Perhaps rip my balls off with one hand. It wouldn't have been the first time a woman tore me a new one.

"You know what? Fuck you, James. I'm outta here."

With a quick flick of her hand, she stormed out of the restaurant. And my stupid ass chased after her.

Let her go. This is what you want.

But I ignored my rational self. Maybe it was my irrational self. Who the fuck knew anymore. Bond had me completely twisted inside and out.

I found Bond outside typing away something on her phone. Probably calling for a driver.

Fuck, she looked so good too. Her dress was royal blue with silver strappy heels and matching jewelry. I'd never seen her so dressed up. My heart beat so hard against my chest that it hurt.

Why was I out here? I never cared before.

"Bond…"

CHAPTER 19

Jane

"BOND…"

I gripped my phone tightly in my hand as I hired a driver to take me home when he said my name, always refusing to call me Jane like I was perpetually a joke to him. A way to keep me at arm's length.

I really tried to keep this on the down low. Not to make this growing thing between us more than it was. But when I asked him to have some real sex, he fucking made love to me. Those blue eyes looked like he might've cared about me, even just a little, as he held me close, slowly pumping into me like I fucking mattered. Like I became the center of his world.

Those bubbling emotions that were growing blew up that night. He came to meet my parents for my birthday, and then we made love. For the first time, I thought, we shifted into something more real. That we finally passed the friends-with-benefits phase.

I guess I'd left him alone too long afterward. We hadn't seen each other for a week because he had a deadline, and I needed to find his proof of the cheating. Maybe it gave him too long to stew over things. But then he called me to come out with him for a date with Brody and Penny. My sister helped me look my best for him tonight. We talked about the possibility that James and I were connecting.

Then all those growing feelings for him exploded like an over-inflated balloon, talking about me as if I was nothing. To Brody, no less. I shattered, going from the hope of expanding this budding relationship, to anger and now hurt.

How could I possibly believe I'd be the one to get James, the manwhore, and have him fall for me? How stupid. I wasn't a supermodel, some famous actress, or a CEO. I was just an ex-cop, trying to make it as a fledgling P.I. There wasn't anything wrong with me, but girls like me didn't catch men like James.

My lips quivered as I fought to keep the tears from shedding. The last person I wanted to see me upset was James Clery, Attorney Douchebag at Law. But my heart told my brain to kiss off.

"Bond," he said again.

Without looking up from my phone, I turned my back on him, so he couldn't see my pain. My humiliation. Always an object to men. I knew better with him, but I became one of those people who ignored the warning bells clanging in her head. It was my fault, really. I fell for the old 'alpha bad boy' trick hook, line, and sinker.

"Go back inside, James. I'm leaving." It took everything I had to hide the quavering in my voice.

"Please, let me—"

"Let you what? *Explain?* Spare me. I don't need or want to know."

I waved him off, still not looking at him. "Don't worry. I'll finish your precious job. I'm a professional, after all."

He touched my shoulder, trying to turn me to face him, but I wouldn't budge. Of course, since I couldn't hide from him, he walked over to face me.

I quickly swiped at my eyes, hoping my makeup wasn't running. "Go inside, Clery. I'm a big girl. I mean, it wasn't as if you lied to me or anything. You've always been honest about who and what you are."

He sighed. "No, I never lied."

"But how could you say that to Brody? I at least thought we were friends. That you had a tiny fraction of respect for me."

"I *do* respect you. We *are* friends."

I finally looked up at him, just in time for a tear to betray me. "Are we? Regardless, I have no control over my heart, no matter your promises of who you are. I shouldn't like you, but I do. There. I said it. You're like one giant big red flag waving in my face, but I stopped caring about that. You're arrogant, narcissistic, and too damned honest sometimes, but you have this tender side. You understand what I want and take care of me without demands or conditions. So, I don't know what to tell you, James. Feelings slipped in when I wasn't looking, but I won't apologize for it."

He wiped my tears away with his thumb, but I didn't pull away. "I'm... confused, Bond. I'm not used to spending so much time with a woman I'm sleeping with, but I enjoy your company. When you mention dates with other men, I get... jealous for some reason. It's not a sensation I'm used to."

"I know, James. Because you always hold all the cards in a two-player game. You control the show. Everything is according to *your* rules. I'm not sure why you're like this. And quite frankly, I'm done caring. I can't do this. Let's part ways now. Hearing you want me out of your system got you out of mine."

He looked pained, but his sky-blue eyes never wavered from mine. "I didn't mean it like that... I did. But I didn't finish what I was going to say before you arrived. I'm not sure I *want* you out of my system. Let me... try."

I shook my head as my lips quivered again. Fuck it all. I couldn't do this. I wanted a man who was certain about me. It was fine when we fucked around. But everything changed the score of the ballgame when feelings got involved, and it was inevitable when you spent so much time with your fuck buddy. But once the feelings arrived, that was it. I wouldn't settle with a man who was confused and unsure about me. If James didn't know if he definitely wanted me by now, he never would, and I wouldn't stick around to give him time to figure it out, wasting my time.

I wiped my face dry, stood tall, and straightened my dress after stepping back from him. "I'll keep you informed of anything I find on Newall."

"Bond... please. Don't."

I shook my head. "No, James. If you have no feelings for me by now, you never will. And that's okay, too. I can't make you like me. But I deserve better than this feeble thing you're attempting. I deserve better than you. Let's chalk it up to a fun time that's now ended."

He winced, and before he could reply, my sister stormed out while Brody tried to hold her back.

"Brody, so help me... let me go, so I can kick his ass!"

"Pen... let them handle it. They're grown adults."

"You cocksucker," she yelled out, fighting off Brody's grip. I covered my laugh with my fist. God, Penny was pushy as hell, but she'd tear the world apart to protect her family.

James looked downright terrified. I would be, too.

"It's fine, Pen. I've got it. Go back inside and enjoy a nice date with Brody. I'll call you later, okay?"

Penny released her fists, and her anger morphed into sadness. "Are you sure?"

I nodded and gave her a reassuring smile. "I'm sure."

When she and Brody headed back inside, a little calmer, I turned to face James, whose face wore a multitude of emotions. I almost felt sorry for him, knowing this was completely new to him. He didn't know how to handle these feelings, and I was sure he had some for me. At least, I hoped so. But it wasn't good enough. I was tired of being tossed around by men. Now I needed to go back to being single, focus on my career, and make sure Penny stayed out of my love life.

Right then, my driver pulled up to the curb.

I reached for the handle to the door, but I turned around to face him. He looked dejected and confused, with hands shoved into his pockets. "Take care of yourself, James. I'll be in touch with the case."

"Jane," he said before I climbed into the car, making me pause. My eyes welled again, dammit. He called me Jane. Not Bond. What did that mean?

It means nothing.

Leave.

I didn't turn around and instead climbed into the car, shut the door, and when the driver took off, I didn't look back.

When I got home, I tossed on a pair of pajama bottoms and my oversized red UMass sweatshirt with Sam the Minuteman blazoned on my chest. I refused to wallow and, instead, decided to work.

I dug in my fridge, pulled out a bottle of Sauvignon Blanc, and poured myself a glass. Then I pulled out my leftover General Tso's chicken, eating my dinner cold out of the cardboard container.

I brought my wares downstairs to my office, dropped everything on my desk, then flipped on my laptop and sat as my computer warmed up. Taking a chunk of chicken out of the container with my chopsticks, I stood and faced my war board. It sounded cool, anyway. I had pinned pictures of Anthony Newall with everyone he'd met since I'd been following him, along with locations he frequented. I couldn't find any patterns. Nothing that stood out, anyway. And, believe me, I looked.

Anthony Newall was highly intelligent. He had to be, being so successful at such a young age. If he really used Rikke Madsen as a beard and cheated on her, he had a lot to lose, so he would use his brains to ensure no one ever caught him. There was nothing wrong with being gay, but being gay, cheating on your wife, and lying about it could ruin him, especially with having such a high-profile wife. And she definitely wanted him ruined.

If I were a smart woman, I'd toss this back to James and tell him to fuck off and do it himself, but I was invested now. And, as I told him, I was a professional. But doubts plagued me. I struggled to believe this man was cheating or gay. It wouldn't be the first time a spouse got frustrated with marriage and wanted to take their partner for all they were worth.

My phone buzzed. I reached for it on my desk when I saw the message was from James. Part of me wanted to delete it, but I couldn't afford to if we were still working together. He paid me a lot to answer his calls and messages.

James: Rikke is headed out of town for three days. Follow him.

That would give Newall a reason to be more careless if his wife was out of the picture. While that was good news for us, part of me was pissed that he was all business, which was what I wanted. Still, he could have tried a little harder.

Bond: Noted.
James: I'm sorry, Bond.

At least he apologized, but it didn't matter because it changed nothing. But secretly, I was pleased he made some sort of effort.

Bond: For what exactly? For being honest? For not liking me? You never lied to me.

There was a long pause before he replied.

James: For hurting you.
Bond: Here's a harsh truth for you since you love them so much. I don't need your apology. I'm a big girl, and doing just fine without you.

The tears threatened again. Goddammit, Clery. Despite my anger, it still hurt like hell.

James: I know you are, and you were right earlier. You deserve someone better than me.

No shit. I tossed my phone on my desk, not wanting to talk anymore.

God, I was so over men.

CHAPTER 20

James

I REPEATEDLY TRIED TO REACH OUT TO BOND OVER THE PAST TWO DAYS in the guise of work, then I'd slip in something personal, but she'd shut me down every time, sticking straight to business as promised.

I had always believed I was a smart man. But if I were, I'd recognize and accept that what Bond did to me was exactly the shit I put women through.

No. I was a fucking stupid man when it came to personal shit.

They say the third time's the charm. Bond became my third time as soon as she'd grown on me. After two previous disasters, I got sucked in again. As soon as she stepped into the car that night, without looking back, I realized what I'd lost. We weren't just fuck buddies. We weren't just friends. We grew to be more than that. Somewhere down the line, our friendship turned into something profound that I fucking shit on because I was a coward and afraid.

If I could be brutally honest with others, it was high time to turn that brutal honesty on myself.

While Daniel had struggled with the loss of Luke, who'd left him before they finally worked things out, he confessed he fell in love with a man for the first time. As usual, I gave him my brutal honesty, and in return, he asked, *"Can you handle harsh truths about yourself because we can go there too?"*

I brushed him off, but he was right. I told him I would face it as soon as my narcissism ran low. Apparently, it crashed, burned, and the remnants of my shattered ego blew away, never to be seen again, thanks to Bond. She slowly broke down my carefully constructed walls, brick by brick, until I laid bare before her. And it scared the piss out of me. After what happened in my youth, I fought so hard never to have to go through that again.

After we made love on her birthday, she became mine, and I fought those feelings every step of the fucking way, which had already developed, but it wasn't until that day that things became clearer. The fog in my brain dissipated, revealing the potential for something more with someone. It didn't matter if I told her I was confused. There was no confusion about wanting her, but I was sure as fuck confused about what to do. It wasn't as if I had experience with having a serious relationship. Or that I knew how to love someone.

Those never-ending fears and lack of trust persisted. Not to mention my own failings. If I only slept with women, I wouldn't have to worry about failing anyone except the periodic disappointment. Deep down, it was probably one of the biggest reasons for my powerful career drive and work ethic. I only had myself to contend with if I avoided relationships, so I didn't want to disappoint myself, either.

What a clusterfuck I was.

I'd been content with the status quo for so long that it was easy to ignore deep underlying issues.

Until Jane fucking Bond.

My average girl wasn't average at all. She outshined all those other women I'd been with. Blew them away with her smarts, perseverance, confidence, and natural beauty. My girl next door. The girl next door with a naughty side, willing to give in to me so effortlessly. So responsive.

But she wasn't mine, and that was the fucking problem.

I'd been so determined not to hurt again, and I'd been fucking destroyed that I'd hurt someone else. Deeply.

And she made it clear we were done. I'd lost her, and didn't know what to do about it.

I was at work, and normally, I'd call Sam in to talk to her. But this time, I think I owed it to Daniel to open up to him. He poured himself out to me, and all I did in return was give him brutal honesty, if not a bit dismissive of what he went through. I just wasn't good at this shit, and he called me out on it. I could talk to Ronan, but he was more closed off than me. He wouldn't be helpful at all. So, now I needed to tuck my tail between my legs. I needed my best friend.

I quickly dialed his number before I took the coward's way out.

"Hello?" said Georgie in her cute, princess way. And a princess she was, thanks to Daniel and Luke, after finding her being verbally abused by her foster father. The same foster father who raised Luke and Daniel. He hadn't been just an abuser but a sexual predator. Daniel finally ended him with a bullet to his head, saving Georgie from further abuse. It didn't take long for the little girl to open up and blossom.

But fuck, why did she have to answer. Damned kids. They stressed me the fuck out, but I did my best around the children of my friends.

"Hi, Georgie. I'm looking for your daddy, Daniel."

"Who is calling, please?" So formal, yet sassy for the seven-year-old.

"It's James, sweetheart."

"Uncle James! Hi! Do you know what happened in school today? Toby is like this really mean boy, and he pushed my friend Tommy off the swing, and…"

"Georgie, honey… I'm sure there are some mean boys at school, but I really need to talk to your daddy."

"Okay!"

And just like that, I heard the phone slam down, and I sat in silence for far too long, wondering if she even told Daniel I was on the phone.

A few minutes later, he finally answered. "Sorry, James. I was in the shower. Georgie's not supposed to answer my phone, but she does anyway."

"You know there are safeguards, right?"

"Yeah, but she seems to figure that shit out. Who knew she'd be so damned smart. Anyway, what's up?"

I swallowed my pride and jumped right in. "I need to talk to you."

"Sure, I've got some time now."

"No. I need to talk to you in person… Alone."

"Mysterious. Is something going down that I'm not aware of? Are you in trouble?"

Yes, but not how you think.

Daniel wasn't only best friends with Ronan and me, but he was Ronan's bodyguard, so he was always prepared for the worst. Ever ready to protect.

I gritted my teeth, not used to being so vulnerable. I usually made it my mission not to be. "It's… personal."

"Okay. When and where?"

And that was why Daniel was one of my best friends. No questions asked. He'd just be there for you, no matter what.

"Can we meet for a couple of drinks tonight? I realize it's a school night, but I won't keep you."

"Sure. Luke is off tonight. He can watch Georgie."

"Great. There's a place not too far from you called *Ice House*. Some new beer joint."

"I'll meet you there. Does eight work?"

"Perfect. And… Thanks, Daniel."

"Sure thing. See you soon."

I turned to a clap on my shoulder. Daniel sat on a stool next to me at the bar. He looked good. Honestly, I was just grateful he lived after the Bratva decided to take potshots at my friend's. Both Daniel and Callum almost died.

He wasn't overly tall, but was bulky with muscle, stretching the brown Henley he wore that matched his pale brown eyes.

"Hey, what's up?"

"Thanks for coming."

"You know I'll always be there. What's good here?"

He looked at me up and down, scrutinizing my face. I didn't blame him. I didn't talk about personal stuff to anyone. And who knew how I looked? I wasn't as put together as I usually was. Shit, and I rarely *needed* anyone.

Once he deemed me well enough, he lifted the beer menu, reading the long list of craft beers.

"This is my first time here, but I ordered Boulevard Deep Dive Fresh Hop Ale, which is pretty damned good."

"Looks too dark for me. I think I'll stick to old school." He got the bartender's attention with a wave. "I'll have a Sam Adams Boston."

When he got his beer, we clinked bottles and took in the crowd before talking. I had to gather my thoughts. This was seriously vulnerable and awkward for me. Painfully so.

"So, what's bothering you, James? You're obviously not yourself."

I scoffed. "That's an understatement." I took a long swallow of my beer. "First... I'm sorry."

"For?"

"I was a dick when you needed me that night when Luke left, and here you are for me when I need you."

"Oh, please. You *were* there for me. Yeah, you gave me some harsh truths and made me think about things. But you came through for me. You arrived when I was at my lowest and helped me get back on my feet. If I recall, you literally got me back on my feet because I was drunk as hell. You fed me, took care of me, and listened. Trust me, I appreciated the hell out of it."

"I dismissed you when you mentioned being gay, or... what did you call it? Being pansexual? I dismissed it. I'd been so used to seeing you with women. I should've listened better. You asked me to look at myself, basically accusing me of not being strong enough, but not in so many words. You were right."

I picked at the label on my beer bottle, unable to look at my friend. It took Bond and losing her to realize the great family and friends I had and took for granted. Maybe I wasn't such a good friend after all, despite being honest with them. I'd always prided myself on being truthful, even if it hurt others, believing it was in their best interest.

"Somewhere along the line, I've lost my sympathy and empathy."

Daniel put a hand on my shoulder and rubbed it because he was a great fucking guy who *did* have empathy and sympathy, even working for the mob. He had a fucking hard life and came out glowing. Whereas mine turned me cold and bitter.

"Hey, that's bullshit. Yeah, you come off as brutal, but sometimes we need a harsh truth. A kick in the ass. You're good at getting people to wake up and get their heads out of their asses." He gripped my shoulder tighter. "Seriously, what's going on? What's bringing all this on?"

"I... think I fucked up something really good."

He winged a thick, dark brow. "Is this a woman?"

I nodded and took a sip of my beer.

"Would this be Jane? The one you brought to Georgie's party?"

"Yep."

"Huh. Well, this is a first for me, so bear with me. As long as I've known you, you've never been interested in a woman for more than a one-night stand. Let me ask you... what makes her so special that you're willing to pour your soul out?"

Fuck, I felt like a pussy. I hated this vulnerable shit, but I swallowed and sucked it up.

"Honestly, I don't fucking know. Yeah, she's pretty and shit, but she's... not like those other women I drag into my bed."

Daniel blew out a laugh. "What? Those superficial women you choose? Let me guess. You choose them, so you don't have to get close."

"Bingo."

"James, what happened? Who made you this way? If you're this distraught and can't figure out shit when you actually like a woman, something must have caused this... distrust or whatever the fuck is going on. No offense, but this isn't normal. Here all this time, Ronan and I thought you were just some manwhore for fun, but now I see something deeper is going on."

I waved a dismissive hand. "I'm not going to talk about it. If I do... it will be with her. It should be with her. Do you think if I told her, she'd forgive me?"

"First, you have to tell me what you did to upset her."

After our second beer, I finished my story. I told him everything about Bond and me since the day we met. "So, what do you think?"

"Man, that's a tough one if she refuses to talk to you. Yeah, for as honest as you are, you were lying to yourself, thus lying to her. The only thing I can think of if she gives you the time of day is to turn that brutal honesty on yourself. You're going to have to lay yourself bare to her. I doubt she's going to take anything less."

I lifted my bottle up to the bartender to order another. "That's what I was afraid of. But she's all business now. Bond has to talk to me because I gave her a job, but beyond that, she refuses to acknowledge me when I try to direct the conversation to more personal matters."

"I don't know, man. I never had good luck with women. They always felt I was too nice." He did air quotes when he said that.

"And I'm too dickish."

He patted my back... hard. I tried not to scowl at him because I hated being touched like that. "Maybe it's time to stop being dickish then. One thing's for sure; if you like her, then go get her. Do whatever it takes without being a creepy stalker. Tell her you're willing to give more of yourself. Shit, it even took Luke a long ass time to open up to me. But once he did, our world completely changed." He clinked my bottle sitting on the bar with his. "Nothing died. Nothing blew up. And everything came together for the better."

"Before she turned her back on me, I told her I wanted to try, but she still said no."

Daniel scoffed. "Yeah, because didn't you say you were confused about your feelings for her? She wasn't wrong when she said if you really wanted her, you'd know it. There wouldn't be any confusion."

"I'm only confused about how to handle things. It's been... a long ass time since I've had something real with a woman. How I feel about her is real enough."

"Then start with that."

I blew out a laugh and took a long gulp of my beer. "Yeah, if she'll even listen."

CHAPTER 21

Jane

RIKKE MADSEN HEADED OUT OF TOWN FOR A FILM SHOOT, LEAVING Anthony Newall to have a little more freedom in his movements. I hoped this was it because the clock was ticking. If Newall had an opportune moment to cheat, now was the time. That wouldn't mean he'd be careless, but he wouldn't be as anal about it. If he was cheating at all, and a big *'if'* at that.

All I wanted was to wrap up this job and finally be done with James. I hated that this job kept us tethered despite the good money. But I needed to be professional, not only because of my work ethic but hopefully for some good referrals.

And hell, he kept texting me, trying to talk. I shut him down every time, giving him a status update on Newall. He hadn't given up, but I wouldn't yield and give in to him. Sometimes, he'd send me a long text, and I'd just delete it unread. I didn't want to read his excuses. Maybe he cared, or perhaps he wanted to try with me. But at the end of the day, he slept around for almost two decades for a reason. He had his own demons to deal with, and he needed to face that before I even thought about accepting him at his word. The last thing I needed in my life was a man in doubt of us. To constantly question what he felt.

I wanted… No. I deserved a man who knew exactly what he wanted. That he knew, for sure, he wanted me. Sure, in the beginning, there were always doubts and insecurities in every relationship. But James and I already established a pretty good friendship.

Ugh. I just needed to get him out of my fucking head. I'd spent too long thinking about him, and I was so over it.

I sat parked a block away from Newall's place in the late morning as I shoved a couple of antacids in my mouth. My dinners as of late hadn't been exactly healthy as I'd been rushed to get answers, spending most of my waking moments stalking Newall. Not to mention all the damned coffee I'd been choking down. My stomach was now pissed off. I'd worry about eating healthier when this job wrapped up in the next few days.

As I chewed the chalky cherry-flavored medicine, a town car pulled up to the front of the house. Shortly after, Newall stepped out and got in. I took a few shots of him with my camera, then once the car pulled out and drove off, I followed closely behind.

We drove through the city and into the Fenway area, which had some of the nicest restaurants and shopping. Strangely, crime-riddled the area, and the mob had a strong presence here, right under the noses of tourists.

Finally, the car pulled up to an Italian restaurant. Newall climbed out, and the car drove off. I parked my car and jaywalked across the street toward the restaurant.

Inside was dim and Frank Sinatra was playing over the speakers. Rich aromas of basil, oregano, and garlic filled the air. I inhaled deeply with a watering mouth, but my stomach couldn't handle anything heavy today. The place wasn't too busy, so hopefully, I could get a table close to Newall.

As the hostess led me to a small table by the window, I passed by Newall and an older gentleman sitting across from him. Good, the table had a perfect view of the two men.

I tried not to stare too hard as I took in the other gentleman's features, looking vaguely familiar. He had black hair with gray threaded through it, was tall and fit, but lean, wearing a crisp navy suit and burgundy tie. He was a handsome, older man of about fifty.

After glancing back and forth at him and my menu, recognition hit me. He was Senator Maxwell Barkin. Everyone called him Senator Max. He'd served two terms already and was up for reelection. The people of Boston loved him for his community improvement efforts, and he did his best to provide for his constituents. A rare treat in politics. Hell, I voted for him, too.

What were he and Newall up to? Perhaps they met up to talk about a building plan for the community.

I pulled out my phone and took a couple of clandestine photos. That's when I noticed it. The Senator's hand reached under the table to touch Newall's knee. Newall responded by placing his hand briefly on top of Barkin's. It was quick, and both pulled away before anyone noticed, but I did.

Holy shit.

This was fucking big.

I had no idea Senator Barkin was gay, despite never marrying. He wasn't exactly open, but it showed Newall that the two men had something intimate going on. No wonder Newall had been so careful. Their movements were subtle but intimate.

When they did it again, I managed to take a couple of pictures.

My stomach turned again, and this time it wasn't just about my poor diet. Could I do this? Turn over everything I'd learned, outing a fucking Senator? This could also make or break me.

Fuck!

I had a job to do, too. I couldn't just quit because it made me uncomfortable. If I were still a cop, I'd have to follow through with my case and close it, no matter my feelings about it.

As the two men ate and talked, I drank some water and ate about a loaf of bread. My stomach rioted, but eating pasta was out of the question. When they wrapped up their meal and paid for the check, I waved the waiter over to pay for mine. I dumped some cash on the table as the two men stood and shook hands. To anyone else watching, it looked like two businessmen brokering a deal, but I knew better.

We all headed outside into the midday sun, and I tossed on my sunglasses, staying out of sight, and rushed to my car across the street without being obvious. They chatted for a bit as they waited for their cars, then shook hands again. The Senator climbed into his car after he gave a quick, tender touch to Newall's hand.

Once Newall got in his town car, I followed him again. Would he meet up with the Senator privately? Would he head home? Regardless,

I had some evidence. It wasn't outright proof Newall was having an affair with the Senator, but those touches appeared intimate enough to raise questions.

After driving out to the suburbs, the town car pulled up to a gated home that opened when he arrived. I was stuck on the street, unable to go any further as the car drove up the long driveway to the mansion. I took a quick picture of the house and texted it to Colton, along with the street address, to look up ownership.

A few minutes later, he texted back a name.

Senator Maxwell Barkin

Oh, they were definitely having an affair.

Fuck me.

I waited for two hours in my car with my camera ready. Newall finally stepped out of the house, and I put my DSLR camera with a telephoto lens to my eye, taking several shots. He looked sexed with a missing tie, rumpled suit, and wrecked hair.

Shit. What was I going to do? Regardless, I had to call James.

I pulled my phone out from my back pocket and called him.

"Bond," he breathed out as if waiting for my call. "Please tell me you're calling to talk."

"Sorry, Clery. This is all work. But if it makes you feel better, I've got something on Newall, and it's a doozy."

He was silent for a moment before he said anything. "Okay, tell me what you've got?" he asked, sounding disappointed, of all things. I thought he'd be excited.

"Do you know who Senator Maxwell Barkin is?"

"Shit… Let me guess. Newall's having an affair with the Senator. Fuck me. So Rikke was right. Well, at least she'll feel validated."

"Right…" In the meantime, we were about to destroy a Senator, and a good one at that, along with a respected architect.

"I assume you took pictures."

"Yep, but they aren't perfect. Just enough to raise questions."

"That's good enough. I'm going to meet with him and see if I can get more proof now that you've got some pictures. If we can get him to open up, perhaps we can reach a settlement and not even bother with a court case."

"Sure."

"What's wrong?"

"Nothing."

"Finally, now I don't have to worry about my damned job. Even without direct evidence, this will at least buy us some time. Meet me over at Newall's place after dinner. Let's catch him off guard."

I didn't like it. "James, this isn't standard procedure."

"Fuck procedure. My livelihood is on the line… Sorry. I'm… not upset with you. I've just been nail-biting over here, and… missing you."

Time to divert this puppy. "What time tonight?"

"Eight-thirty."

"I'll be there."

"Bond…"

I hung up before he could get personal.

By the evening, I pulled up my Honda in front of Newall's home, turning off the engine. My stomach still turned, but it grew worse at the sight of James' Mercedes. Though I couldn't see him through his tinted windows, I felt him looking over at me.

Here we go. Game time. Now I only had to keep James from getting personal and keep things professional.

I popped two more antacids in my mouth, got out of the car, and walked over to him. When I reached him, he opened his driver-side door and stepped out. It always hit me hard how attractive he was. He at least seemed no worse for wear with perfectly combed blond hair, cleaned up scruff, and wore dark gray slacks with a pale blue button-up with the sleeves rolled just below the elbows.

"Bond," he said, narrowing his eyes at me while scanning my body. "What's wrong? You don't look so good."

I waved a dismissive hand. "Something I ate. I'm fine. Let's get this over with."

"Bond…" He grabbed my elbow as I walked off.

"Jesus, James. I just want to get this over with and crawl back into bed."

I shook off his hand and made my way to the front door, and rang the bell.

CHAPTER 22

James

SO MUCH GUILT. IT TORE THROUGH ME, MAKING ME ACHE FOR HER. Guilt for what I said to Brody. Guilt for letting her go so easily. Guilt for pushing her to work so hard that she made herself sick. I had to find a way to fix all this. I needed her back in my life. But first, I had to get Newall to talk and get a settlement. Once I secured my job, then I'd do what I could to get Jane back.

After she rang the bell, Newall himself answered the door a minute later. Interesting. I would have thought he'd have house employees.

He was an attractive man, wearing crisp jeans and a v-neck sweater with bare feet.

"Yes?" He asked, glancing back and forth at the two of us.

"Mr. Newall, sorry to disturb you so late, but this is important. I'm Investigator Bond, and this is James Clery, Attorney at Law."

The man stiffened and frowned. "What's this about?"

"May we come in? It's best we talk about this in private."

He stood, blocking the door for a moment, mulling it over. "I need to see I.D.s first."

"Understandable." Bond pulled out her wallet and showed him her Private Investigator's license. And I showed him my driver's license and gave him my business card.

He nodded and stepped back, letting us through. I didn't think he would've let us in if Bond were a man. We followed him to a comfortable living room. While the neighborhood was highly expensive, the homes weren't massive, though it was still bigger than my place and decorated with contemporary furniture. It was warm and inviting and tasteful and expensive.

He waved a hand at the loveseat. "Have a seat."

Bond and I both sat down, but she moved as far from me as possible. I tried to hide the hurt by focusing on the man seated across from us with crossed legs, but he was stiff and distrustful. I hardly blamed him.

"Excuse me for not offering refreshments, but let's not waste time. Something tells me you're about to tell me something that I'm not going to like."

I let Bond take the lead first, since she tended to be more delicate than me. Once she got him loosened up, I'd take over.

She pulled out her phone, opened it, and scrolled through her photos. Then she handed him the phone. "We know about your affair with the Senator."

So much for being delicate. How could I forget she was once a detective? She could be direct and brutal if she wanted to be to get the truth.

Newall deflated, scrolling through the few images with trembling hands. "This is circumstantial at best. He touched me by accident, and I moved his hand away."

"I witnessed you come out of his house looking rather more rumpled than when you entered it." Before he could interrupt, she held up her hand. "Look, you're going to be outed. Your wife knows, though she has no proof yet. There are signs. You're careful, but you're not careful enough. Not only does she believe you're cheating on her, but she believes you're gay, too. I can understand where she's coming from. I mean, if my husband not only cheated on me but used me as a beard, lying about it, I'd be furious. And Rikke is furious. Now's the time to come clean and try to reach a settlement before she destroys you. And she will destroy you."

I glanced at Bond with renewed respect. To see her at work first-hand was impressive. I wouldn't have mentioned anything about Rikke, but dumping everything Bond had on the guy would tighten the noose. Corner him with feelings of no way out.

"Anthony. She's out to ruin you."

"Tell us what happened, and I might get her to back down and agree on a settlement instead of dragging you through a very public court case that could affect your business," I said. "She wins, I win, and you get out relatively unscathed."

The man literally melted into his chair then leaned into his hands, and fucking cried.

Shit.

"I can only imagine how hard this must be for you," Bond said with a much gentler tone.

He looked at us with anger on his wet face and red eyes. "You have no fucking idea. None."

Leaning back in his chair, he stared up at the ceiling and wiped his face. "No fucking clue. Max and I have been together and in love for thirteen years. I was with him way before I even met Rikke. It's been so fucking hard. The hiding. The lies. The secrets." He scoffed and stood to pour himself a whiskey while leaning against the bar. He took a sip as we waited for him to finish his story. "Honestly, it's a relief to be found out. I'm fucking exhausted from it all. I didn't even want to get married, but Max saw how interested she was in me and pushed me… to hide us. To fucking protect him… and me. Neither of us is out."

He took another sip, then looked at us. "Fuck it. Do you all want a drink?"

We both shook our heads.

He shrugged and resumed talking. "We met at a charity event, and to say I was instantly smitten was an understatement. He was hand-some and a freshman Senator. He exuded confidence and grace. So beautiful. I've known I was gay since I was a kid, but my parents were ultra-conservative and anti-gay everything. Hell, if I'd come out. They would've disowned me. But I would've come out for him had he asked. I would do anything for Max."

Newall downed his drink and poured another. His eyes reddened again, and his lip quivered, trying to control his emotions. "We talked that night and hit right off. I became a shameless flirt when no one was looking, and it was so unlike me. To my surprise, he liked me too. It started out with sex. Clandestine meetings for fun, but eventually, our relationship grew to so much more." He wiped his face as tears fell once more. "I never pressured him to come out. Never questioned his reasoning. I love him. He had an image to protect. Hell, so did I. This could ruin him, and I love him enough never to force him to come out. But, god, I'm tired. I never get to see him enough. I'm sneaking around more than ever because I agreed to marry Rikke. What a mistake. She's a horrible person. Demanding, snobbish, and entitled. No, I'm happy to divorce her finally. So, what's the plan?"

I took that as my cue. "Well, I'll bring this all up to my boss and see what he says, but what will probably happen is you and I will first talk about a settlement, then I'll broach the subject to Rikke, talk her into taking it, or listen to her counter offer. I'm confident I can talk her into it and not take you to court."

He nodded at me. "I only ask one thing."

"What's that?"

"Please don't bring Max into this. I beg you. It will ruin him. Me? I can build again. Him? No, it will ruin his chances. Especially, since he's going to make a play for the U.S. Senate, and eventually the Presidency. I can't have him destroyed like that. And Rikke *will* ruin him. It's what she's fucking good at."

"If he's going forward with such lofty goals, he needs to come out. The press has a way of digging deep the higher you get in office," Bond said.

"I've told him this already, but he's so established in the political game, he feels it's a little late." He shrugged and downed his drink again. "It's out of my hands now."

I glanced at Bond. She was stone-faced, and while she couldn't quite hide her emotions, she said nothing.

"I will do what I can to keep things quiet, but she may demand to know who you're having an affair with. If you don't reveal it, she may take you to court, anyway."

Newall slammed his glass down hard enough to shatter, but it held strong. "Then fucking lie! Say you don't know who he is. Something! Anything! I beg you... leave Max out of this."

"I'll do my best. What are you willing to offer her?"

"Let me talk to my lawyers and accountant. I'll draw up an agreement and send it over to you to look over before you meet with Rikke. I assure you, it will be generous because I want out of this living nightmare and farce of a marriage. God, and having sex with her is pure torture."

After exchanging information between the three of us, Bond and I left, standing outside in the warm evening, feeling as if I could breathe again. As if I'd been holding my breath the entire time. Finally. We would reach a settlement, Rikke and Anthony could move on with their lives away from each other, and I'd get my promotion. It was almost over.

I turned to face Bond, who had her arms wrapped around her, staring at the ground.

"Thanks for this, Bond. You did amazing work."

She looked up at me with a fire in her eyes. "You need to drop this case, James."

What the fuck?

"No. What the hell, Bond?"

"Dammit, James! Yes, he was cheating on his wife, but imagine what it's like for Newall. For Senator Barkin. Always hiding from prying eyes. Having to keep their love a secret for fucking thirteen years! Why? All because so many in this country are still homophobic? How fair is that? I mean, you have gay friends, for fuck's sake! We have no right to out the two men!"

"This isn't about them. This is my entire career on the line. Something I've worked my fucking ass off for." I calmed myself, not wanting to snap at Bond. I got where she was coming from, but I wasn't about to toss my career in the shredder over this. "Look, if I lose this client, I will not only *not* get the promotion I've been working so hard for, but they'll fire me."

"Then get another job! Anything!"

"I can't."

"So, is money worth more to you than doing the right thing? Is that it?"

Now I was the one angry. I wanted Bond in my life, but not if she was going to force me into this. This was my life. My career. I hadn't worked so fucking hard to reach the top just to toss everything away. I would figure something out to keep the Senator's name away from Rikke.

"Why do all you women insist on changing me? You want me in your life, but only under certain conditions. Everything is a fucking condition. This is who I am, Bond. Call me a bastard. Call me greedy. I never pretended to be a fucking saint."

Her face morphed from anger to sadness, nodding.

"You're right. You do you, James. But I won't help you with this any longer. I won't be your witness. I won't hand over the pictures. And I'll return all your money. I am not about to destroy that man who only wanted to love openly with his lover. A man who was forced into this cruel and unaccepting world. Who has done everything possible to protect his partner? Yes, it was fucking wrong for him to cheat on her. Hell, it was stupid of him to marry. I'm sorry, but there are worse things than a cheating spouse. We would be destroying two men's lives."

"Look, if I don't do it, someone else will. She won't give up."

"Then make her give up, James! Tell her there's nothing to find. Hell, let him admit to the cheating, but keep his sexuality out of it."

This was it. I understood right then, if we didn't come to some sort of agreement; we were permanently over. I would never stand a chance to be with her.

"Let me ask you this, Bond. Would it matter in the end?"

She furrowed her brows. "What would what matter?"

"Us. It seems, no matter what I do, you aren't going to accept me. Do we have a chance? Do I?"

"Are you seriously fucking telling me you'll agree to this if I go back with you?"

"Hell, no. But I want to know if I will matter to you after this. I won't toss my career for nothing."

She scoffed. "For nothing? Jesus, James. How about it will make you a good person."

"A good fucking person? Jesus. Yes, it would be for nothing. I'm not going to toss everything away for a case. I worked for nearly two decades to get where I am. You asking this of me is a big fucking deal. Answer the question, Bond. Will it matter to you in the end? To us?"

She looked up at me with watering green eyes but said nothing.

No. No matter what I chose to do, she'd never accept me back. She didn't need to utter another word. Her face said it all.

Crushed, I stormed off to my car, got in, and drove the fuck out of there.

CHAPTER 23

Jane

NOT EVEN MY SCENTED CANDLES, HOT BUBBLE BATH, AND A GLASS OF Chardonnay calmed me down. I was still fuming a day later over James and his arrogant, greedy, selfish, egotistical ways. Fuck him. I'd already been upset after what he said to Brody, but now he just pissed me off. The willingness to destroy lives for a job.

Surely, James exaggerated about getting fired if this case didn't work out. Fine, if I'd been a cop, and this was a case I'd been investigating, I'd have to follow all leads and build my case, but I owned my business, enabling me to bow out if it grew too uncomfortable. Shit. Would he really lose his job over this?

But those poor men. Imagine living so long with a secret that could destroy you. And Newall would give it all up just to protect his lover, the Senator. I had to admit, how they went about protecting themselves was fucking stupid. But I just couldn't be responsible for outing them and destroying their lives. Let someone else fucking do it. I was sure James would be just fine in that regard.

I climbed out of the tub, dried off, and blew out all the candles. Now the flower scent turned to an acrid burning that matched my mood. I grabbed my robe from behind the bathroom door, put it on, and tied it.

When I walked to my bedroom, I grabbed my phone and scrolled through some songs to play over my wireless speaker, picking, *'Where Did All the Love Go'* by Kasabian. Completely apt. I shook my hips to the upbeat tempo, digging in a drawer to find panties, trying to force the frustration and sadness out of me through music.

At least my stomach felt much better, but I still had some acid reflux. Eating some roasted pork chops and steamed vegetables helped.

I planned to hit the sack early tonight, so I'd be one hundred percent tomorrow and work on a new case I was hired for this morning. A mother's son ran away when he had a fight with his stepfather. While the son was nineteen and an adult, she only needed to find out if he was okay. Then, she'd try to bring him home on her own.

A loud sound, possibly a crash, startled me. I quickly shut off the music, and held my breath to listen, suddenly alert to every sound. Instincts told me to get my gun out and look around. That sound wasn't normal. So, I opened my safe, grabbed my gun, shoved a clip into it, turned off the safety, and pulled a bullet into the chamber.

I steadied my breathing and made myself stay calm and focused. Padding barefoot out of my bedroom, still in my robe, I held my gun ahead of me with two hands as I inspected my small apartment, checking every room and every dark corner.

After checking all the windows because the noise sounded like breaking glass, I saw they were all intact. The one over the fire escape always concerned me.

Nothing. I still had to check the downstairs office. With a quick flick of the locks on the apartment door, I opened it to a darkened hallway and stairway. I remember vividly turning on the lights, always keeping them on. Not for security measures, but in case I had to come down to my office at night. I didn't want to trip and fall.

Flipping on the switch on the wall did nothing, leaving the area still covered in darkness. My heart raced, as I struggled to breathe, but I calmed myself, allowing my years of training to take over. As my eyes adjusted, I slowly walked down the steps, keeping my gun trained straight ahead.

I flinched when the old step creaked, and I froze for a moment to make sure no one came rushing at me from the sound. It was a dead giveaway as to my location. When nothing happened, I continued down and down until I reached the front office. On my right was my personal office, and on my left was the restroom and a storage room with a copier and files.

I didn't relax as my stomach churned with an uneasy feeling. With one bare foot, I eased the bathroom door open, keeping my gun steady. There were too many fucking dark corners and way too many places to hide. This wasn't exactly the safest neighborhood, and I mentally repri-manded myself for not installing a security system. I'd intended to, but hadn't gotten around to it yet.

The sound came from behind me. Small and unrecognizable, but I heard it all the same, with the sense that someone was behind me. But as I spun around, a sharp pain hit me from the side, along with getting the wind knocked out of me. One minute I was standing, and the next I was sprawled on the floor, gasping for breath followed by the warmth of blood.

Once clarity hit, I realized I had dropped my gun. Fuck. Then someone came barreling at me. I quickly rolled out of the way and leaped to my feet. If they had a gun, I'd already be dead. A glint of metal from my attacker's hand reflecting from a sliver of light from the streetlamp shining through my blinds showed they had a knife. I needed to find my gun.

They lunged at me, but I dodged their attack, feigning left, then caught them in their midsection with my leg. The gasp of breath slam-ming out of them showed I made my mark. When they dropped, I tried to kick their head, but they dodged.

I kept a close eye on them and their attacks as my eyes scanned the floor for my gun. Everything was too dark, and my blinds kept most of the light from outside at bay.

My attacker was a few inches taller than me, bulky, and wore all black with a ski mask. Beyond that, I wouldn't have been able to pick them out in a lineup. I'd worry about why they attacked me later, but I knew this was definitely personal. Someone wanted me to hurt and to die slowly, hence the knife.

I made my stance, fists out and legs evenly spaced, ignoring I was half-naked, still only wearing a robe. As soon as I turned my head to quickly scan for my gun, they came at me again. It had to be a he, judging by his physical shape and size. He was fast, with a body heavy enough to knock me onto my back again before I could use my fighting skills. My first kick must have shown him I could handle myself.

The knife slipped into my side, right under my ribs, with searing pain. I cried out as he sat on top of me. I fought the panic as I lifted my hips, forcing him to brace himself as he fell forward. I shoved him off of me and rolled out of the way. But he recovered too fast. Fuck.

He grabbed a fistful of hair by the back of my head, yanking me back. Then his fist slammed into my face several times before I reacted. Blackness threatened to overtake me, but I shook it off, along with the stars that flashed in my vision.

I twisted my body, forcing him to let go of my hair, and tackled him, getting a few punches in myself, ignoring the pain in my knuckles. Then I saw it. A flash of light on my gun against the wall. One more punch and I rushed off him on hands and knees to get it, dripping blood from my nose all over my new flooring.

Before I reached it, he grabbed my head and slammed it on the ground, nearly knocking me out. More stabbings in my back after I fell on my stomach. The fight and wounds quickly took their toll on me, weakening my body. I had to move if I didn't want to die.

Move, move, move.

Another stab to my back, up higher. Hard to breathe. He hit a lung. I was fucked. With the edges of my fingers, I finally grabbed the handle of my gun. I flipped my bleeding body, seeing him hover over me with his knife held high.

Flashes of light from the two rounds to his chest and one to his head lit up the room. The sound of gunfire resonated against the walls as he dropped the knife, then he dropped on top of me. I already struggled to breathe as it was. Gasping, I tried to shove him off, but I couldn't. I was too weak, and he was too heavy.

Blissful blackness came before I died.

CHAPTER 24

James

I TOLD RONAN AND DANIEL THAT LOVE LED TO ALCOHOLISM BECAUSE when the chips were down, both men resorted to drinking excessively. And here I sat, embracing hypocrisy by doing the same thing. I normally didn't drink over three alcoholic beverages, preferring to maintain control. Plus, drinking too much leads to sexual dysfunction. But since I wasn't fucking anyone, least of all Bond, I poured my fourth bourbon of the night the day after our meeting with Newall.

I had two more days before Rikke returned, demanding answers, or else they'd fire me from the case or fire me from my job. I drunkenly wallowed at my crossroads, teetering on the edge, not wanting to go in either direction instead of plowing my way forward as I'd done my entire life, hacking and shoving away obstacles.

Fuck, and I missed her.

I missed her crooked smile, coy dark green eyes, that little mole near her sweet pussy, fisting my hands in her silky strands, spanking her gorgeous ass, making her beg for me. Most of all, I missed her company. And that was how I knew I loved her.

Love had always brought me nothing but grief, and why I avoided it like the plague. And it was no less painful with Bond. But I enjoyed being around her beyond the sex.

I poured my fifth drink and dumped my ass on the couch, flipping on the television, turning on some cop show for some background noise as I decided between Fuck My Life Drive and Loneliness Boulevard. Either direction sucked.

Did I really want to give up everything I worked for and achieved for a girl? For love? Was it all worth it in the end? What if I did toss my career down the garbage disposal? There were no guarantees Bond and I would work out, not that she wanted to fucking talk to me. Did I even want something serious? I loved her, sure, but that didn't mean I wanted to jump on the marriage, house, and kids bandwagon.

My past still determined my future—more like controlled it—and all that remained was the dull ache. Then I'd get those pesky little triggers that tried to keep me on my current course. But Bond derailed that fucking shit.

I downed my drink, starting to feel a little woozy. Before I could pour another, my phone buzzed. I lifted it, and with blurry eyes, I saw it was Callum.

"Whassup brotha man," I said when I answered.

There was a snort of laughter on the other end. "Are you fucking drunk, James?"

"So what if I am? Not drivin' anywhere."

"Fair, but you don't get drunk, at least not as long as I've known you."

"Is there a reason you're callin', or are ya just gonna be smartass as always?"

"Actually, I have pretty serious news. I found a hit on your girl. Someone is desperate to take her out. Luke is on his way to get her out of there as we speak and stash her somewhere safe until we can deal with this."

If that didn't sober me instantly up, nothing would. My heart palpitated painfully in my chest, and my stomach clenched. "Fuck. Who? Who put a hit on her?"

"Unknown as of yet. I'm digging, but trust me, I'll find them. I had her name flagged on the dark web because I worried about retaliation from her boss since he'd gone through so much trouble keeping his secret. And it could very well be him. After all, we sort of stirred up a hornet's nest by dumping the data into the laps of Internal Affairs and HR. I have no proof yet, but I'll get it. The only thing I *do* know is that someone took the contract, and the hit is supposed to happen within the next few days."

"Shit, I need to get to her. What if something's already happened?"

"Luke will get her out of there. He's qualified for this. No offense, but the last time I checked, you weren't exactly a combat expert."

I hung up, not caring if Callum wasn't done talking to me. I stood, wobbled a bit, and headed to the kitchen to drink a gallon of water. Then I sent a quick text for Luke to grab me on the way, using the adoption of Georgie that I put on the fast track as a favor owed. He sent a quick message back that I was a dick, but he'd be here.

Once my stomach was perfectly sloshy with water, I took a quick shower. I wasn't quite sober, but it was enough. I grabbed my keys, phone, wallet, and pistol and left my condo to wait downstairs. Ten minutes later, Luke pulled up to the curb, and I quickly jumped in.

Daniel's husband was dressed in combat gear in all black. As a former Marine, he was perfect for this job. His piercing hazel-green eyes bore into me. "I don't appreciate you using Geo against me, so just stay the fuck out of my way, Clery."

"I'll do what I need to."

"What, are you going to question him to death if there is any 'him?'"

I pulled out my gun from my holster, double-checking I had the safety still on. "I can handle myself with a gun."

"I repeat, stay out of my way, and don't fucking shoot me."

We sped through the city streets, weaving in and out of traffic fluidly. There wasn't too much traffic at this time of night, especially as we reached the less friendly parts of town where Bond lived and worked. I gripped the handle over the door to keep from getting tossed around as we sped around corners. My stomach reeled, and it could've been from the amount of alcohol I drank, but it was more likely from my fear for Bond's life.

On the outside, I may have appeared calm, but on the inside, a storm raged. If she got through this, I'd tell her everything, just as Daniel suggested. I took calming breaths as I told myself I was getting worked up over something that may not even have happened yet. We'd reach her, get her out... probably kicking and screaming, but she'd be safe.

I pointed to my left. "Her office and apartment are over there."

Luke took an immediate left and pulled to a stop a block away. "I don't want them to know help has arrived. It's best to catch them by surprise."

We both checked our guns again and jogged the block to her place. Before we even reached her office, I knew we were too late.

Her front door was wide open, and the glass was shattered everywhere. My stomach bottomed out.

"Fuck, Bond."

Luke held me back before I could rush in like an ass and get us both killed. For the first time in over two decades, fear for someone else took over. All I thought about was getting to her.

"Stay back and let me lead," he whispered.

It took every ounce of willpower not to run in there like a fool.

Luke held his gun and a flashlight with two hands and slowly stepped inside, sweeping his light and gun in every dark corner. As soon as his light swept over the floor, I saw her there, looking entirely too dead with a body on top of her.

"Bond…"

"Check on her while I clear the building to make sure there are no other assailants."

I nodded and rushed to her, dropping to my knees and shoving the dead man off of her. My hands shook, and my stomach felt nauseous. I couldn't lose another. Not again. This was why I didn't fall fucking in love. But it was too late. I already loved her.

"Bond… baby," I whispered, checking for a pulse in her throat. It was there but weak. Opening up her robe, I saw several stab wounds. How was she still alive? Barely alive.

Thank fuck.

Luke quickly came back. "It's all clear. This must be the only asshole. I'm impressed she took him out. Stay here, and I'm going to get the car. It will be faster to take her over to Doc Miller's since it's down the street."

I covered her back up, tied her robe, and sat her up, pulling her close to my chest. I held on to her and prayed to everything I didn't believe in that she'd live.

"You're going to be okay, sweet girl." I kissed her forehead with a promise that I didn't know I'd be able to keep. But I did promise her one thing. She would know me. All of me… if she lived. Then I'd kiss her ass and beg for forgiveness and to give me a chance.

Luke rushed back in, and we both gently lifted her and laid her on the back seat; then we rushed down the street and lifted her out. He must have called ahead because Jonas, José, and a pretty black woman, Dr. Cook, waited for us. We put her on the gurney, and they rushed her off to the operating room.

Luke gently clapped my back and steered me over to the waiting room. "She's going to be okay, Clery."

I said nothing, not wanting to jinx shit, and pulled out my phone, texting Brody and Penny. They should be here for her. As I waited for them to arrive, Luke and I had to get our stories straight. We couldn't let on that we learned about her attack or how. Besides the obvious, Penny would flay me alive.

After an hour and no word, I sent Luke home to Daniel and Georgie. There was no need for him to stay.

"Call Danny or me with any news," he said, and with a brotherly grip on my shoulder, he left.

I drank too much coffee, pacing, trying not to fucking lose it as I waited. Surely, she was fine, right? They would've told us by now that she hadn't made it, right?

The first threads of sunlight brightened an overcast sky, shining through the windows. Early shift staff arrived before the crowd of those in need showed up to heal injuries, help sniffling children, or give vaccinations.

Two hours later, Penny hadn't arrived yet, but a worn and weary black woman stepped out into the waiting room. She removed her surgical cap, exposing swirls of curls. I stood and approached her, knowing this was about Bond.

"Good morning," she said, shaking my hands. "I'm Dr. Cook. So, Jane is out of surgery. Are you… family?"

"I'm her husband, James," I lied because I knew she wouldn't tell me anything without Penny being here.

"Well, James, she sustained several lacerations from a knife. We had to repair one of her lungs and stitch up her other wounds. The wound to the lung was the worst. At least she didn't need a blood transfusion. She should survive it all as long as she doesn't succumb to infection, but we've got her on fluids, pain medications, and antibiotics. Right now, we have her in the ICU."

I was relieved, but ICU wasn't a guarantee she'd survive. "So, she's going to make it?"

"Time will tell, but in my professional opinion, she should make a full recovery, eventually."

"And I'm not sure if your wife's told you, and she might not even be aware either, but our blood work showed she's pregnant."

Pregnant?

As my world closed in around me, and the panic threatened to constrict my heart and lungs, vertigo tried to topple me over.

I blurred out everything the doctor said, hearing only snippets.

Around two weeks

Won't know if it's fine

Will have to wait

Uterus uninjured

I had to sit before I dropped.

With hands running through my hair, I asked, "Is… is it alive?"

"As I said, we won't know until later on. It's too early to know, but the knife never entered the uterus, so it should be fine, but I make no promises."

My world was crushed.

A baby.

My baby. It had to be since I never let her date anyone else and saw her nearly every day.

And that changed everything.

Thirty minutes later, Penny and Brody rushed in, looking worried and sick. She was carrying a duffle bag, tossing it on a chair.

"What's happened? We would've been here earlier, but I had to grab some things for her in case she was here for a while," Penny said.

"Someone attacked her. I'd been… upset about us not working out and had been drinking tonight, so I called a friend of mine to pick me up and take me over to Bond's place to talk things out. We found her front door shattered. She was on the ground, and a dead man was lying on top of her. The clinic was right down the street, so we rushed her over here."

Penny grabbed my hand with one hand and Brody's with her other one. "Thank god you decided to be a creep, James. Normally, I'd rip you a new one for that, but you probably saved her life," she said, breaking out into a sob and burying her face into Brody's side, who wrapped his arms around her.

I didn't tell her Jane was pregnant. She'd find out soon enough. The last thing I needed was Penny flipping out that I'd lied to get those details from the doctor.

CHAPTER 25

Jane

I'D BEEN AWAKE FOR FOUR DAYS, HURTING LIKE HELL, ESPECIALLY THE wound to my lungs, and madder than a hornet. I hated being sick and injured. Being incapacitated and useless. I had to call clients to inform them that I wouldn't be able to do the job for a while, so I lost all my damned clients. They understood and empathized, but many were under time constraints, especially the mother looking for her son.

Once I got out of ICU, they moved me to Massachusetts General Hospital. My family came and went, and Colton stopped by a few times, sneaking me treats.

But James never left my side, taking a leave of absence from work. He told me he got a reprieve from his deadline with Rikke Madsen when he told her he had something on her husband. I wanted to be angry, but his being here reminded me of our friendship. Though we weren't together, he still sat by my side.

Then there was the pregnancy. I hadn't lost it yet, so we all held bated breaths until we could get proper scans in about four to five weeks. I didn't know how James took the news, though he hadn't said anything one way or the other. If it survived, I planned on keeping it. I didn't go through hell and back, only to give it up. James would just have to deal.

He stepped into the room with a cup of coffee for himself and some iced water for me.

"Hey, you're awake," he said. "I won't ask you how you feel. It's written all over your face." He gave me a small smile and set my cup on my table.

Since I was awake, and he was here, I supposed now was a good time to talk about things. "James?"

"Yeah?"

"First, I realize I didn't thank you for saving my life and... being here for me."

"God, Bond. It's the least I can do, since I probably caused all your problems. I shouldn't have butted into your case with the deputy superintendent."

"You just tried to help. I appreciate the effort. It's not your fault, but his. We still don't know if he's the culprit, but I wouldn't put this past him if he felt the walls were closing in. He's the one who should be blamed. If he hadn't been this way, nothing would have happened to me in the first place. Hell, I'd still be working as a detective."

Already I was out of breath, and my voice sounded rough and wheezy from the intubation. Though talking for long periods was hard, I was tired of sitting in silence, and James and I needed to clear up some shit.

He took my hand in his and played with my fingers. "What's the second thing?"

"We need to talk about this baby."

He set my hand down, withdrew into himself, and leaned against this chair, running a hand through his hair that hadn't seen a comb in a few days. That should have told me right then that he cared about me.

"I know we do," he finally said.

"You don't... need to be a part of its life... if it lives. I know you don't want kids, and I'm not sure if you even like them. It's—"

"Stop. It's... not what you think."

James grabbed my hand again in his clammy ones, unable to meet my eyes. I wasn't sure I'd ever seen him so vulnerable. Sure I had glimpses of it, like a quick flash, but then it was gone.

"What is it, then?"

"Can you stay awake long enough for a story?"

"So, the truth finally surfaces."

He blew out a depreciative laugh and gave me a small smile. "It does."

I gripped his hand to encourage him to talk.

"God, I was just a fucking kid. Only seventeen. Denise... I called her Denny, who had been my girlfriend since we were fourteen. Like she was *'The One'* kind of girl. She had light blond hair and amber eyes. So damned pretty. I was the luckiest guy. We'd do everything together and talk about a future of marriage, what colleges we wanted to go to, everything. We were tight. Or so I thought."

I squeezed his hand again, seeing the strain on his face. "I can see where this is going."

"You'd think, but you'd be wrong. No one could have foreseen the disaster that would unfold in my young life."

He let go of my hand and took another sip of coffee. "So, she grew up wealthy, and me... not so much. Her parents didn't care for me because of it. Dad worked—still works—at the textile factory in Lawrence. Mom worked at a diner, but she's retired because of bad knees after years of being on her feet. I... try to send them money regularly. Anyway, that's why I always felt so lucky. She didn't care how I grew up when she had everything. Stupid. I mean, I didn't have anything to offer her. It's an age-old story.

Things were great. We had lots of friends; I was at the top of my class; I played football; she was the cheerleader. Then our junior year rolled around, and everything changed. I headed over to my best friend Dalton's house. It was around early February, right before Valentine's Day. He struggled with his chemistry, and I was going over there to help him. I'm sure you can guess what happens next. I won't go into the gory details, but he definitely wanted me to come over to catch him and Denny fucking. He probably wanted to give her an ultimatum. Her parents would have been thrilled since his father owned the factory Dad worked in."

"I'm sorry she cheated on you."

"That's just the beginning."

Things got worse? Shit.

"Apparently, they'd been sleeping together for months. She slept around with both of us, but he knew, of course, while I sat completely in the dark. She never gave me a reason to distrust her."

"She chased after me when I stormed out, begging me to forgive her. Fuck that. I may have been poor, but I had enough self-esteem to tell her to fuck off. The school year was awkward as hell. She dumped

Dalton for setting me up, and I dumped her for cheating and Dalton for being a fucking dick. A few months later, she came knocking on my door while my parents were working. The year was almost over, so why did she want to talk then?"

His hands shook as he took another sip of coffee. I had a feeling the cheating was nothing compared to what was coming.

"Denny came by to tell me she was having a baby. And I said, good fucking for her. When I tried to shut the door on her, she yelled out that it was mine. Despite her sleeping with both Dalton and me, there was a chance the baby was mine. I told her I'd help out, but first, we had to do a paternity test. No way would I contribute shit if it was Dalton's kid. But she swore it was mine and begged for me to take her back. The fucking tears tore at me because I still loved her. We'd been together for three years. But I couldn't ever take her back. We had the test done and waited over a week to get the results. Today, they're quick… we've done them enough for clients. Anyway, the baby was definitely mine."

Shit. I hoped this wasn't going to go in the direction I suspected. I swallowed my fear for him and tried to remain alert because I was growing tired. "So, you stepped up then?"

"I did. I kept my promise to help and sent her what money I could from the job at the quickie mart I worked at. She didn't need it. Her parents were rich, but I kept track of every cent I gave her. To show that I would be a man and do the right thing. In all honesty, I was excited to be a dad, despite being so young.

We were having a boy. I told my parents they were going to be grandparents, and while concerned for us, they were proud that I did the right thing. But as she got bigger, she grew more frantic with me, begging me to be with her again and to marry her. That she didn't want to be a single mom. Her parents grew angry and impatient. Then they started calling me to man up. Fuck them. I *was* manning up. But I wouldn't marry her. Not after what she did to me… repeatedly. I didn't trust her and never would.

During the summer she came over to my house again, as she'd been doing over and over, begging me to take her back. That her parents were getting angrier and angrier. I was fucking sick of it and I finally lashed out at her. I'd been silent about her cheating since I dumped her, but I couldn't take the pressure anymore. Short of marriage, I did everything possible to do the right thing. I yelled at her, Bond. I screamed at her, telling her to go find her fuck toy, Dalton, to marry. He was a better fit for her, anyway. I said I would only put up with her for the baby and to stop hounding me. That hell would freeze over before I took her back. She hurt me. Crushed me. I would never forgive her, just like I wouldn't forgive Dalton."

James sat up and ran a shaking hand through his already wrecked hair, grabbed my lidded cup of water, and fed the straw to my mouth. "Sorry... I was getting lost there." I took several long sips, and the cold water woke me up a bit.

He set the cup back on the table and resumed his story. "Don't worry. It's almost over."

"So, Denny ran away sobbing, got in her car, and that was the last time I saw her alive. They say she drove to the Central Bridge, got out of the car, and jumped. It wasn't that high above Merrimack River, but the water's shallow in parts. She died as soon as she landed on her head on the river bed. By the time they found her, she and the... my son were dead."

James pinched his eyes closed with his fingers and took a few deep breaths. "It was... my fucking fault. I killed them because I was young, stupid, and stubborn, and I should have tried harder."

"Oh, sweetie, I'm so sorry. It wasn't your fault. By the sound of things, she was facing stress, pressure, and depression. What a big responsibility for two kids. And her cheating wasn't your fault. You did what was best for you. You had no way of knowing she'd take her own life. Have you carried this around with you all this time?"

"Oh, eventually, everything grew numb. After that, all I wanted was to get the fuck out of Lawrence. No one faulted me if I wanted to take time off from school, but I was determined to bury myself in good grades, graduate at the top of my class, and go to Harvard. And I did. They wanted me to do a class speech, talk about suicide, blah blah blah. Hell, no. What did I know about it? Nothing other than I lost my child because Denny took her own life. I refused to talk about that shit.

And I made it to Harvard finally, and the start of a new life. I felt healed enough that I wanted to try dating again. It'd been over a year by then. That's when I met Bethany. She was cute, with black hair and brown eyes, and bouncy. And smart as hell. We dated for about seven months, and once again, I fell in love. But I caught her cheating too. Thank fuck she wasn't pregnant. But catching her at a frat party with some dude was enough to trigger me. I fucking lost it. Since that day, I swore women off. I just couldn't take another relationship. The only two I ever had were fucking disasters."

James gave a small laugh and glanced up at me. "Until you, that is."

He stood and kissed the top of my head. We still had a lot to talk about, but I couldn't keep my eyes open any longer. They burned and were heavy. Plus, my chest was tight and achy. "Get some rest. I'm sorry it was such a long story. But we can talk more later."

CHAPTER 26

James

TELLING BOND MY STORY COMPLETELY WIPED ME OUT MENTALLY, physically, and emotionally. I hated reliving it. But now more than ever, I had to face it with her being pregnant... if it lived. I couldn't lie; the very idea of having a chance to be a father again scared the piss out of me. But I wouldn't leave Bond to handle it alone, no matter if we were together or not. But when we talked again, I wanted to convince her to give me a second chance. Or was it a first one, since we hadn't been exactly official?

I'd also been getting to know her family, who seemed appreciative of the effort of staying by her side and taking time out of my busy schedule. Their words. It was the fucking least I could do. Just like Denny, Bond getting hurt fell on me. If I hadn't probed into her personal business, she wouldn't have been attacked.

After I had breakfast, I headed to take a shower, shave, and put on some clean clothes. Before I headed back to the hospital, I stopped by the florist to get another bouquet for Bond, as I'd done every day since she went to the hospital.

Bond was awake when I came in. I set the flowers on the table with all the others. It looked like the florist shop I had just left.

"You don't need to bring me so many flowers, James. It's turning into a jungle in here."

I smiled and kissed her head. "The place is depressing. We don't give the sick flowers out of kindness. It's to keep visitors from getting depressed."

She laughed. "Stop. I know you're not as cynical as you make yourself out to be."

"Wrong. I'm the very definition of cynicism. My face is in the dictionary. You're looking better today."

"I'm feeling better."

"Are you up for talking?"

Why the hell was my stomach in knots? What happened to my damned confidence?

"Sure," she said, pushing the button on her bed to raise her.

When I sat down, I looked into her forest-green eyes. "I would like you to give me a second chance. I really want to try something real with you, Bond."

Tell her you love her. But I couldn't. I had too much underlying fear and uncertainty. I needed to know first if she was going to give us a try. "I'm so sorry for what I said to Brody. After everything that's happened, I know this is what I want. I think we could have something great."

The look on her face told me I was dead wrong. I closed my eyes and waited for the hammer to drop on my head.

"James…" I had my answer. It was all in her voice. "You got hurt. I completely understand that. But… you used your pain to hurt others. You blamed pretty much all women for what happened to you."

"I know, but—"

"I appreciate and understand what you told me. God, I'm so sorry you lost your child. But it changes nothing between us. I understand. I really do. Two women destroyed you. They hurt you enough that you completely changed your ways to protect your heart. Here's the brutal truth, since you enjoy honesty so much. If we try something together, what's going to happen to us when we get into a fight? Are you going to run to the first woman to open up to you? Are you going to leave me because you don't trust me? Don't even get me started on you denying me dates even though we weren't committed to each other. On top of everything else, you never got therapy. You never tried to fix your heart and pain. Instead, you participated in reckless behavior out of fear. As I said; I get it. That doesn't mean I'm going to allow you back into my life."

My heart ached, and I wanted to scratch it out of my chest. I understood there was a chance she'd turn me down. I hadn't exactly been my best around her, and she deserved better than me. But she was my chance. My second chance to heal. And she was worth it.

"What if I got therapy?"

She shook her head. "I think you should get therapy for yourself. Not for me. That would be great if you did that. In the end, I… don't trust you to stick around for the child… should the baby survive. Those fears run deep enough for you to change your entire life and outlook for almost twenty years. That's… big, James. Don't even get me started on the job we did together. You've said nothing about leaving the two men alone."

I pulled my hand away from hers, and she let me. I had to get the hell away. Standing, I straightened my T-shirt, bent down, and kissed her head again.

"I get it. Get better soon, Bond. Please keep me up-to-date on the pregnancy."

"I will."

"See you around, Jane."

"Bye, James."

I gripped the steering wheel as I headed somewhere. Anywhere. I didn't give a fuck. After pouring my goddamn soul out to her, she still rejected me, and for the first time since walking in on my girlfriend and best friend, I felt insecurity consume me. I spent my entire life, since college, redefining who I was. Made me into a highly motivated, career-oriented, confident man who knew exactly what he wanted. Now, uncertainty and a sense of failure threatened to choke me. Like when I came to my crossroads, I took the wrong path, and now I was paying for it. Perhaps I'd always chosen the wrong path, and that's how I ended up here.

As I drove, I put in a call. There was only one thing that would fix Bond's problem and get the anger, frustration, and despair out of my system.

"James."

"Meet me at my place in an hour, if you can. I have a job for you."

"Give me two, and you have me the rest of the day."

"See you then."

After I got home, I made myself some lunch as I waited impatiently. Soon, the doorman to my building buzzed that my guest had arrived. A few minutes later, there was a knock on the door. When I opened it, there stood the massive man at six feet five inches and all muscle. He was also the only one with red hair out of all his brothers, looking like their mother, whereas the other brothers looked like their father.

"Brady. Thanks for coming."

Brady, Ronan's brother, worked periodic jobs to extract the truth out of clients after he'd been 'The Negotiator' for the O'Callaghans. Their father trained Brady in the most brutal, psychological ways to extract information from their enemies. It wasn't until the torture and loss of his gay lover four years ago that sent Brady spiraling with crippling PTSD. Eventually, he married Charles, Ronan's former PA, and quit the family torture in order to recover since torturing was triggering.

But I needed him.

I stepped aside and let him walk in. "You're not looking so good, James. What's going on?"

I waved a dismissive hand. "Don't worry about me. This is about my friend Bond, the woman you met at Georgie's birthday party."

Brady didn't bother sitting. He stood with arms folded and was all business.

"She's a former homicide detective, now a P.I. But it wasn't something she wanted or planned, feeling she had to quit after the deputy superintendent sexually harassed her. That wasn't the bad part. After she filed a complaint, his harassment grew, but not sexually. He made her life a living hell, turning the rest of the department against her. Instead of fighting it, she moved on, believing that he had too much power."

"Okay. So, what's the problem? If she's moved on; why am I here?"

"I almost called Cian to take him out, but I would rather put the fear of god in him, so that's where you come in. This asshole didn't only ruin her life. When I had Callum do some digging on this Eakin, he found a pattern with other women, so we sent off what we'd found to HR and internal affairs. They must have questioned him, triggering his rage. Callum and I believe he sent out a hit on her. But not just any hit. He wanted her to suffer, and she fucking did. They nearly killed her, but she shot her attacker. Luke and I reached her just in time. The problem is we have no proof. Callum is digging, but I'm fucking done waiting. I want this bastard to admit what he's done; we record it, and make him suffer."

"I don't do this anymore, James. It's triggering for me."

I raised a hand to stop him. "I'm aware, and I don't want you suffering. But you are good at getting information out without pain. I can handle the dirty stuff."

Brady's gray eyes scrutinized me. At least he didn't tell me to fuck off and leave. "Are you sure about this? Hurting someone else is no walk in the park. I was trained for it at a very young age. It desensitized me... until... Anyway, I'll help you, but I can't make him bleed."

"Done. Now we need to get him when he isn't protected by his fellow officers. Somewhere alone."

CHAPTER 27

James

WE PARKED BRADY'S NONDESCRIPT SUV A BLOCK FROM THE POLICE parking garage and waited. Thanks to Callum, we learned Eakin was due to get off in ten minutes., though it didn't mean he wouldn't choose to stay late. Anything could happen in those ten minutes.

"How's married life?" I asked.

"Better than expected. Charlie's a handful, but that's why I love him. He keeps me on my toes."

Brady and Charles couldn't have been more different. I suppose opposites did attract because those two men were polar opposites. Whereas Brady was a former MMA fighter, massive, and a killer. Charles was sassy, sharply dressed, and thin.

"Good." I had no idea what else to say. I didn't talk about these things period, but since Bond, thoughts like these had been at the forefront of my mind. Not marriage… maybe. Fuck if I knew. The only thing I understood was that I had to have her in my life, but that ship sailed since my failures. I hadn't realized how much I let my past rule me until I met her. Before, I accepted the way things were because I refused to change. Now all I wanted to do was be a better man… be a good father.

"She means something to you."

"She means everything." I was done denying it. So be it if everyone told me karma had come to bite me in the ass. I didn't give a fuck anymore.

Brady glanced at me, then nodded. "Good," was all he said.

It took twenty minutes for the fuck-face to make his way out of the building and to the parking garage. Callum informed us to look for a red Mustang GT. Eakin was probably making up for his tiny dick. It definitely explained the sexual harassment.

"Showtime," he said.

Brady started his car, and as soon as Eakin pulled out of the garage in his car that could be seen for miles, we followed, staying far enough away not to be spotted. Thank fuck for egos bigger than mine.

"Plug in his address into the GPS just in case we lose him," Brady said. "There's an unused road he'll take about ten miles outside the city limits. We'll get him there."

I said nothing as I did as Brady asked. Then I sat back, keeping my eyes on the road and not losing sight of Eakin while my mind wandered to all the shit I planned to do to him. Once he admitted what he did to those women, then I was going to destroy his career. It wouldn't bring Bond back to me, but Eakin wouldn't get away with attacking her. I'd thought about it being Newall or the senator, but this seemed in line with Eakin's dirty tricks against women who defied him.

"Hang tight," Brady said, pulling me out of my thoughts. "We're reaching that road soon. I'm going to speed up. It's rural enough there should be little traffic. We can't afford to let him reach his home."

"What's the plan?"

"I'm going to run him off the road. When he's dazed, I'm going to force him out of his car and inject him with a sedative. Grab it out of the glove box."

I found a box with several syringes ready and filled with a clear liquid, and took one out.

"That will save us from having to fight him. Then I'll toss him in the back. You'll get in his car and follow me back to the city and to my little warehouse, which I used to use for gathering information from… unwilling participants. There are also tools there to hurt him if you're so inclined."

"I'm inclined."

As soon as we turned right onto the road, Brady sped up.

"I don't see any cars," I said. "It's all clear."

He gave me a tight nod and gripped the wheel, keeping the SUV steady.

The drawback to this move was Eakin would know we were after him. Sure enough, he caught sight of us and sped up, but not before Brady gunned the SUV and clipped the Mustang on the corner, forcing the smaller car to spin until it stopped on the shoulder.

"Quickly." Brady shot out of the car like a light, and I was close to his tail.

He opened the car door, pretending to be a caring citizen. "Sir, are you okay?"

Eakin looked dazed and too slow to react.

"What the fuck…" Before he could finish, Brady grabbed the syringe from me and injected the man, and waited until he was out.

"You know what to do," he said to me. "I'll get him in my car."

I hopped into the Mustang, thanking luck the airbags didn't deploy. The car was still running, so I put it in gear and eased my way off of the shoulder. The car was banged up but drivable.

Once Brady was ready, I followed him close behind.

We had Eakin tied to a chair by the time he came out of his sedative, groaning and mumbling.

"Fucking head… what happened?"

"It's the sedative. It'll wear off soon," I said, standing in front of him, wearing a ski mask. Brady and I didn't intend to kill him, but if we needed to hurt him, he couldn't know who we were.

Brady sat in a darkened corner, ready to intervene should he need to.

"Who the fuck are you?" Eakin struggled in his bonds, finally realizing that he was in a vulnerable position. "Let me go! Do you have any idea who the fuck I am? I'll fucking destroy you when I get out of here! They will find me and kill you."

"Nice try. We've swept your car and body for bugs and cameras."

"Who are you?"

"As if I would tell you."

I grabbed a baseball bat off the table covered in torture devices and instruments made to inflict fear and harm. I wasn't sure if I could smash him with it because I wasn't a killer, nor did I hurt people for a living as the O'Callaghans did.

When I moved back in front of him, I dragged the bat onto the ground, making sure he knew what it was and its intention.

"You're so fucking dead!"

"Actually, you have no idea who *you're* dealing with. You see, you messed with a friend of mine. Someone I care about. She almost died because of you, and you *will* pay for that, but first, it's confession time."

"What confession? I've done nothing wrong. I'm the goddamn deputy superintendent with the Boston PD!"

"Does Jane Bond ring any bells?"

"What about her? She used to be a detective, but she quit."

"Yes, because you kept harassing her."

"Bullshit! She came onto me. I warned her, but she refused to back down, so I had to reprimand her. She didn't like it, so she fucking left. End of story."

A simmering fire grew into a rage. "Is that what you told the rest of the team? That she fucking wanted you? Give me a fucking break. Who'd want you? You're pudgy," I said, poking at his belly with the bat. "You're only a fraction better looking than Harvey Weinstein. I'm sure your dick is small too."

Brady chuckled behind me. Eakin quickly looked up in search of the other perpetrator, but it was too dark.

"Bond would never hit on you. Even if you were attractive, she has too much integrity."

The man narrowed his beady brown eyes under thick, bushy brows, saying nothing.

"Here's how this is going to play out, *Josh*. You're going to confess to the harassment claims filed by Bond and admit to the harassment of the other women. I have a list of them already, but I'm sure there are more women who stayed silent. Then you're going to admit you hired a killer to take out Bond. We all know you did, but you need to confess. If you can do this, we'll let you live with only one or two broken bones. Maybe minus a finger, but at least we'll let you live."

"Fuck you! Help! Help! I'm in here! Anyone! Call the police!"

Brady outright burst into a full-bellied laugh. "Oh, that's a classic. Sorry, bud. No one's out there to hear you. No one but us and the rats."

"We have no problem dumping your corpse in the river," I said. I placed the tip of the bat on his chest and pressed down, so he could feel the weight of it. To remind him how much damage I could cause to his flesh and bones. "Jane Bond means something to me. She nearly died, and while she's too pure and good to seek revenge, I'm not and more than happy to give it to her. She may not forgive me, but it will be worth it to see you suffer. How you suffer is your choice, which is more than you gave to Jane. You can suffer from the loss of your career. Or you can suffer a painful death. Pick."

Eakin spat at my feet as an answer. I swung the bat like a baseball player about to hit the ball pitched to me, but instead, I hit his arm, relishing in the crunch of bone. His screams were music to my ears, but I had to be careful with the bat shit. That was how Brady's previous lover died. I didn't give a shit about Eakin, but I didn't want to stress Brady out.

"Fuckfuckfuckfuck..." he whimpered as sweat poured down his face. No doubt he was in pain. Hopefully, it was enough. Men like him were cowards, pretending to be wolves, but were only sheep.

"You ready to talk yet?" Brady said from his dark corner. But with his words came a scraping noise. I knew what it was because he had told me his plan. The sharp blade of his knife swished and scratched over metal as he sharpened it.

Eakin whimpered again. "Wha-what's that?"

"Pain," Brady said.

His brown eyes were wild, ping-ponging all around, looking for the source of the sound, but it bounced off the walls in the empty warehouse, so it was hard to pinpoint.

I pointed the bat at him again, inches from his face, drawing his attention back to me. "Ready to confess?"

When he didn't answer, I looked back at Brady, though I couldn't see him either. "Tell me, friend. What happens to those who don't talk? You're the pro here. What do you do when they remain stubborn?"

"First, it's all talk. I tell them what I'm going to do to them in detail. If they haven't pissed in their pants at that point, I start slow. Painfully slow. Usually, it's ripping off a fingernail. My favorite is taking off the shoes and socks, then slipping a thin blade between the toes. Such a small thing, and after a few times, they end up singing. But there are always those who are strong, like Vinny Vinci, who didn't whimper once. Not even when he drew his last breath. Do you know Vinci, Eakin? You should, being in homicide and all. Vinny was second in charge next to the Don of the Italian Mafia. He would leave a trail of bodies in his wake. I bet you haven't seen him around for a while, have you? Oh, he was tough until the end. Not once did he scream. Not even after I shattered every bone in his legs. You should be thanking me for taking him off the streets. He was a monster. Now imagine what I could do to you."

"Okay! Okay! Just… wait. Fuck! You took out Vinny? Holy fuck. Who the hell are you people?"

I swung the bat around his face, making sure he felt the breeze of it. "Let's just say we're concerned citizens. You see, we pay your salary through our taxes. We don't pay you to fuck around with women and backstab them. It's time for a demotion. Speak, or suffer. The choice is yours."

Eakin dropped his head as he sobbed. We had him. Fuck yeah.

I kneeled down in front of him. "Don't worry. We aren't asking you to retire. Though they may ask for your badge at worst, demote you at best. Maybe force you to take a little sensitivity training."

"Fine!"

I opened my phone and dialed Callum. "He's ready."

"Excellent work. How badly is he bleeding?"

"No blood at all. But possibly a broken arm."

"Ouch. Okay… I've got the recording equipment on. When we're done, if it sounds good, and he's not giving off hints about what's happening to him, I'll patch it directly through to Internal Affairs."

"Good."

I put the phone to Eakin's ear while he told his sob story to Callum. Several days later, news hit about the firing and arrest of Joshua

Eakin, Deputy Superintendent of the Boston Police Department for sexual harassment, destroying evidence, manipulating cases, and forging documents.

I may have been horrible for women, but at least I wasn't that piece of shit, Eakin.

CHAPTER 28

Jane

I CURLED UP IN BED, FLIPPING THROUGH TV SHOWS, TRYING TO FIND something remotely distracting, but nothing appealed to me. I'd been at my parents' house since yesterday, at Mom's insistence, so she could fuss over me. While annoying and missing my independence already, I also liked not being so alone.

Just because I chose not to have James in my life didn't mean I didn't hurt like hell when he walked out that hospital door. It was for the best, but those feelings I had for him lingered, no matter if he was good for me or not. I really enjoyed his company... and the sex. God, I missed the phenomenal sex. But I couldn't let that rule me. I was smarter than that.

I rubbed my flat stomach. And how the hell did I get pregnant? Sure, birth control wasn't one hundred percent, but it was damn near close. I must have forgotten to take a pill or two. I tried to hammer my brain to remember if I had hit the birth control alarm to snooze. Or if I didn't hear it on my phone. Things had been crazy between setting up my office, working the case, and spending all my spare time with James.

It was too late now, and I'd already decided to keep it, which would make being a businesswoman with no staff difficult, but I'd figure it out. I had no plans to shut out James from the baby's life if he wanted to be a part of it. But he probably didn't. At first, I thought he hated kids, but now I knew the truth. Poor young James and what he went through. Imagine blaming yourself for two decades for the loss of your child and the mother. I ached for him and understood where he came from, but to change yourself so much and live that way for so long? No. It was too risky. I wouldn't be able to trust him to stick around. He'd feel trapped, eventually.

Then there was the ethical issue of the case. I refused to budge on that, which was a deal-breaker for me. In a few days, I'd return his money and be done with the job. Those poor men. Sure, Newall shouldn't have married Rikke. It was deceitful to use her as a beard, but I also understood his reasoning.

A knock on my door had me turning off the TV and tossing the remote on the bed. "Come in."

Fiona came in, carrying a tray of food and waddling in with her growing belly. Shit, that was going to be me soon enough… if the baby lived. The doctors were confident everything was fine. Was I ready for that? Hell no. At least I had my baby sister to give me all the answers as I progressed.

"Hey," she said, setting the tray on my dresser. "Mom sent me up to bring you lunch. She's made you some tomato and basil soup and a grilled cheese sandwich."

"Thanks."

I pushed myself upright with some difficulty, wincing from the pain. It still hurt like a bitch, but I was getting better. The stab wounds weren't so bad, but getting stabbed in the lung was a bitch.

"You're looking better today."

Once I got comfortable, she brought the tray over and rested it on my lap. I took a spoonful of the soup and sighed. So good. Mom took time off of work to help care for me.

"Where are the boys?"

"Downstairs with grandma. She's got them helping her make cookies."

I nodded and took another bite of soup.

"How are you doing, Jane?"

I shrugged. "Been better, I guess. Getting stabbed sucks. Remind me never to do that again."

"Did they find out who that guy was who attacked you?"

I shook my head. The police took my report a few days ago while I was still in the hospital. Though I didn't know my attacker, after James told me he and a friend gathered data to show a pattern of behavior against my former boss, we both agreed it was probably him who retaliated. I left that part out to the police, not wanting to alert Eakin that I figured it out, only for him to come after me again. But something would have to be done. He could try to have me killed again once he learned I didn't die.

"Nothing yet. He had no identification on him, but I'm sure they'll figure it out."

"It's not the safest neighborhood, Jane. Maybe you should move."

"First, I can't afford it. I dumped most of my money into the place. Second, I don't think he was a regular criminal looking for cash for drugs or theft. The attack was way too personal."

"Well, at least the bastard is dead."

"Yeah..." *Except that it's not over yet.*

"How are you and James? He hasn't come by to visit in a while. Is everything okay? Is he not excited about the baby?"

Stupid leaking eyes. I wiped at them and took another spoonful of soup. "I'm not going to have a relationship with him, Fi. His not visiting is my choice. He'll help out with the baby. At least he said he would. I just—"

My phone buzzed, interrupting us.

I picked it up from my nightstand and saw it was Penny.

"Hey, Pen."

"Turn on the news."

"What?"

"News! Now!"

I grabbed the remote from the bed, careful not to dump my tray of food, and turned on the TV, flipping the channels until I found a local news station. There on the screen was the Boston Police Commissioner with breaking news, addressing a crowd of journalists.

"*—the evidence has been gathered and poured over by Internal Affairs. Deputy Superintendent Joshua Eakins has been arrested for inappropriate behavior among some of our female officers, for evidence tampering, and for the attempted murder of former Homicide Detective Jane Bond, who fortunately lived. And I assure you any cases that were affected by his actions will be closely looked at. If a case* *results in a trial and prosecution, it will have to be retried. We've been working closely with the District Attorney on this issue."*

The crowd burst into a flurry of questions and photos. The Commissioner waited until it died down before he finished.

"I would like to extend an apology to the women of the Boston Police Department for not being believed and being harassed. In particular, it was Detective Jane Bond, from homicide, who quit over this after Eakin tried to ruin her career for having the guts to come forward. Her bravery should be a beacon to all women. I vow to ensure that all female officers are protected from within, and that we will require sensitivity training to ensure this never happens again."

I turned off the television, stunned. How the hell did they finally get Eakin? How did they know he tampered with evidence or hired someone to kill me? I had a feeling he attacked me, but now that proved it. Even more important, I was safe. I didn't have to worry about being attacked again.

"Jane? Are you there?"

Oh, I'd forgotten Penny. "Yeah, I'm here."

"This is amazing news. Finally!"

"It's a damned relief. Thanks for calling, Pen, but I've gotta go."

I hung up before she could argue.

"This is great news, Jane," Fiona said, gripping my hand.

"The best news. Thanks. Can you… give me a moment?"

"Sure, just text me if you need anything."

After she left, I called James, who answered on the first ring. "Bond."

"Hey."

"Hey."

"Did you do that? Did you destroy Eakin?"

"Would you hate me if I told you yes?"

I picked at a loose yarn thread from my old quilt. "No."

James blew out a sigh as if relieved by my response. "He deserved it, sweet girl."

My eyes watered at his other moniker for me. Normally it was arousing. Now it just hurt. "So, it was really him who almost killed me?"

"Yes. He confessed."

"How? What did you do to get him to confess? Specifically, what did you do to *him?*"

"Does it matter?"

It would've mattered if it were any other person. That Eakin tried to kill me... he could fucking rot in hell for all I cared. "I suppose not."

Another sigh of relief from him.

"You can go back now. You'll be safe," he said.

"I can't. Everyone turned their backs on me. I'll never be able to trust them out in the field... except for Colton. The only one who had my back the entire time."

"I've got your back, too, Bond."

I wiped a stray tear, saying nothing. We were silent on the phone for so long, too afraid to speak. Too afraid to hang up. At least for me. He wasn't good for me. I had to remind myself of that. Regardless, I missed him.

"Bond," he finally said, breaking me of my indecision.

"I need to go."

"Wait—"

I turned off my phone before he talked me into taking him back. Red flags, deal-breakers, and all that.

CHAPTER 29

James

MY HEART POUNDED IN MY CHEST, BUT I KEPT MY BREATHING STEADY as I ran on the trail. Everything was lush and green. The morning was beautiful, with an orange sky as the sun made its way to greet the day. But my normal routine and the scenery did nothing to assuage my growing apprehension and anxiety. It seemed like everything was coming to a fucking head, and the crushing weight of life-changing decisions made it difficult to breathe.

After Denny, I knew exactly what I wanted to do with my life. I had a single focus. Graduate college, go to law school, find a reputable firm, and climb my way to the top. Oh, and never lose. Now, after everything I'd achieved, it was all slipping through my hands like sand... because of fucking love.

I wanted to say I wish I'd never met Bond, but that would be a lie. It'd been two weeks since I'd seen her, and two weeks without her reporting anything new on the Madsen/Newall case. Everything was at a standstill as I grappled with indecision.

For the first time in my life, I thought about letting everything I worked for go. Let it all go for Bond. Let it all go for the baby.

One thing I knew for sure; Bond would never take me back unless I dropped the case, which would have my world crashing down if I chose that path. Again. More fucking crossroads, and I kept choosing the wrong road, leaving me with constant indecision.

But the idea of becoming a father was terrifying to me. The triggers of grief kept hitting me, despite burying that pain so deep; it hadn't seen the light of day until recently. If I chose that path, I'd have to marry Bond... if she'd even have me. And while terrifying, I found myself not as afraid as I once was.

Bond was right. I had to be certain. There was no 'just trying,' especially with a baby coming. I had to put on my big boy Clery pants and suck it up. The only thing keeping me from freaking out was my love for Bond, which was how I knew she was the real deal. That she was it for me. I couldn't go back to my old ways. Not after her.

If that was my route, then I'd have to seek therapy to deal with my past. To finally face it instead of burying myself in work and career goals and pussy.

After my run, I was no closer to an answer than before. I did a few stretches and when my heart settled down a bit; I sat on a park bench and observed others running. Were they also faced with an existential crisis? All I understood as I watched people go about their day was that whatever my choice, my life would never be the same.

My phone rang, and I didn't bother looking to see who was calling when I answered.

"James."

"It's Ronan."

I leaned back on the bench and ran my fingers through my sweaty hair. "Hey."

"Hey? That's it? No grumping about disturbing you? No questions about what I'm going to invite you to next?"

Normally, I jump on his case in defense, but I just didn't have it in me this morning.

"No."

The silence was so long that I pulled my phone from my ear to check if we'd been disconnected, but he was still there.

"I've apparently shocked you into silence," I said.

"That's an understatement. What the fuck is going on with you? You sick?"

"If only."

"Something big must've gone down. What's going on?"

"I'm going to be a father," I blurted. It was probably too soon to say that, since we still didn't know if the baby would be okay. We still had another three weeks until Bond had some scans done. "Maybe."

More silence. I knew he didn't leave this time, but was processing what I'd just told him.

"Maybe? I can't believe you weren't careful. That's fucking unlike you."

"No shit. And not helpful."

"Is... is she going to keep it?"

"Yep."

"Was this some hookup? Is she trying to get money out of you? I'd get a paternity test first."

"I would if I wasn't one hundred percent it was mine. And no... Bond wasn't a hookup."

"I'm not understanding."

For the leader of the Irish mob and for how smart he was, he sure could be fucking slow on the uptake sometimes. Fuck if I didn't love him, anyway. "I'm not understanding, either. All I know is you fucking jinxed me. You said my time was coming, and well... it came and slammed me over the head with a cast-iron skillet straight out of a Looney Tunes cartoon. I... love her."

I leaned forward and rested my elbows on my thighs, staring down at the ground. Fuck, I couldn't believe I was telling Ronan this. "For the first time in my life, I'm not sure what to do." I waited for him to tell me karma was rubbing it in my face.

"Have you told her?"

I was floored. I deserved his taunts after years of bullying everyone with my version of the truth. It wasn't until Bond that had me really looking at myself and how I treated people. But Ronan only asked a simple question.

"No. She hates me."

And just like that, I poured out my story to him. He was my best friend, and I hadn't been able to tell him or Daniel for some reason. He sat on the phone listening, not interrupting or swearing like a sailor, which threw me completely off kilter.

"I don't know, James. I'm shit with these things, and I leave relationship intelligence to Cat. It fucking sucks you had to go through that. All I can say is what I know Cat would tell you. That if you want her badly enough, you'll do anything it takes to have her. I'm just grateful Cat accepts me as I am."

"Bond accepts me as I am. She didn't give me an ultimatum or ask me to change. She only explained that I'm not the kind of person she wants, and I can't fucking blame her. This was just one of the many fucked up things I've done."

"Maybe it's for the best. She's an ex-cop, James. An ex-cop with morals. If you two become fucking tight, what happens when she learns who we are?"

And a good fucking point. Another notch to add to the list of life questions.

"Noted."

If I chose her above all else, I'd have to be as honest as always and tell her the truth. It'd be a massive gamble because she might have us all arrested.

"Fuck, if I'm not tired of all this shit, anyway. This mob shit. I never wanted it, but I felt entitled to it since we all fucking suffered. My brothers were forced into it, and look at them now. Brady struggles with PTSD. Our father ruined Cian beyond repair, and he would've committed suicide if Addy hadn't intervened. Callum almost fucking died and had to learn to walk again. I'm... fucking sick of it. I thought I was cut out for this shit since it's all I've known. Dad beat it all into us. But once I took over, it'd been one disaster after another."

That piqued my interest. I sat up, suddenly more alert and less pouty than before. "What are you saying?"

"I'm not sure. Giving up my leadership role and pulling my brothers out won't keep us safer. There will always be those who will want us dead, anyway. But I'm almost ready to make Callum wipe us all clean and start fresh. We've got more money than we know what to do with. We also have legit businesses going too. I could sell it all off to the highest bidder, but fuck if I'll sell to my enemies. My best option is to find someone to take over."

"Do you have someone in mind?"

"No. Not yet. I've been keeping my eyes open for potential leaders. Those who are quickly moving up in the ranks. I haven't decided shit yet, but it's on the table."

Fuck me. If Ronan could give up everything he'd worked so hard for and suffered for so easily, could I?

"I just want to focus on my family now. Not sure what Cian will do. Killing is all he knows."

"Have you asked him?"

"I haven't talked to any of my brothers about this yet, but perhaps I should. Maybe they've got some ideas."

"Good plan."

Ronan burst out into a laugh, surprising me.

"What?" I asked.

"You. Jesus fuck... Normally, you're full of harsh truths and sage advice. I just don't know what to think. It's weird as fuck."

I smiled despite myself. "I'm currently on overload right now. Who knew trying to see hard truths inside yourself was so fucking difficult."

"Ain't that the fucking truth. I had a rude awakening after Cat. But when she and the baby almost died... Nope. I would move the earth to keep her. Once I realized I would do anything for her, no matter what, I knew she was it for me. Ask yourself if that's how you feel about Bond."

Surprisingly, Ronan helped put things more in perspective for me.

Once I hung up with my best friend, I put in a call before I changed my mind.

When the knock sounded on my door at my condo, I walked over and answered it. Standing there was Anthony Newall. He looked nervous, but he shook my hand, which I offered anyway.

"Thank you for coming," I said.

"Max will be here soon. We... felt it unwise to come together."

"Good call. Come on in."

I led the man through the foyer and into the living room, offering him a seat of his choice. He sat on the sofa, crossed his legs, and visibly tried to relax.

"I'm assuming you chose to meet us at your home for a reason. It's most unusual not to meet at your office. Though I'd been waiting to hear from you regarding the settlement and if Rikke accepted."

I nodded. "We will talk once the Senator arrives. In the meantime, can I get you a drink?"

"Uhm, sure. Bourbon, if you have it. On the rocks."

I left him as I headed to the bar area next to the kitchen and made him his drink, and made one for myself. "Do you know what the Senator likes?" I called out.

"Oh, he won't drink until we get to the bottom of this. He likes to be clear-headed."

"Good man."

As soon as I handed Anthony his drink, there was another knock on my door.

I opened it to a lean man, but taller than me. He wore jeans, a polo shirt, and a baseball hat, presumably to mask his appearance.

Once he stepped inside, he removed his hat, and we shook hands.

"It's a pleasure, Senator Barkin. I voted for you, by the way."

He gave me one of his smiles he was famous for. If he was as nervous as Newall, he showed no sign. Then again, the man could campaign like no one's business. He had a lot of charisma.

When we stepped into the living room, Newall stood but was tightly wound, as if holding back to keep himself from rushing to the Senator.

"Believe it or not, this is a safe place here," I said. "If you... need comfort from each other, I won't say anything." When they looked skeptical, I smiled. "I already know, so there's no point in hiding it if you don't want to. Besides, my best friend is married to a man."

The Senator sat on the sofa with Newall and grabbed the younger man's hand, threading their fingers. Newall relaxed and looked at the Senator, filled with love and longing.

"I realize you both are stressed, so I won't beat around the bush. I'm dropping your case."

The two men looked at each other, eyes filled with doubt. It was probably hard to trust, especially with someone who had been out to get you at first. I was the attorney for Newall's wife, after all.

"Rikke won't let this go."

"Probably. But I'm done. My partner... the woman you met convinced me to let this go. She was right. Your cheating was wrong... hell, marrying Rikke was a bad call. You're smarter than that, Senator."

At least the man had enough intelligence to look contrite. "It seemed like a good idea at the time. But you're right. Tony has been absolutely miserable, which is all my fault. Not my proudest moment."

"Rikke may not stop, so I suggest you divorce her, give her a good payout, and move on with your lives. Thank god there aren't kids involved."

"She never wanted any," Anthony said. "But you're right. I will do what you suggest."

"What do you get out of this?" the Senator asked.

I blew out a laugh and took a sip of my bourbon. "Absolutely fucking nothing. Ms. Bond was right. This is the right thing to do. I'm sorry, people like you have to hide who you love. Life isn't fucking fair sometimes. I understand the importance of careers very well, and I've worked my ass off for mine, but... It doesn't matter. What matters now is that you have a little bit more freedom to spend together. Just stop fucking getting married unless it's to each other."

The two men chuckled and agreed.

"I'll do my best to talk Rikke out of pursuing further investigations on you."

"I... don't know how to thank you," Newall said as both men stood to leave.

"I don't need thanks. Just divorce her. That's all I ask."

Newall turned to me as the two men headed toward the door. "It's her, isn't it? The lady you were with that night."

I gave a tight-lipped smile. "And I wish it were enough. Regardless, it's the right thing to do. Honestly, I may not have done the right thing had she not pushed me. I'm a single-minded man."

The Senator clapped me on the back, which I always fucking hated, but maybe not so much anymore. "Don't let her go then."

I wish it were that simple.

Bond made it clear that no matter what I did, we would never be.

CHAPTER 30

James

It was five-thirty Monday morning as I sat in my office, twiddling my pen between my fingers and resting my feet on my desk. I wanted to stare at my office longer while I still had it, but I was too lost in my mind. Strangely, I wasn't as upset about it as I thought I'd be. That probably had a lot to do with Bond, despite never having a chance with her. She was thrown into chaos with the job she loved, forced to quit and make something of her life all over again. She did that all on her own. Sure, it upset her, but she kept pushing herself.

Maybe I'd take this opportunity to steal Sam and start my own firm. It wouldn't bring me the money I'd come to enjoy, but at the end of the day, everything I'd accumulated was just stuff. I'd been so entrenched in that 'stuff' along with every pussy I could get my hands on for so long that I didn't know how to live a different life. But perhaps it was time. Not that I had a choice. By giving Newall and the Senator a free pass, I threw away my career as if I didn't spend over twenty years working my ass off for it.

Twenty years of dedication. Twenty years of one direction. Twenty years of knowing exactly what I wanted, along with a hefty price tag on my education.

I hadn't even had coffee yet as I stared out at the slowly creeping morning, watching the city come to life. My eyes burned from a lack of sleep, and I stifled a yawn, but I couldn't be bothered with making myself caffeine.

A knock on my door stirred me out of my growing depression.

"Come in."

The door opened, and Sam walked in. "James, I saw your car in the garage… and… it's early… even… What's happened?" she asked, scanning me. I probably looked like a disaster with my wrinkled button-up, I wasn't wearing a tie, and my feet were in socks only, resting on my desk. My hair probably looked like a wreck as I kept running my hands through it.

I waved a dismissive hand at her concern. "Nothing that a new life won't cure."

"I'm growing increasingly concerned by the second, James. Tell me what's happened."

"Fucking Bond happened. She completely upended my life, and I don't hate her for it."

"Give me a second." Sam left my office, and several minutes later, she returned with two steaming cups of coffee, setting one mug on my desk. I took a tentative sip, sighing at the needed jolt.

"Now... start from the beginning."

I barked out a laugh, startling her. "Sorry. My career is fucked." I told Sam everything from the pregnancy, to me dropping the Madsen/Newall case, to quitting my job soon. "I've never lost or failed at anything after my last girlfriend in college, and I've been one-track-minded ever since, succeeding at everything I've ever done. This is the first time I've ever lost. I'm about to lose my job, and I've lost Bond."

"Give me a fucking break," Sam said. Her tone and swearing snapped me out of it. She never swore, so she currently had my full attention.

"You making life-changing choices isn't losing, James. You're just changing your path. That's all. It may seem like you're losing, and starting over is never easy, but you already have ideas on what direction you want to go in."

I pondered Sam's words. Perhaps she was right. I made a choice. A difficult choice, but it was still under my control. My decision. "What about Bond?"

Her hazel eyes bore into mine as she folded her arms. "Since when has James Clery given up so easily?"

"Excuse me? She said she didn't want me. She was loud and clear."

"I've never seen you tuck your tail and run before. James Clery is a man who gets what he wants through grit and hard work. He doesn't just give up when he's told no. Now, I'm not saying go be a creep about it. But you need to go to her and tell her that you want to be a part of her life and the baby's life. Tell her what you've done here. That you're trying. Lay it all out on the table for her, James. Let her see the man that I see. Not the one who hides behind sex and career goals."

"I did lay it all out to her. I poured my fucking soul out." So what if I sounded like a whiny child?

"You told her your story. You never told her how you felt. And you need to tell her what you're willing to sacrifice for her."

I stared out at the bright morning. Tucking my tail was exactly right. If I wanted Bond back, I'd have to do just that. It wasn't something I was used to. I was confident in all that I did, not used to this insecurity and uncertainty shit.

Sam stood and approached me behind my desk. "Stand up, James."

I did as I was told, sulking as I did so.

"Now, I know you hate being hugged, but you're going to deal with it."

She reached around me and pulled me into a tight hug, and I hugged her back. When she pulled away, she gripped my biceps, then she fingered my hair, smoothing out the strays. "Now, you're going to finish your coffee, put yourself together, and explain to the bosses what's happened. Afterward, you're going to march your ass to go see Jane and get this relationship fixed if you want to be a part of her and the child's life."

"Yes, ma'am."

Her smile was crooked, and her eyes twinkled. "And if you ever call me that again, I'm going to smack you."

"So violent, Sam."

"Once you find a place to get settled, career-wise, you give me a call, and I'll be there."

"What would I do without you?"

She gave me a wink. "Still be pouting."

"So true."

———

Leo's assistant opened his office door for me, and I stepped inside. Ian Levitt was there too, per my request. I owed my bosses the truth. Ian was our corporate attorney and the opposite of Leo. While Leo looked more like some Italian mobster, Ian looked more like he belonged in IT. He was only ten years older than me, and I'd hoped I would work alongside both men, but it wasn't to be.

For the first time since—I couldn't even remember—butterflies ate away at my gut, along with a gallon of coffee. I've stood in front of doubtful juries, difficult judges, and lying witnesses. Now my body was betraying me.

"Thank you for seeing me, gentlemen."

"James, are you unwell?" Ian asked.

"Not in the viral sense, but... there's a problem with the Madsen/Newall case, and I thought I would give you both a heads-up."

"Then why did you ask for Ian? He's not even involved in this case," Leo asked.

"You know me. I don't like to beat around the bush. The fact is, I'm dropping the case."

Leo leaned back in his chair and crossed a leg over the other. "Did you not find anything on Newall? I was wondering since it's taken so long."

"No, there is."

"I don't understand."

"Newall is indeed cheating, and he is indeed gay. But... it's complicated, and I'm sworn to secrecy. I will tell you if you force my hand, but you'll both have to sign an NDA."

My bosses glanced at each other, but other than that, I struggled to get a read on them.

"That means Newall is having an affair with someone important." Leo guessed it, as I knew he would. He didn't get to where he was by being dense.

"Very important," I said. "More important than Rikke Madsen. He could destroy this company if he so chooses."

"Is that why you're dropping it? Did this man threaten you?" Ian asked.

I raised my hand to stop him. "No. This is solely my choice. Honestly, Newall was... relieved it finally came out. I'm dropping this because it's the right thing to do. Newall was tossed unwillingly into a marriage he never wanted to... cover up the relationship between the two men. If we go forward with this, we will essentially out both men on their sexuality, which, quite frankly, isn't up to us. But that knowledge will destroy both men. There's a reason they haven't come out."

"I'll sign the NDA," was all Leo said.

"Agreed. Me too. For us to further assess this situation, it will help to learn who this other man is."

I nodded and slid the men two folders with the documents enclosed. They read over it and signed them.

Leo put down his pen and steepled his fingers under his chin, scrutinizing me. "I understand now. A senator who has aspirations for the White House. He's going to have to come out before he runs."

"He's aware, but that should be his choice, not ours. Newall has agreed to pay Rikke's legal fees, give her a hefty settlement, and get a divorce. He's eager to. Hopefully, this will make her happy. But... I just wanted you both to understand that she might press forward, but I refuse to give her any details."

Those butterflies turned acidic in my stomach. I sighed, weighing my words. "My decision puts this company at risk. She might try to hurt you if she doesn't take the settlement. She could retaliate. I hope she doesn't, but I also understand that by doing this, I lose any chances of moving up within the company... at best. I also understand you may want me to leave. Regardless..." I slid them both my resignation letter. "I'm resigning."

Leo looked sharply at me with narrowed eyes and a furrowed brow, while Ian read my resignation letter.

"Now hold on," Ian said calmly. "First of all, if we feel you dropping a case is valid, there's no need for firing or preventing anyone from getting promoted. Granted, we could lose a lot on this deal, and there's no guarantee she won't use another firm. While it's great we won't lose money on this, she might still hurt us. With that said, and I'm sure Leo agrees with me, we agree with your judgment, even if it's not in our best interest business-wise. In the end, sometimes we have to make difficult choices. We aren't a dirty law firm that takes any case and doesn't care whom we destroy. That's not who Meyers and Levitt are. There's no need for you to resign."

Leo nodded. "Agreed, Ian. We will talk to Rikke and figure this out."

I let out a breath of relief. While I would love nothing more than to stay and pursue my goals, Bond was it for me. She needed to know how much I'm willing to risk for her.

"I can't tell you how much I appreciate that, but I'm resigning all the same. This isn't just about the case, but a... new trajectory. A new road in my life. This case... was eye-opening in so many ways. I appreciate everything you both have done for me."

Leo grabbed both copies of my resignation letter and shoved them in a drawer without signing them. "James, I'm going to hold on to these for now. Take some time off. Take a month if you have to. Think hard about things. Talk to friends and family. See what they say. Ian and I don't want to see you go. You've been a great asset to this company."

I couldn't remember when I had such an overwhelming sense of respect for someone else. I always respected both men, but this situation sealed it for me. Also, the surge of emotions was killing me. I struggled to keep my eyes from fucking leaking, but I managed.

When I stood, I shook both men's hands. "I agree to your terms and will take some time off to think about it longer. Thank you both so much."

Brody stormed into my office without being invited. He looked pissed too. I sighed and waved my hand at the chair for him to sit on.

"What can I do for you, Brody?"

"What's this taking a month off bullshit I just heard?"

"I see the gossip mills are running smoothly."

"Knock it off. What's going on with you?"

Well, he'd learn anyway, so I may as well have told him. Plus, maybe I could glean some information about Bond out of him if I played nice.

"How's Bond doing?" I asked.

Brody softened. "She's good. Her recovery is going well. Man, what the hell happened with you and her? I thought… I don't know. I just thought you two had something there for a while."

"We did." No point in denying it any longer. "I'm not any good for her. She also made that abundantly clear."

"You could suck it up and apologize to her. She's a reasonable woman."

"That's the plan."

Brody's eyes bugged out, and his jaw dropped. "No fucking way. Are you seriously going to end your womanizing ways?"

"Jesus. Remind me why I talk to you again?"

"Because I'm amazing like that."

It took all my power not to roll my eyes at him. I'd been childish long enough. I stood and packed up my things to leave for the day. No. For the month. It took me most of the day to clear out my calendar and dump some of my cases on other associates.

"Anyway, I need to leave and clear my head." I ended up not bothering to tell him I was thinking about resigning until it was definitive. I was so certain I would until Leo and Ian talked me out of it. Their… response to all this was surprising. I wasn't so sure I'd have been so lenient had the roles been reversed, but I wasn't such a good guy.

I offered Brody my hand to shake. "Talk to you soon, Brody."

"Call me if you need anything, or have Penny talk to Jane on your behalf."

"No. Please, for the love of all that is sane, don't let Penny get involved anymore. I'm a big boy."

Brody clapped me on the back, and I bit back a snide comment. He was a good person, even if he annoyed me now and again.

CHAPTER 31

Jane

IT HAD BEEN THREE WEEKS SINCE MY ATTACK, AND THIS TIME NEXT week, I get the first scans of my pregnancy. While recovering, it had been rough going mentally. I worried over and over if it would survive. Every day I didn't see bleeding was one extra day of relief.

Lying in bed for two weeks also left me thinking too much about James. I ached for him and didn't think I'd miss him this much, making me realize my feelings for him were stronger than I first thought. I guess denial was a powerful thing, trying to keep those growing feelings at bay. It wasn't quite love, but I fucking missed him. A lot. How could I possibly miss that ego? But I did. God, and the sex. I'd never been so sexually satiated.

After too much pain, worry, and stress, I left my parent's house and headed home. Now I was back at work and on my first case. It wasn't anything big, but perfect, since I still wasn't one hundred percent. It would be a mistake to overdo things. Regardless, I needed to earn money again, and it wasn't like I had any insurance at the moment, so I had a lot of doctor bills, except for the clinic down the street. They refused to charge me, stating the bill had already been covered, though they refused to tell me who paid. Probably James.

The early summer morning was muggy and warm as I walked up the steps to the colonial home in an upper-middle-class neighborhood with well-manicured lawns and trimmed bushes.

I rang the doorbell and waited. I knew he would be home since I had been staking out his place for the past couple of hours.

An attractive older man in his mid-forties answered the door. He'd cheated on his wife, and she was serving him his divorce papers. That's where I came in. One of the low parts of my job.

"Can I help you?" he asked, scanning me up and down. One benefit of being a woman in this line of work is that men frequently underestimated me, and I also posed little threat.

"Mr. Isaac Donovan?"

"Yes?"

"I have a delivery for you. If you could sign here, please?" I handed him a receipt and a pen. He quickly signed it, and then, I handed him his large envelope. "Congratulations. You've been served."

I left him standing at the door, looking down at the envelope. I didn't stay and wait for his response. My job was done.

As soon as I climbed into my car, I got a call from Colton. I put him on speakerphone and answered as I drove off.

"Hey, Jane."

"What's up, Colt?"

"How are you feeling?"

"Much better. Still a little sore and get a little winded, but I'm almost right as rain. Soon, I'll be able to work out again."

"I'm glad. Don't scare me like that ever again, got it."

"Yes, boss."

"It's so weird around here. Eakin packed up his shit after being fired. Everyone's pissed. Not just because he lied to everyone, but now we all have to go through sensitivity training."

"I'm sorry. Perhaps it's for the best. I hate to see you go through it, since you don't harass others. But those other guys... I don't know. They... Well, it doesn't matter now. It's finally over, and Eakin got what he deserved."

"They're talking about prison time, Jane."

"Good. He shouldn't have tampered with evidence, tossing out who knows how many cases."

"Yeah, we're all under the magnifying glass now."

"You could always come work for me. I tease, but I'm serious, too."

He laughed. "It's a thought, but you can barely pay your bills now as it is, let alone pay me."

"Yeah, no shit. I'll get there, though."

"When you do, hit me up. Maybe I could help bring in extra work.

But if you need anything on the side, let me know… within legal parameters, of course."

"Of course."

"When's your scan?"

"Next week."

"Do you… would you like company?"

God, this man. If he weren't gay and in a loving relationship, I'd jump all over him. "You know, I'd love that. Thanks, Colt."

"How's the piece of shit father? He bothering to care at all?"

"Be nice. This was my choice. But he's been sending me money already, and I've created a separate account for it. And to be fair, he's the one who helped get Eakin behind bars. Don't ask me how because I have no idea, but he found all the evidence and sent it to Internal Affairs."

"Seriously?"

"Yep. So, please cut him some slack. He's not a bad guy… just… too many red flags. He's not a man I can get involved with."

"Alright, I'll back off my caveman ways."

I laughed. "I appreciate that."

"Anyway, I'm about to go on duty. Text me the time and place next week, and I'll be there."

"Love you, Colt."

"Love you, partner."

After I sent the invoice to my client for today, I sorted through my email, which was more spam than job offers. When I finished, I turned off my computer. I really needed to finish fixing up the place, but my body couldn't take it yet.

At least the front office was done. James had gone out of his way to get me a new glass front door, clean the blood-stained flooring, and set up a high-end security system thanks to the same friend who sent details to get Eakin fired and arrested.

Shit. James had done so much for me, even after I pushed him away. Maybe he wasn't as red-flaggy as I thought. Whatever. It didn't matter now. We hadn't talked since that day I discovered Eakin was finished with the police on the news.

It was late afternoon, but with no other jobs currently, I decided to call it a day. I was tired anyway.

As I turned off the light to my office, the rapping on my door startled me, but I soon filled with anticipation, hoping for another job. I headed to the front office only to stop in my tracks to see James of all people standing there carrying a box.

Was it wrong of me to wish the box was full of food? Yeah, I missed him, but I was hungry. My stomach suddenly growled to prove the point. That along with my sudden flurry of butterflies. Yikes. That wasn't supposed to happen. It only proved that I definitely had a lot of lingering feelings when it came to James Clery. Did I ever mention how stunning he always looked?

I flipped the lock and opened the door. "James. What are you doing here?"

"Bond. Jane Bond."

My usual eye roll had gone out the window in favor of a smile. I even missed that stupid phrase, but only from him. Anyone else who said it, I wanted to throat punch.

"That's not answering my question, Clery."

I couldn't remember ever seeing him appear so uncertain before. Like he was ready to bolt at any second. "Uhm, can I come in?"

"Fine, but only if you have food."

That uncertainty suddenly vanished and morphed into his cocky smile. "No food, but if you let me, I plan to take you out after I tell you why I'm here."

"I'm only doing this with promises of you feeding me."

His smile wavered only slightly when I stepped aside to let him in. "How are you feeling?"

"Not too bad. A little tired, but each day is better than the next."

James stopped in his tracks, looking thoroughly confused. I suppressed a laugh as he mulled through my words.

"If you're still feeling—"

"It's a joke, Clery."

"Right."

James came in and walked straight to my office, switching the light back on. "Do you have a shredder?"

"Uh, yes. It's over there in the corner. Surely your law firm can afford such trinkets."

"Ha. Ha. You're full of jokes today. In case you haven't noticed yet, I'm here making a grand gesture."

"What gesture?"

Instead of answering, James took his box and turned it upside down, letting all the papers spill to the floor. "It's the Madsen/Newall case. All the documents from the contract to the evidence you gathered to the emails. Everything."

"W-what are you saying?"

"Do you want to shred them together, or should I do it alone?"

"James, you're not making any sense."

"I didn't tell you before because, in the end, I didn't think it would matter. That you wouldn't change your mind about us. But Sam, my assistant, reminded me that I'm not prone to giving up." When I still appeared confused, he sighed and finished. "I had a meeting with Newall and Barkin two weeks ago. I told them I'd call off the case under the agreement that Newall had to divorce Rikke and give her a decent settlement. Regardless, you were right. It wasn't our place to out the two men. If my friends found out I did something like that, they may have forgiven me, but they wouldn't be happy with me."

"Wait... you didn't tell Rikke anything about them?" My heart hammered in my chest and those pesky butterflies returned. "I hate to say this, but you didn't do this to get me back, did you? I'd rather you choose to do it because it's the right thing, not because you gain something out of it."

James took three strides to reach me. He took my face in his two large hands. "You know, Bond. I'm beginning to think you don't respect me, and I aim to remedy that. I do have some morals left, and I've risked my career for this... willingly. In fact, I told them I quit, so I could... figure out shit. I chose to do this, knowing you wouldn't take me back. But I'm here now trying to do just that and to prove to you that maybe I'm not so bad. To ask you to bet on me, despite it being a high-stakes game because somewhere down the road, I fell in love with you. You're mine, and I don't let go so easily of what's mine. So, take this how you will. The case is done, and I'm on a leave of absence to think over things... my bosses' orders."

Did he really risk his entire career over this? A man so driven, he couldn't see those he drove off the side of the road? "James—"

"I love you, Bond. I'm not expecting you to say it back. Just know that I'm fucking over denying it. That these feelings no longer scare me. I can't promise I'll always be perfect, or I won't have issues, but I'm going to do my damnedest to do right by you and the baby if you'll have me."

Annoying leaky eyes and hormones. He loved me? Before I could respond, he pulled me to him and kissed the hell out of me, as if sealing the deal of his words. His promise to me.

"Y-you love me?" *God, stupid question. He told you that already. Twice.*

"Yes. That night we made love in your childhood bedroom proved that. To me, anyway."

"Why do you always call me Bond, then? You never call me by my name as if you're trying to keep up walls between us."

He stroked a thumb across my cheek to catch a stray tear. "Haven't you figured it out yet? Me calling you Bond is a term of endearment, not a wall. It's not my way of keeping me from getting attached."

"You love me?" *Shut. Up.*

"Yes," he said again, undeterred. Then he kissed me once more.

CHAPTER 32

James

"Let's eat first; shred later. I'm *starving*," she said.

"Too bad you live in such a shitty neighborhood; otherwise, I'd order us some food. But there's a little diner not too far from here."

"If it has food, then I'm golden."

I blew out a laugh and took her hand. I was about to put everything on the line. "Before we go, there's another truth I need to tell you. It's something that could... make or break us. I realize you haven't committed to me yet, and that's fine. Take all the time you need, but this will probably factor into your decision-making."

She wrapped her arms around herself and took a step back. This was going to be a rough ride because I struggled to see Bond regularly hanging out with a bunch of criminals. At least Ronan was prepared for it, willing to risk it because we were brothers, and family always came first. "Do you remember going to that birthday party for Georgie?" When she nodded, I plowed on, ripping off the proverbial band-aid. "They aren't only my best friends. They belong to the Irish mob. In fact, they lead it."

"What the fucking hell, James? You brought me to a mob house?"

"If we are to work out, you need to know everything and be prepared."

She took another step back, but it might as well have been a mile.

"That's how you found out about Eakin. How you learned of my attack."

"Yes."

"Why are you telling me this? You realize I could destroy you and them. I'm an ex-cop, for fuck's sake! Are you crazy? What the hell are you running around with the mob for, anyway? Oh, god... what have I done getting involved with you? Oh, shit... we had sex on a mob boss's desk!"

I grabbed her arms to stop her pacing. "Listen. Please. You don't understand. This mob is what saved you. This mob is what paid for your treatments at the clinic. This mob installed your security system. This mob found out about the hit on you and took care of Eakin. This mob did this without asking for anything in return. They accepted you, knowing you were a cop because they trust me. I understand this goes against your moral code, but... I realize this sounds cagey and probably a bit stupid, but they're different. The four brothers you met never wanted this life. They were forced into it thanks to their abusive father. Their leader is already talking about leaving it for good. They're tired. And just so you know, they don't murder innocents and family, nor do they do prostitution or sex trafficking."

I had to sell them in any way I could to get her to accept me, and them. Bond didn't move, but she also didn't pull a gun on me, nor did she rush to her phone to have me arrested. I took that as a win.

"Vinny Vinci is dead thanks to them. One of the worst mafia members. He was brutal. Thanks to them, they took the Bratva off the streets, who trafficked little girls. Thanks to them, they destroyed even their own. Seamus Delaney. They're just four brothers trying to survive and thrown into a world they never wanted. You met them, Bond. They're good men. They're just trying to protect each other and their families. Give them a chance to move on and allow them to go legit. Please."

I unbuttoned my shirt and exposed my chest, pointing at the tattoo. "This symbol here means family. We all have one. We're united through our past, present, and future. That's what the three wolf heads represent. I would die for them, and they would for me too."

I held my breath as I waited for her response. *Please accept this.*

Bond reached out and gently traced my tattoo with her finger. "Do... do their wives and girlfriends know?"

"Yes."

"And, Cat? She knows?"

"Yes. Ronan saved her life and her baby, which wasn't even his."

Bond dropped her arms and gave me a curt nod. "Okay."

My heart fucking stopped. "Okay?"

"I'm choosing to trust you, James. I know you didn't have to tell me. That you took a big risk. It seems you're doing that a lot lately for me, which says something. You're risking your friends, family, and career. So... I'll take a risk for you in return. Please, don't make me regret this."

"I make no promises other than always giving you the truth and loving you."

"Deal."

I took her hand and led her out of the office. "Now let's get you fed."

After she locked up her office, I drove her to the little place where Cat used to work and the very diner Ronan met Cat for the first time. It seemed so long ago. If it was good luck for them, perhaps it would be for me too.

When the waitress took our order, my gut turned. While telling her I loved her had been easier than I thought, we still had another elephant in the room to face. It was more my elephant than hers because this was a massive leap for me. Beyond all my sudden sacrifices, this was a step toward something I never thought I'd do. Regardless, I was determined and would accept whatever she said.

I reached into my sport coat pocket and pulled out the small black box, placing it on the table in front of her. Not the most romantic of things, but I hoped she understood me enough to realize that I wasn't exactly the most romantic person. She looked at me wide-eyed.

"Before you say anything, I'm not outright asking you to marry me... yet. Just that... my offer is on the table. I'm not expecting you to suddenly fall in love or say yes. I just want you to understand that the offer is there if you ever want it. All you have to do is put the ring on, and I'll know. It could be next month or ten years from now. This is my way of making a promise to you and the baby. And believe me when I tell you I am serious about this. If you don't accept, that's your choice, but it won't change how I feel about you nor keep me from being by your side."

She stared at the box but didn't reach for it. "Wow, when you said you were making a grand gesture, you weren't kidding. I should've known your grand gestures would be epic. This is… a lot."

Before I could say anything, the waitress brought us our food, and we sat in silence as we ate. Well, I ate. Bond scarfed.

"God, why am I so freaking hungry? I guess I should be grateful for not having too much morning sickness."

She ate every crumb, and I worried she'd lick the damn plate, but instead, she took my hand. "Don't give up your job. Not for me. I appreciate what you've done here and for those two men, but if your bosses want to keep you, you should stay. I also appreciate you wanting to take care of the baby and me… well if it all works out. And I appreciate you being honest. I realize none of this was easy for you."

I took her fingers and threaded mine with hers, then I pulled her hand and kissed her knuckles. "Will you give me a chance to prove to you how serious I am?"

Her smile was soft, and she reached for my face with her free hand and cupped my cheek. I leaned into it when she said, "Oh, James. You've already proven it. Yes, let's give *us* a chance."

All those butterflies that had been going to town on my gut finally settled. A calm wave washed over me, and I found myself finally relaxing.

"And if you ever decide to officially quit your firm, I know of a private investigator who sure could use someone like you in her business."

I smiled and pulled her across the table to kiss her. "I will keep your offer in mind."

Bond grabbed the little black box and slipped it into her purse. "I won't look at it yet. Not until that day, I decide to accept your proposal."

She didn't say she wouldn't accept it, only that she would eventually. That worked for me.

"Ready to shred some papers with me, Bond?"

She smiled up at me and bit her bottom lip, shaking her head. "I can't believe you did this."

"That makes two of us."

We sat on the floor together and tore through every single piece of paper I brought with me that had to do with the Madsen/Newall case, as I sat and quietly wished the best for both men. Rikke, too.

"It's done," I said, sitting on the floor and leaning against the wall.

"There's only one thing left to do?"

"Oh?"

"Yep."

Bond got on her hands and knees, my favorite position of hers, and crawled toward me. When she reached me, she straddled my lap as I ran my hands along her sides underneath her T-shirt, feeling her soft skin. This wasn't only a promise of some sexual fun, but showed that Bond was mine again. That I succeeded in bringing her back into my life.

She pressed her lips to mine, and I swallowed her smell and taste. God, I missed this. Missed her. All those other women in my life were forgotten the day I met Bond.

As our tongues and lips explored, she unbuckled my belt and unzipped my jeans. "Need him."

"Oh, are we personifying my cock now?"

"Yep."

She pulled me out and gave me a few languid tugs, not that my dick needed encouragement. As soon as she was on my lap, it craved her.

After sliding off of me, Bond bent down and slipped my cock into her mouth. Yes. The wet heat of her mouth was like coming home. Yep, I fucking missed her.

She ran her tongue up and down my shaft, curled it around my cockhead, then dug into my slit. I hissed and threaded my fingers through her hair. Once the ever-familiar tingling and tightening of my balls hit me, I eased her off.

"I need to be inside you."

I stood and slipped my cock back into my pants, then I helped her to stand. "Let's do this right and show me your bedroom, Bond."

She locked up the office, set the security alarm Callum had set up for her, and led me to her apartment. I supposed we would need a new place for the baby. Her apartment was too small, and my place wasn't really catered to children. I could buy us a house somewhere in the suburbs. I shuddered at the thought. Maybe not. Surely I could find a house for sale in the city.

"What was that shiver for?" she asked when we reached her bedroom.

"Envisioning us living in the suburbs."

"Ugh. No."

"And that's another reason I love you."

I slowly peeled off all her clothes, then removed mine. After easing her onto the bed, I hovered over her and gave her a few tender kisses. "We're going to save the naughty games for another night. I want to make love to you, Jane."

Her breath hitched, and her eyes watered, but the tears didn't spill.

"The last time we did that, it ended me. The old me. It was then I realized I wanted you in my life. It scared the fuck out of me, but I'm not afraid anymore. In fact, I've never been so sure of anything in my life."

Before she said anything, I kissed her and plunged into her tight warmth. Her mouth wrapped around my cock earlier wasn't coming home. No, this was. This was where I belonged.

I pressed soft kisses to her face, ears, and throat. Anywhere I could reach as I thrust in and out of her. Her legs wrapped tightly around me, and her hands trailed soft strokes across my back.

The surge of emotions coursed through me that she accepted me, cared about me and took me back left me vulnerable, but it enhanced our lovemaking. There was no blind rutting and games. Just Bond and me. And, at least for now, we were the only two that existed in this world.

She squeezed me tighter with her legs and arms. "More, James. I need you."

"You have me."

As I picked up speed and depth, she reached between us to stroke herself without being told. I lifted myself up by my arms to watch her writhe underneath me. Her eyes fluttered closed, and her plump, swollen lips parted as her breathing grew heavier.

Her pussy tightened around me and leaked, allowing me to glide in and out of her effortlessly.

"That's it. Come for me, Jane. Explode around my cock."

Her head thrashed back and forth, spreading her hair around her pillow like a curtain. When she bit her bottom lip, she groaned and squeezed the fuck out of my dick from her tight pulses, sending a wave of euphoria through me. The tight grip sent the orgasmic pressure down my spine and exploded from my balls into her.

Her body lay limply as I chased my climax with wave after wave of shudders until I couldn't take anymore. When I had nothing left to give, I slipped out of her, fell to the side of the bed, and pulled her with me. I kissed her head, trailing gentle fingers across her back, trying to regain my breath and calm my heart down.

Bond traced the tattoo on my chest and blew out a laugh.

"What?" I asked.

"You know, if we get married, you could take my name and be known as James Bond."

"Yeah, that's not happening. Only you get to be the butt of Bond jokes. I loathe being teased."

"Spoilsport."

"You will forever be known as Bond. Jane Bond to me."

"I guess that's not so bad. Who knew I would actually like that? But only from you."

CHAPTER 33

Jane

JAMES SAT NEXT TO ME, HOLDING MY HAND AND KISSING MY KNUCKLES, while Colton sat on the other side as we all waited in silence for the doctor to come in.

I lay on the bed dressed only in a hospital gown as nerves filled me, worried about how the fetus was doing. I hated having to wait so long before the ultrasound, but the day was finally here.

Glancing at James, he had his jaw set tight, but he gave me an encouraging smile. He mirrored my nervousness, and he had a lot to lose, too, especially after what happened to him all those years ago.

"It's going to be okay, partner," Colton said.

I just nodded.

"Colt, if... if it all turns out okay, would you like to be the godfather?" Then I glanced at James, forgetting that he was part of this decision process. "Sorry, is that okay?"

"Of course. You decide."

I looked back at Colton, who beamed at me. "I would be honored, partner."

My doctor finally walked in and shook all of our hands. She was a short thing with a mop of brown hair threaded with silver, like she couldn't be bothered and cut it herself. Then again, she probably worked long-ass hours.

"All your blood work came back normal, Jane. Now, I'm sure you're eager to see what's going on, so let's get started."

The doctor opened up my gown from the front to expose my still flat stomach and squeezed a tube of warm jelly on me. She pressed the wand on my stomach and started searching for something that probably wasn't bigger than a bean.

After some scanning, the doctor finally found it. She said nothing as she took measurements and made a few prints. We all held bated breaths, waiting for the results.

"Well, Jane, it looks like all is well, the fetus is growing normally, and I see no problems. You're about seven weeks along. Now we need to put you on some prenatal vitamins, and I need to see you once a month. Your next scan will be at twenty weeks, at which point, you can choose if you want to learn the sex of your baby."

"Thank you, doctor."

When she left, James leaned over and pulled me to him in a tight hug. "It's all good. It's all good."

I couldn't stop smiling if I tried, unable to contain my excitement and relief. Even James looked relieved and hopeful.

Then it was Colton's turn for the bear hugs, squeezing the life out of me. "I'm so happy for you, partner."

"Thanks, Colt."

After I got dressed, we all stepped outside on a warm and bright day. Colton shook James' hand, and he must have squeezed it hard, judging by James' wince. "You be good to our girl. I mean it."

"She'll have the best," James promised.

"Good."

We said our goodbyes with promises of catching up with Brice, then James pulled me against him. "I think Colton broke my hand."

I snorted a laugh. "I'm sure you're fine, but yes, he can get a bit protective of me, like the big brother I never had."

James held on tight and kissed my head. "I never thought I'd hear myself say this, but I'm... excited about this. For the baby and having a life with you. But I'm also terrified as fuck. I keep getting hit with little fears that something's going to happen to you and the baby."

I cupped his face. "Hey, nothing is going to happen. We're going to be fine."

"Jane, you nearly died already."

Jane.

He rarely used my first name except when he was trying to make a point or feeling vulnerable.

"And you took care of that. There are no more threats against me."

"I haven't told you yet, but I've set up some time with a therapist to deal with my past."

"Good. I'm proud of you."

What a night and day difference James had become. This one-eighty he'd done was proof enough that he'd be by my side. I trusted him. Though, I was also worried about all this change. It was a lot for him, but he seemed to be coping well enough.

"Just make sure you do it for yourself. Not me. Okay?"

"It is."

We walked hand in hand to his car, and he leaned against it, pulling me with him. "Listen, I want to take you to Lawrence this weekend to meet my parents. It's time. I've been rather neglectful of them. I send them money once a month, but I don't call them nearly enough, and I haven't been to visit them in a couple of years. It's not that I don't love them. They raised me well enough. It's being in Lawrence that I don't like."

"I would love to meet them."

James breathed out a laugh. "Boy, are they going to be fucking shocked after I tell them they'd never be grandparents?"

We drove in silence past old brick factories with towering smokestacks that darkened back to the days of the Industrial Revolution. Some were well-kept, while others fell into ruin. There was something nostalgic yet sad about the area. Parts of downtown struggled to thrive. Some quaint shops and restaurants went in, trying to gentrify the area. As we moved on, we drove past strip malls, and way too many gas stations, and eventually reached a lower-class neighborhood full of homes in various states of repair and disrepair.

James pulled to a stop in front of a little one-story house in a pale blue color, and though you could tell it was old, probably dating back to the thirties, it was well cared for. The yard was neat with pruned shrubs, and the plant beds had a border of white flowers. All were tucked inside, surrounded by a chain-link fence.

"Well, here we are. This is where I grew up."

"The house is cute."

"Yeah, I paid it off for them. I tried to get my parents to move closer to the city, but this is home for them. Honestly, it's close enough that I can visit whenever I want, but…"

He left his words hanging, having already explained why he hated coming back here.

"My parents always understood and didn't nag me to come home. But after everything recently, I'm feeling guilty, and I miss them. This isn't an emotion I'm overly familiar with. You know… being a narcissist and all."

I took his hand to hold since he wasn't in a rush to get out of the car. I used to believe he was narcissistic too, but most of his behavior was a wall to hide behind. After everything we'd both been through and how James had allowed those walls to drop, I understood and saw the real man. Or who he could be. I didn't pretend that all would always be perfect or that he wouldn't fall back on bad behaviors, but I chose to trust him. He'd earned it.

He gave me a small smile. "Ready?"

"I think the better question is, are *you* ready?"

"That's why we're here, right?"

He climbed out of the car, and I followed close behind. Hand in hand, he opened the gate, and we walked up to the front door. James tested the doorknob and opened it.

We walked into a modest home with old but neat furniture in the traditional style. Dated floral wallpaper covered most of the house, but they installed laminate flooring, which looked like hardwood floors. Pictures of a little blond-haired boy of various ages hung on the walls. Some were of him on a lake, and there was one with him wearing a baseball uniform at about the age of ten. And another of him playing football in high school.

James was adorable as a kid. He smiled in all the pictures, but something changed in him by his senior year and graduation. He had sadness in his eyes, and he didn't smile at all.

"Hello? Mom? Dad?"

Instead of answering, a short and plump woman in her late sixties came to greet us. Her hair was a dark blond like his but with streaks of silver. James looked a lot like her too, though he was about a foot taller.

Following close behind was a man of James' six-foot height, but with a little bit of a belly. He was around his mother's age, with a thick head of hair cropped short and completely white.

"James?"

"Hi, Mom."

His mother pulled him into a tight hug, resting her head on his chest. "James…"

He enveloped her in a hug, too.

"I missed you so much, son."

"I missed you and Dad, too."

James' father also pulled him into a hug. Both of his parents tried to hold back their emotions, but you could tell how much they loved James and missed him.

"Mom. Dad. This is Jane Bond, my girlfriend. Wow, I think that's the first time I've said that out loud."

I gave him a playful shove and then shook their hands. "It's a pleasure to meet you both." His mother also surprised me by pulling me into a hug.

"A girlfriend. I never thought I'd live to see the day."

"You and me both," James quipped. "But Bond beat me into submission."

I burst into a laugh and rolled my eyes.

"Actually, I'm here for you to not only meet her, but we have news. Can we sit and talk?"

"I'm making dinner, so we can talk in the kitchen. You're staying for dinner, right?"

"We're actually thinking of staying the night here in my old room if that's okay. Unless you turned it into a gym or office or sewing room."

"Oh, of course, you can stay. It's a guest room now, but I've kept some of your things from when you were younger."

We sat down at the kitchen table, and James' dad handed him a beer. He offered me one, but I declined. He pulled the tab back on the can and took a long sip. "I want to first tell you how sorry I am that I haven't visited more often. I—"

"Son, you don't need to apologize. While we've missed you, we've always understood your need to be away from this town. And maybe we reminded you a little bit of that day, too, which is why we didn't come to Boston either."

"Just the same, I'm sorry. I'm going to do better. I promise."

"James, what is going on, honey? You call us out of the blue, ask to visit, and you have a girlfriend. We may not see you often, but I know my son. Something is going on."

He took my hand and threaded our fingers together. "Apparently, I lied a few years back. Jane and I are going to have a baby, and you're going to be grandparents."

James' mother was freaking adorable. She put her hands to her mouth as her eyes watered. "I'm going to be a grandma? Did you hear that, Frank?"

"I did, Chrissy. Congratulations, you two."

"Thank you," I said.

"I... I never pressured you about settling down and having kids. I always knew why you didn't, but... this surge of happiness is quite unexpected." She fanned her face as her eyes leaked. "Oh, I'm so happy for you both."

"Are you going to get married, son?" his dad asked. The question was expected because he told them he'd never marry.

James looked at me, then addressed his father. "We're talking about it, but right now, I'm trying to get used to having a relationship. I want to do this right and not go head first into something I've been avoiding most of my life."

"I'm so proud of you, James." His mother rushed him and pulled him into another hug, and then she hugged me again. God, his parents were so sweet and supportive, and kind. It gave me hope for James and our future.

CHAPTER 34

James

"DO YOU LIKE THAT, BAD GIRL?"

"Yes. Harder."

I smacked her ass harder as I pounded into her tight pussy from behind. Bond was bracing for impact on the wall, shoving herself back on me.

"Deeper."

I'm trying, sweet girl. I'm fucking trying.

Smack, smack, smack.

Good thing I worked out and ran because I would have keeled over and died by now. Sweat dripped down my face and onto her back, which was already covered in a sheen of sweat. I was out of breath, pounding the life out of her. Despite my stamina and strength, my leg muscles felt the burn. We'd been at it for an hour now. And though Bond came twice already, she wanted more.

Her ass turned bright red, and I was afraid I'd injure her if we kept this up, but she was… persistent.

At first, I worried I'd hurt the baby, but she insisted the baby wouldn't care. My woman was hornier than a bonobo monkey. Once she hit her third trimester, she wanted it two to four times a day. I bought her a box of toys to use on herself, or for me to use on her, to give my poor, raw dick a rest.

Smack, smack.

"When are you going to learn to be a good girl?" I asked, nearly out of breath.

She shoved her hand between her legs, rubbing one out. Thank god, because that meant she was wrapping it up.

"I like being bad for you."

"And I like bad girls that I can punish."

"Yes, I'll take my punishment and learn."

I couldn't help but smirk despite my exhaustion. Bond really embraced the spankings, and I was happy to accommodate her. We even tried a crop, a paddle, and my belt. She ate it up. Well, her ass did.

"I'm coming!"

"Come for me, sweet girl."

Her pussy gripped me like a vise as she pulsed and writhed. Once she finished chasing her climax, I was completely spent. No more. If she asked again, I was going to sob.

I pulled out of her and fell on my back onto the floor, struggling to get my heart rate back to healthy levels.

Jane hovered over me, her swollen belly and breasts grazing my torso. Her sweaty hair stuck to her face, and she was also out of breath. And the most beautiful thing I'd ever seen at that moment.

She leaned in and gave me a wet kiss full of tongue. My hands gripped the back of her head and gave the kiss my all. Then she pulled away and curled up on her side, facing me.

"That was amazing," she said. "I mean, sex was good before, but now? Holy hell. But I probably won't be able to sit for a week."

I glanced at her, full of concern. "Bond—"

"Don't. I'm joking."

"Regardless, we should probably back off soon. The last thing I need is to get arrested for domestic abuse when you give birth, and your doctor sees your poor ass."

She laughed. "God, can you imagine? But you're right. We should probably take it easy since I'm so close."

Once my breath calmed the fuck down, I turned to face her and combed her wet hair away from her face. "I never thought I'd see the day when I said there's such a thing as too much sex."

She snorted a laugh and patted my chest. "Well, you better enjoy it while you can because, after the baby, we'll both be too tired to do much else."

"Come on." I stood up and helped her to stand, then led her to our bed. We probably needed a shower, but I was too fucking tired.

Bond draped a leg over mine and swirled fingers through what little chest hair I had.

Everything had gone surprisingly well between us. We dated for a few months, and falling into a pattern with her was surprisingly easy. She was smart, sassy, fun, and sexy. She made getting along easy and never ever put up with my shit.

At the beginning of November, I let her pick out a house and bought it for her. It was an old farmhouse that came up for sale recently for a cool one million, but it'd been completely refurbished, so we didn't have to do any work. While it was a house, and we planned to raise a family in it, it sat within the city limits. As soon as she saw the house, she fell in love. And I could afford it, especially after making a partner at Meyers and Levitt.

Now we lived together, and the baby was due on Valentine's Day, believe it or not. We didn't know if we were having a boy or a girl, and because it didn't matter to us, we chose to be surprised.

She never did put on my ring, but I never asked her to, and I refused to pressure her. She would put it on when she was ready. If she didn't want to get married, I was fine with that too. I knew she loved me as much as I loved her. She told me enough.

"We still need to pick out names," she said through a yawn.

"We can talk about it tomorrow. Let's get some sleep."

"I can't believe the baby will be here in three weeks." Her words were slow and groggy.

I moved my head to her stomach and kissed the baby through her tummy. "Our world will never be the same," I whispered to her leveled breathing. And I was more than okay with that.

I stirred from that state between wakefulness and dreaming. A wet heat surrounded my cock, and I looked down between my legs to see a head bobbing up and down from underneath the blankets. My smile was crooked from the pleasant wake-up call.

I was oversexed, but sometimes it was nice not to have to do anything but lie there.

I whipped off the covers to find Jane going to town on my dick like she worshiped it. Her delicious tongue wrapped around my cockhead and dug into my slit. I hissed and gripped her hair on instinct.

I was too big for her to shove down her throat all the way, so Bond stroked me as she played with my balls, gently tugging on them. Then she licked the sensitive underside of my shaft before she slipped me back into her mouth and sucked me for all she was worth.

I couldn't help but thrust in her mouth, making her gag, but she kept at it like a champ.

"Like that, baby. Keep going. Right there."

My balls grew tight as fuck, ready to release before they burst. The pressure was strong, and I gave her a little warning, but she always knew when I was close. My dick swelled and let loose load after load that she swallowed down. Then she licked me clean.

I just woke up, but now I was ready for a nap.

"Good morning," she said, curling up to my side.

I gave her a lazy laugh. "Morning."

She swirled her hand over my chest, so I grabbed it to kiss. But I stopped myself when I saw the ring. My ring. I didn't go overboard with the design because Bond wasn't complicated. It was a band of small diamonds with one larger one in the center.

I flipped her over onto her back and stared into her green depths. "Do you mean it? You want to get married."

She bit her bottom lip and nodded.

Before, I didn't care if she wanted to marry or not. Marriage had never been a priority in my life, but once she put that ring on, it was like she was marked as mine. I found something primal about that. Every man would see she was mine. For the first time in my life, I looked forward to committing to someone wholly.

"I love you so fucking much."

She cupped my face like she always did, filled with patience. "Are you sure you want to do this? It's okay if you're still uncomfortable with marriage. I know you're committed to me."

"Are you talking me out of this, Bond?"

Her smile was broad. "Definitely not."

"Then I definitely want to marry you. I'll do my best not to blow it."

"Marriages are never perfect, James. You understand that. We need to make sure to keep our love growing. To tend to it like a lush garden. Things won't always be easy, but that's okay too."

"And I trust you to tell me when I'm being an ass."

"That's a promise."

I gave Bond a quick kiss and climbed out of bed to take a shower. It was Saturday, and we had a week left before the baby came, though there was no guarantee it would arrive on that specific date, so we planned to take it easy.

After my shower, I tossed on some boxer briefs and joggers, leaving my shirt off, and headed to the kitchen and pulled out some eggs, cheddar cheese, sausage, onion, and red bell pepper. Bond loved my omelets, so I made them for her on the weekends.

After chopping up the bell pepper into tiny pieces, I diced the onion.

"James?" Bond called out from our bedroom.

"In the kitchen."

"Can you come here, please?"

I put down the knife, washed my hands, and then headed to the bedroom.

"Need help?"

Bond stood there with spread legs, looking grossed out. "I, ah, think my water broke."

My mind went instantly blank. "What?"

"James! You know how this works. I'm going to get myself cleaned up. Can you please get my bag and warm up the car?"

"Wait. It's time? But it's early."

She rolled her eyes at my confusion. "It's not that early. Only a little. Regardless, the baby is coming."

My brain finally took over as my heart did somersaults in my chest. Shit, it was time. I rushed to my closet and pulled out a shirt and sweater, tossing them on. I grabbed some socks and put on my shoes, then I pulled her already packed bag from the closet and ran downstairs, snatching my wallet and keys from the front table.

When I ran out the door, I nearly slipped on the ice. Dammit! It was supposed to have melted already. We'd have to be careful getting Bond to the car. I tossed her suitcase in the trunk and climbed in the car to start it, turning the heat on full blast.

I ran back inside and found Bond waiting by the front door. I took her hand, trying not to panic, but my heart refused to stop racing, and my stomach was doing something awful in there. The poor thing waddled, trying not to slip on the ice, as we made it to the car.

Twenty minutes later, we made it to the hospital and got Bond all checked in. Shit, I was going to be a father soon. While pregnant, the thought was almost abstract but now soon to be a reality. The entire thing terrified me, yet I was excited to meet my child. All I could do was hope I'd be a good father and didn't ruin the kid.

As we waited for the doctor, I texted everyone the baby was coming. And by everyone, I meant her family, my parents, the O'Callaghans, and their partners, Brody, Colton, Brice, and Sam.

I sat in a rocking chair and spent a few minutes with my son in the nursery as Bond slept. The amount of love and emotion coursing through me was overwhelming and unexpected. I knew I'd love him, but I didn't think it was possible to love something even more. He was so fucking cute, too. And so tiny. He had very little hair on his head, but what he did have was blond. I wondered what color eyes he'd have. Would they be blue like mine? Green like Bond's? Or would they be another color?

The birth was long but uneventful. Bond's entire pregnancy and birth went smoothly, and thank fuck for that. After the last time, I wasn't sure I could take any trauma, despite all the therapy I'd received.

Greyson Alan Clery

That was the name we picked for him. Completely *not* Bond movie related.

I imagined his future attending the best schools, having lots of friends, going to a good college, and succeeding in anything he chose to do. Hopefully, his biggest worry would be a breakup with a girl he liked.

And as I rocked my sleeping infant son, I suddenly didn't miss my past. That life before Bond. Everything became a blur and meaningless. But everything I'd been through culminated to this moment. This sheer love and happiness. And because of that, I had no more regrets. Sure, I had that lingering grief from my youth. I would forever wonder what would have happened if I had that child.

"You're going to do great things, Greyson," I whispered.

THE END

Please enjoy a special Kings of Boston epilogue for FREE, by joining my newsletter!

https://BookHip.com/KSFDKQD

ACKNOWLEDGMENTS

I would like to first personally thank you, the reader, for sharing in the journey with me. Kings of Boston has been a wild ride! I still can't believe it's over now. Well, at least for this series. But I have so much more to look forward to!

Though I still haven't been writing for a very long time, I've been learning with each book to keep pushing to do better. I don't think I could have done all that without the help from my beta reading team who tell me like it is. And I love that!

But not only is this the end of a book series. It's the end of a genre for me. In Vindication is the last male/female romance I'll be writing. I will now only stick with male/male romances which I've learned that I prefer writing. Even my team agrees I write better with this genre as well. I hope you continue to follow me along as I grow and push my writing skills.

ABOUT THE AUTHOR

Thank you for reading *In Vindication*.

Courtney W. Dixon loves to write steamy romance, but in each story, she gives her characters challenges and struggles. She writes m/f and m/m stories within one series to add a variety to her characters. And she writes her characters as having flaws, imperfections, and who don't always do the right thing. Humans are never perfect, and make a lot of mistakes in their lives. In the end, she tries to help them grow to be better as they achieve their HEAs.

You can find Courtney working in Central Texas with her husband, two boys, and two crazy dogs, none of whom know how to knock on a door while she's working.

She's an independent author. As such, she needs you to help her grow and thrive. She is always appreciative of feedback from you, the reader. Good or bad, if you have the time, please leave a review. Ratings are good too, but reviews say so much more. This helps her learn what you like to make her books more enjoyable.

You can also send feedback via email at courtneywdixonauthor@gmail.com

Connect with me:
www.courtneywdixon.com

Courtney's Corrupt Readers Facebook Group
Courtney's Corrupt Readers | Facebook

Made in the USA
Columbia, SC
01 February 2023